Double or Nothing

CARI Z
L.A. WITT

ISBN-13: 978-1720864660
ISBN-10: 1720864667

Copyright Information

This is a work of fiction. Names, characters, places, and incidents are either the product of the author's imagination or are used fictitiously. Any resemblance to actual persons living or dead, business establishments, events, or locales is entirely coincidental.

First Edition.
Copyright © 2018 Cari Z & L.A. Witt

Cover Art by Lori Witt
Editor: Leta Blake

ISBN-13: 978-1720864660
ISBN-10: 1720864667

DOUBLE OR NOTHING

Chapter One
Rich

"Join the U.S. Marshals," they said.

"It'll be fun," they said.

I glared around the dimly lit hotel room. If this was anyone's idea of fun, they were crazy.

Three other deputy marshals loitered in the room with me. Greg Rogers, who was basically my mentor, sat back in the chair by the curtain-covered window with his suit coat unbuttoned and his nose buried in a paperback. Alan Holloway, an ex-Marine like me, stood rigidly against the wall, a seemingly contradictory mixture of cable-tight tension and excruciating boredom. Sam Miller sat on one of the two beds, back to me, talking quietly into his cell phone.

And me, I was kicked back in one of the not very comfortable chairs at the table near the door and trying not to fuss with the tie I'd been wearing for too long. My phone was facedown and quiet on the table next to the thick file folder. I'd been through the file enough times to know everything I needed to know about our witness. And

I'd been to every end of the Internet on my phone. Now I was just…fucking…*bored*.

I'd joined the Marshals for the same reason everyone did—to chase down bad guys and bring them in. Especially with the FBI shifting its focus to antiterrorism, we had plenty of work to do. Lots of fugitives to keep us busy. All through training—all twenty-two weeks of it— I'd been chomping at the bit to get out there and do my job.

So imagine my surprise when my assignment had come in. I didn't mind the location—I could deal with Chicago—but WITSEC? Seriously? I went through all that shit, including kissing Senator Broadwater's ass so he might eventually nominate me for Presidential appointment to be a district Marshal like my dad, to babysit witnesses? What the ever-loving fuck?

"Just hang in there," Dad had assured me. *"They're hard up for witness security right now, but you won't be stuck there forever."*

Easy for him to say when he'd been on the tail of his first fugitive almost immediately after graduation. He'd been dropped right into an active case, and he'd slapped cuffs on a *fucking serial killer* within *weeks*.

I'd been doing this for just under a year, and I hadn't put cuffs on anyone. Well, aside from that guy I'd hooked up with on vacation last summer—Phil? Paul?—but as fun as that was, I hadn't exactly been hauling him off to federal prison.

No, I'd spent the last eleven months babysitting. Sticking with protected witnesses until they testified, and then helping them transition into their new lives. It was theoretically dangerous work because witnesses wouldn't need protection if they weren't testifying against people who'd want them dead or otherwise silenced, but the Marshals were pretty fucking good at hiding people. Once we had them, nobody was finding them. Hell, *I'd* gotten lost on the way to a safehouse a couple of times because they were so well hidden.

So we protected witnesses as if every supervillain in every comic universe was minutes away from busting down the door, hid them like we were giving the Easter Bunny a run for his money, and then almost keeled over from boredom because nothing happened.

Which was good for the witness. And for us. I guess. Nothing happening meant nobody dying. I didn't want anything to happen to our witnesses or to any of us.

But holy fuck, BABYSIT—err, WITSEC—was going to kill me.

"*Join the U.S. Marshals,*" they said.

"*It'll be fun,*" they said.

Sam abruptly stood from the bed where he'd been sitting. "He's on his way in."

Immediately, Greg and I were on our feet. So was Alan, but…well, I wasn't sure he knew how to sit down and get comfortable, so yeah, he was already standing.

Anyway, we were all instantly on alert, the room silent and each of us craning our necks to hear what was going on outside. Greg absently checked his sidearm. I realized I was doing the same thing without even thinking about it. WITSEC detail was kind of like combat. Ninety-five percent boredom, five percent sheer terror. Well, okay, it wasn't really sheer terror. More like ten minutes of excitement while a witness was handed off to us, since that was when he'd be the most vulnerable. This guy had been at a meeting with the District Attorney, and now we'd be taking him into protective custody until the trial. Let the babysitting begin.

Sam's phone buzzed. He looked at the screen, then at Greg, and they exchanged nods. I was still learning the telepathic signals passed between deputy marshals, but I knew the routine well enough to know what happened next.

As expected, Greg and Alan stepped out. There was some activity—movement and voices—but nothing to raise alarm. A moment later, the door opened again, and they returned with a couple of FBI agents I'd met before, and of course, the witness. There were more agents from both teams lurking outside—in the hall, in the lobby downstairs, in the parking garage—but I couldn't see any of them.

And anyway, I was having a hard time seeing anyone except the witness.

He was dressed down in an unzipped blue hoody and jeans, but I instantly recognized him. Leotrim Nicolosi was not someone whose face I could forget. It wasn't just because I'd been poring over his file for the last twenty-four hours, memorizing details and getting a feel for just how many people wanted to shut this guy up. He was…well, who was I kidding? Criminal or not, the guy was hot.

Nicolosi was one of those people whose ethnicity I wouldn't have been able to guess if I hadn't had a cheat sheet to tell me he was Sicilian and Albanian. He had artfully mussed dark hair, light olive skin, and rich brown eyes that were even more stunning in person than in photos, not to mention full lips framed by a thin goatee.

He was a little shorter than I'd expected. Maybe five-ten or so. But somehow, when his intense gaze landed on me, I felt like *I* was the one looking up. These Mafia guys were something else. That much I'd learned in my short career. The big guys could be teddy bears when their peers and bosses weren't looking, and the smaller ones could be pit-bulls. Or angry chihuahuas in some cases. Something told me Leotrim Nicolosi was nothing that could be described as cute, cuddly, or unlikely to rip off your face with his teeth. I wondered what happened to whoever had busted his nose at some juncture of his life. I had a feeling that had been a *"you should see the other guy"* moment.

One of the agents was speaking to Sam and Greg while I ogled the witness. "Mr. Nicolosi is due to testify—"

"Leo." Nicolosi—Leo—sounded tired and irritated. "For the fiftieth fucking time, call me *Leo*."

Uncomfortable looks passed between the agents and the other marshals.

Greg extended a hand to the witness. "Leo, I'm Deputy Marshal Greg Rogers. My men and I"—he gestured at us—"will be keeping you safe until you testify."

Leo eyed him uncertainly. "They say you'll hook me up with a new name and all when this is over?"

Greg nodded, hand still hovering between them. "Your new identity is in the works as we speak."

Leo chewed the inside of his cheek, regarding Greg and his outstretched hand suspiciously before he finally accepted it. Then Greg introduced him around.

When he got to me, he touched my shoulder. "And this is Rich Cody."

"Rich." Leo shook my hand, his skin a lot softer and smoother than I'd anticipated. "So can I call you Richie?"

"Are you my mother?" I asked, ignoring the *be nice to the witness* glare from Greg.

Leo's dark eyes sparkled with mischief. "Not that I'm aware of."

"Then no. You can't call me Richie."

He chuckled, and when the tip of his tongue darted along the inside of his lip, I realized he hadn't let go of my hand.

As politely as I could, I cleared my throat and loosened my grip. He waited a beat before doing the same, almost like he wanted me to be sure I knew it was *his* choice to break contact. I wondered if he was trying to intimidate me.

I've faced down men twice your size wearing explosives and waving automatic rifles. You don't scare me, punk.

Maybe turn me on a little, but—

I cleared my throat again and shifted my gaze to Greg, hoping my cheeks weren't as red as they felt. "Do you want me to radio for transport?"

Greg shook his head. "It's already scheduled. We've got three hours to cool our heels before the car gets here."

It was all I could do not to groan in frustration. Three more hours in this godforsaken place? I knew there was rhyme and reason and protocol—not to mention the need to avoid getting caught in Chicago gridlock—but I'd been here for too long not to wish we could just *go* already.

Beside us, Leo looked around the room, and a smirk materialized on his lips. "This your whole crew?" As he turned to Greg, his eyebrow rose. "Let me guess—budget cuts?"

"Something like that." Greg chuckled. "Make yourself comfortable, Mr.—Leo. We'll let you know when it's time to leave."

Leo grunted quietly, eyeing the beds. He took the one furthest from the door, flopped onto his back, and laced his hands behind his head. While Greg and Sam spoke quietly with the FBI agents, and Alan stood rigidly by the wall like he'd been doing before, I picked up the folder on Leo and flipped through it again. I'd already memorized every line, but it was something to do besides stare at Leo.

Good looks aside, he was my least favorite type of witness. This wasn't some innocent person who'd been in the wrong place at the wrong time and seen something they shouldn't have. No, Leotrim Nicolosi was a criminal through and through. The mastermind behind the Grimaldi crime family's obscenely successful and highly illegal online gambling operation. He wasn't a made man, but he wasn't an innocent bystander either. Now that the family had turned their crosshairs on him—Nicolosi hadn't been entirely clear why—he was turning state's evidence and planned to bring them all down with his testimony. The man could've gone down for decades upon decades of prison time for his own crimes, but since he was helping us, he'd get the works—federal protection, followed by a brand new life and a clean slate. The fucker was a computer prodigy, too, so he probably even had bank accounts somewhere that no one knew about, which he'd be able to access from his new identity.

I didn't object to protecting innocent witnesses. Unrepentant criminals who were only testifying to save their own skin? Fuck that. I'd joined the Marshals to *catch* assholes like him, not cater to his every whim so he didn't change his mind or die—by way of boredom or a bullet—before he could testify. Being insanely sexy—especially lying back with his T-shirt and Kevlar vest pulling up just enough to bare some skin—didn't negate the fact that he was a *criminal*.

I closed the folder with a sigh. When I eventually got that coveted position as U.S. Marshal—the President-appointed Marshal in charge of an entire federal district like my dad—I'd look back on this and laugh about paying my dues.

For today, though? Fuck my life.

It was finally time to move on. We all checked our weapons, and Sam and Greg radioed the other marshals to tell them to stand by.

Leo had been dozing, and he nearly took Greg's head off when the man roused him.

"Come on," Greg said with his usual endless patience. "You'll like your new digs a lot better. I promise."

"Well shit. Why didn't you say so?" Leo rubbed his eyes as he rolled to his feet. "There'll be food, right?"

"Of course." Greg's brow pinched. "You hungry? You should've said something."

"Meh." Leo grunted like a kid who didn't want to get ready for school. "Let's just go."

After triple-checking we had everything we'd brought into the room, Sam radioed that we were on the move.

As we left the room, the four men who'd been posted outside joined us, and we led Leo to the service elevator at the far end of the hall. It was guarded top, bottom, and inside by marshals, and would take us to the parking garage where the equally heavily guarded motorcade was waiting.

While we waited for the elevator to arrive, Leo glanced around at his growing entourage, and he smirked. "This must be what Beyoncé feels like."

Some of the marshals suppressed quiet laughter. I rolled my eyes. Great. I was stuck for the next several weeks with a man who got an ego boost out of needing an armed security detail. I couldn't wait until this assignment was over.

The elevator finally arrived. The doors started to open.

And as soon as they were an inch apart, all hell broke loose.

"Get down!" Alan tackled Leo. Gunfire cracked, and suddenly there was shooting from both directions. In seconds, the entire hallway was near-silent, men's mouths opening and closing in soundless shouts. My ears were stuffed with cotton, my only sense of each gunshot coming from the muzzle blasts and concussions.

Alan and I dragged Leo to his feet and backtracked to take cover. Men in suits came around the corner. More muzzle blasts. Alan slumped, nearly pulling Leo back down with him. I fired twice, catching one of the men in the throat. The other shot at me, the bullet zinging way too close by my ear, and when I pulled the trigger again, he went down.

I shoved Leo against the wall, shielding him as much as I could. I still couldn't hear well enough to tell if anyone was coming my way. Someone was screaming into the radio, but the transmission didn't make it past the cotton in my ears.

Greg and another marshal hurried toward us, laying cover fire between us and the elevator while I checked around the corner. No one was coming from that direction, so I pulled Leo into the safety of the adjacent hallway. A moment later, Greg joined us. The other marshal didn't. I didn't ask why.

"*Fuck.*" Greg's strained voice was barely audible with the way my ears rang. He clutched his side, and just below where his vest ended under his white dress shirt, a red stain was rapidly spreading. Way too much blood seeped past his fingers. I reached for him, but he waved my hand away. "Go. Take the witness and get the fuck out of here."

"Where do I—"

"Go up. They'll be expecting you to go down." He paused, grimacing. "Once they're off your tail, get out of the hotel, run like hell, and don't let anything happen to—"

Gunfire cut him off. We all instinctively ducked.

"Go!" Greg shouted, and gave me a shove for good measure. "I'll cover you!" My stomach flipped. He'd keep them at bay until he ran out of ammo or passed out, and I didn't want to think about how much time that left us.

I grabbed Leo by the elbow. "Come on! Run!"

"Where the—"

"Just *run!*"

He didn't argue. Crouched low, we stayed close to the wall and hurried down the hall. Bullets flew behind us. A couple whizzed past, way too close, and one pinged off a light fixture.

The floor was ring-shaped, and at the end of this hall was another left turn. At the corner, I swept the perpendicular hall, and when I was confident it was clear, I pulled Leo with me and we sprinted.

I skidded to a halt by the bank of elevators. "In here."

"What?" Leo stared at me as I thumbed the down arrow button. "We're taking the *elevator*? Are you fucking crazy?"

I didn't answer. When the elevator doors opened, I leaned in, pressed the button for the lobby, then stepped back out and motioned for him to continue running.

We found the stairwell and hurried inside. I quickly dropped the magazine from my pistol, switched it out with another, and wedged the nearly empty one under the door. It wouldn't hold forever, but it would slow someone down.

"This way." I nodded toward the stairs.

I could see the question in Leo's eyes—*why are we going up and not down?*—but he didn't ask. He just followed, and we hurried up three floors. Like the floor where we'd been hunkered down with Leo, the two above and two below were empty, and they were supposed to be patrolled by marshals, but I was taking no chances. If our location had been compromised, those patrols were probably dead, their killers waiting to intercept us.

I went up one more for good measure and paused. There were no footsteps anywhere else in the stairwell. My ears were still ringing badly, but I didn't hear the percussion of someone trying to open the door I'd wedged shut, and no voices either. My radio was eerily silent.

I tried not to think about the carnage we'd left behind and how many of my colleagues were dead or dying. Right now, the only thing that mattered was getting Leo and myself out of this building and to safety.

"What now?" Leo's voice just carried above the ringing in my ears.

I was tempted to shake my head and say I wasn't sure, but that wouldn't instill confidence in a man expecting the Marshals to protect him. As it was, we'd already promised him no one would find him, and…here we were.

"This way." I motioned toward the door. I pulled it open and did a quick sweep of the hall. No one except some maids taking towels from a cart parked between two rooms. They glanced our way, but didn't seem to think anything of us. Apparently they hadn't heard anything from the other floor; amazing how much two floors of rooms could insulate from people going about their lives like normal.

We strolled past the maids into one of the rooms.

"Could we get some more bath towels?" I asked casually. "He likes to use three or four to dry his hair."

The maid laughed and handed me a stack.

"Thank you." I closed the door and tossed the towels into the bathroom, narrowly missing some toiletries the actual guest had laid out on the counter.

"What the fuck do we do now?" Leo asked. "How did they find us?"

I was about to answer, but the radio in my ear crackled to life. "All units, respond with status updates."

I held a finger to my lips. Leo scowled.

"Stay quiet," I said. "I'll get us out of here."

"By what? Helicopter?"

Ignoring him, I turned on my radio. "This is Deputy Cody. Over."

"Cody, I read you. Are you all right? Over."

"I'm fine. Got a lot of men down, though. Over."

"We've got medical help on the way. What's the status of the witness? Over."

I glanced at Leo. "No joy on the witness. Lost visual contact during the firefight. Another deputy told him to take the southeast stairwell down and head for the hotel's front entrance. Over."

"Copy that. What's your twenty? Over."

"Sweeping the seventeenth floor. No one here. On my way back down. Over."

"Copy that."

I clicked the radio off again. Leo's inquisitive expression was no surprise. I ran a hand through my sweaty hair. "Our communication channels may be compromised. Anyone who's listening is going to be looking for you on the stairwell and by that entrance."

He seemed to relax a bit. "Okay. So, we just stay here, then?"

I shook my head. "No. We give them a chance to sweep the stairwells, and then we take the northwest stairs down and go out via the side door."

"And go…where, exactly?"

I swallowed. "I'm still working on that."

He eyed me. Then he looked me up and down, and some renewed tension crept into his features. "I'm stuck with the new guy, ain't I?"

"I'm not a rookie, if that's what you're worried about."

"Yeah? And how long have you been 'not a rookie'?"

I glared at him. "You want to go out on your own? Because it's either me or one of the dead guys downstairs."

Leo scowled, but he didn't push.

For the next twenty minutes—which felt like hours—I listened to the radio chatter. It wasn't easy to hear after the gunfire had fucked up my ears, but I was able to parse most of it. No one was calling for medical help or police yet, which wasn't surprising. Everywhere we were supposed to go with Leo had been carefully cleared of people so only those involved with his transfer would be anywhere near him. Even now, no one would have heard anything except my team and our assailants. And since my team wasn't calling for help… well, that told me what I needed to know about their status.

I tried not to think about that, and just listened for the information I needed: when the northwestern stairwell had been deemed clear.

As soon as it was, we hurried out and started down. Sure enough, the stairs were clear, but I kept my pistol in hand the whole way, and we moved as stealthily as we could in the gigantic echo chamber.

The stairs let out at the far corner of the lobby, which was under inconspicuous but heavy guard from all directions. Everything was relatively calm down here. There was a lot of activity near the check-in desk and elevators, but no one screaming or shooting. As far as I could tell, the situation was under control, and everyone was keeping things impressively quiet. Probably to avoid creating a mass panic.

Still, I didn't want to take any chances. Not as long as our assailants could still be lying in wait.

Heart thumping, I strode toward the rear exit with Leo on my heels. A uniformed cop was positioned there, and held up a hand.

I showed him my badge. "I've got the witness in my custody, and I'm taking him around the back to meet his escort at the hotel's main entrance. Radio ahead to Deputy Marshal Scott that I'm on my way to his location."

The cop blinked, stunned by the order. He looked at me, at Leo, at the gun in my hand, and the badge in my other.

"*Now!*" I snarled.

The cop moved aside. As he started to radio Scott, we hurried past him, and I stuck with my original plan— heading for a side entrance. Once we were clear of our location and I was sure Leo was safe, I'd make contact, but for now, I had to assume we were still in enemy crosshairs.

I fought the urge to sprint, and we quickly walked up the sidewalk and away from the hotel. As we merged into the crowd of pedestrians, I scanned our surroundings, searching for anyone who might be too interested in us.

There were dozens of parked cars along the street, not to mention two parking garages in sight, but I ignored them. Stealing a car would be too risky and too conspicuous. Most modern cars couldn't be easily hotwired anyway. I also didn't know this city as well as a local. One wrong turn, and we were stuck behind a construction snarl. Or worse, on a one-way street.

CARI Z & L.A. WITT

If we stood a chance at getting out of here without getting cornered, our best bet was a driver who knew the roads and wouldn't draw attention by driving erratically.

Half a block later, I found a cab idling on the curb. His light was off, so he was probably waiting for someone, but I slapped my badge against the window. He blinked, then nodded, and the backseat locks popped.

Leo and I slid in, and I ordered, "Get us out of downtown."

"Uh, where—"

"Just out of downtown. I'll let you know where to go from there."

The driver jerked the wheel and pulled into traffic. He narrowly missed a minivan, and the driver laid on the horn to let him know how pissed she was.

He ignored her and slammed on the gas. I had no idea where we were going after this. Some place we could lay low. Once we were safely hidden away, I'd get in touch with the Marshal Service and let them know where we were. And then…fuck. I had no idea. Our witness's location had already been compromised once. There was no reason to believe it couldn't happen again.

I pressed my elbow against the window and rubbed my eyes.

"*Join the U.S. Marshals,*" they said.

"*It'll be fun,*" they said.

Chapter Two
Leo

Fuck the U.S. Marshals.

No, first fuck the goddamn D.A., who had smug, careless asshole written all over him from fifty feet away, *then* fuck the FBI for sending agents Tweedle-Dee and Tweedle-Dum to play escort, because those guys didn't have a relaxed bone in their bodies. Seriously, I had never worked so hard to get anyone to say so little, and I'd been raised by the mob. Nothing but, "We can't tell you that, Mr. Nicolosi," or "We don't know the answer to that, Mr. Nicolosi," or my personal favorite, "That would be inappropriate, Mr. Nicolosi." From my perspective, my situation couldn't *get* any more inappropriate than giving up the Grimaldis to the Feds. Calling me by my first name was the least they could do.

And finally, *finally*, fuck the U.S. Marshals for giving me the idea, brief though it was, that they were competent at their jobs before walking me into a firefight. I knew my own people were going to be gunning for me, and I didn't hold it against them—that was how the game went. What I *hadn't* been expecting was for them to have gotten to the Marshals so fast. Someone with a lot of influence on the shiny side of the law had just taken out some of his own guys to get at me.

Part of me wanted to dwell on the sound of gunfire, and the smell of the blood that had sprayed from my first babysitter's neck as he went down in front of me. I shook it off. I'd seen worse. I almost felt guilty for stealing the guy's phone as he went down, but he wasn't gonna need it anymore. I'd already taken the battery out—there was no safe way to use a fed's phone, not right now, not when I had no idea who I could trust. But it might come in handy later.

First things first, though. I had to figure out how to get some distance from that shit show with my new babysitter. Marshal Rich Cody, not Richie, was tall, dark-haired, and handsome, with freckles scattered across the bridge of his nose. He must've been in his mid-thirties or so, and he had the kind of lips that naturally wanted to fall into a pout, and bright hazel eyes that were hard to look away from. The only thing I was almost sure of—apart from the fact that the guy sitting next to me was definitely the hottest marshal on offer—was that he probably wasn't working with whoever had just tried to kill me. Faint comfort, but I could work with it. First I had to stop him from being an idiot, though.

"You should dismantle your phone. And your radio."

He glanced at me with a little frown, almost like he'd forgotten I was there. Angry was a good look for him; he was just rugged enough to come off as "intense" instead of "constipated." "Why?"

"So we can't be tracked." Of course we were already being tracked—this city was full of cameras and the driver could already positively ID us, thanks to Mr. "I'm commandeering this cab in the name of the law" here, but there was no sense in making it easier than it had to be.

"I need to be able to get in touch with my superiors."

"You don't really believe that." I knew that much, at least. "Otherwise you would have been honest with them back there, not sent them running in another direction."

"That was just to get you out of the line of fire," he said testily. "It won't take them long to clean up the mess. Once the Marshals have taken care of whoever Grimaldi sent after you, they'll contact me and arrange for a new safehouse."

What the…what? "Wait. You think whoever was in that elevator was sent by the Grimaldis? And they just, like, *intuited* where and when the best time to go after me would be?"

"You were probably followed from the courthouse."

"Then why not come after me sooner instead of letting us all sit in a room for three hours with nothing to do but listen to your buddy digest his lunch?"

Rich shook his head. "The room was a fairly fortified position. You're more vulnerable when you're in transit. They probably had someone watching us to see when we started to move."

"How'd they get past the other marshals, then?"

"How did *we* do it?" Rich countered. "I hate to say it, but that hotel wasn't exactly an airtight security situation."

"That's just my point! You guys do this all the time, right? You know how to move a witness safely, and your boss, at least, seemed pretty competent." That was the guy who'd told us to run, Greg-something. Rich's expression darkened, and I hurried on to make my point. "You really think a bunch of Grimaldi soldiers are gonna be discreet enough to make it past a group of trained marshals? Especially ones guarding me?" I smirked, because it was better than grabbing the guy's suit lapel to try and shake some sense into him. "I don't know if you know this, but I'm kind of a big deal."

His jaw clenched, and I could almost see him rein in the urge to grab *my* collar and shake me. "You'd better be a big enough deal to be worth the bloodshed."

"I'm gonna be." And I was. If I survived long enough, I'd make sure of that. "But first you've got to make sure we don't get tracked by the wrong people, and right now I don't think either of us knows who the wrong people are. Just—c'mon." I laid a hand on his forearm. "Turn them off. Just for now."

Rich stared at me for a long moment, inscrutable, searching for—what, the truth? A glimmer of honesty? Ha, he could keep on looking. I'd learned to hide everything I felt at the age of eight, and no "I'm not a rookie" marshal was gonna break my winning streak. All he needed to see was earnestness and confidence, and I projected those in spades. A moment later, he nodded. He took the battery out of his phone and shut off the radio, then looked at me again.

"I assume you turned yours off too."

I frowned. "What?"

"The phone you stole from Holloway. You turned it off, right?"

"I—yeah." There was no point in bluffing with an empty hand. But it had been so frantic in that hallway, and he'd been so focused on getting me out—how had he known? When had I given it away? "It's off."

"Good. Give it to me."

I shook my head. "I need a phone."

"Not his. Give it to me."

"I'm telling you, I *need*—"

"His phone is full of pictures of his wife and his new baby girl, and if you think I'm going to let you have access to those, you can think again. Give. It. To. Me." *Or I'll take it from you*, his subtext read loud and clear.

I was a more-than-decent scrapper, but Rich had probably thirty pounds of muscle and four inches on me. He hadn't let himself go, like so many of the neighborhood cops did once they settled into their roles. Even the FBI agents escorting me to the hotel had been on the flabby side, clearly more used to chasing down white-collar bullshit than running after criminals. Rich Cody had the kind of hard edges that his suit couldn't hide all the way, easy to see in his wrists and neck and the sharp line of his jaw. This was a guy who didn't just train because he had to, he did it because he was *driven* to. He kind of reminded me of—

"Fine." I coughed to clear my throat as I reached into the inside pocket of my hoodie and pulled out the marshal's phone. "But I'm going to need to use one within the next two hours. Preferably a new one." Any Walmart would have some for cheap.

"Why?"

"Because if I don't get in touch with my server, it's going to release all of the data that I'm currently holding back and make a lot of mafiosos and lawyers and federal agents really angry." That was key to my deal, actually, the cherry on top of my snitch sundae. I'd had to tell my handlers about it in order to make sure my safehouse-to-be had WiFi so I could log in regularly and keep the data from releasing prematurely and scaring everyone out of extradition range. I'd given the D.A. enough information to know that what I had was damning and that I was serious about testifying against my old keepers, the men who'd made my father, then broken him and sent him away to rot in prison.

No, I hadn't been planning my revenge since I was eight—that would be Machiavellian even for me. I'd settled into the role of good little soldier, second class citizen, someone who would never be pure enough to bring into the family, and that was…well, it had sucked, but it was the best offer I'd had. I'd been eight and completely alone, my mother fleeing back to Albania, my father locked away in a federal penitentiary for crimes he hadn't committed. Any attention had been better than none, and for over a decade, that had been enough. Five years on from that and I'd actually been happy with my life.

25

But then they'd murdered the one man I thought was untouchable, their prince, the Grimaldi family's best chance at creating a new empire in this new century. I could still hear his brother's laugh on the other side of the door.

Fucking Matteo. I was saving a special kind of hell for him, but first I needed to dismantle his safety net. It had to be done carefully. I didn't want to involve their sister, Gianna, in the mess.

Regardless, timing was everything. If my data got disseminated early, a lot of guys would go on the run. Matteo would probably hightail it back to Sicily before anyone could stop him, and he was the most important catch. The don might have ordered the hit, but he'd only done so after his most useless child had dripped poison in his ear. If my info leaked too soon and Matteo and his father got away, then I might as well kiss my ass goodbye, because the Feds would have no reason to help me anymore. Not that they'd done a great job of it so far, but that was a problem for another hour.

"We need a phone. And an ATM, so you can get out as much cash as you can. Different clothes," I added, because his G-man suit wasn't gonna help him blend into a crowd. "And fast, before they catch up to the cameras. And *food.*" I hadn't eaten since breakfast, which felt like days ago and had been nothing but a stale pop tart and a single cup of shitty coffee. "And a basic toolkit would be good."

"Why?"

"So I can get us a car."

"You are *not* going to steal a car. Not on my watch."

"Think of it like temporarily displacing a car, and yeah, I am. Unless you think it's a good idea to keep taking cabs." I gestured to the front seat, where the cabbie had thoughtfully turned the music up a while back to obscure what we were saying. Smart guy. *He* knew how to handle bloodstained fugitives. "Or maybe you prefer to Uber, Richie."

"Rich," he corrected automatically. He looked away, and it wasn't hard to see the tension he was feeling. It manifested in the corners of his mouth and the fine lines around his pale eyes. "Fine. Drop us at the nearest Walmart," he said to the cabbie, who nodded his understanding. Then he looked back at me. "If you try to run—"

"Whoa, I didn't say anything about running, why would I try to run?" Why take off from the *only* guy I could be reasonably sure wasn't trying to get me killed? If I cut out altogether, then that was it—my deal would be done, null, over. I'd never get the law on my side again, and I fucking hated it, but I *needed* them. The Grimaldi family had over two hundred soldiers on the streets, guys just waiting for their chance to prove their mettle and get made. I'd never make it through all of them on my own. If I could have, I would never have contacted the fucking D.A. in the first place.

"Uh-huh." He continued like I hadn't even interrupted. "If you try to run, I will hunt you down and cuff you to me. If you try to run a second time, I'll shoot you in the leg, *then* cuff you to me. Got it?"

"Yeah." It didn't get much clearer than that. I knew violence—boy, did I ever know violence. I was the nephew of one of the most notorious Albanian hitmen in modern history, and before the Italians had subdued that side of my family, I'd learned a lot from the guy. I knew violence, and I knew how to gauge a bluff, how to look for tells. All I got from Rich was cool, solid determination. He'd do it.

I could respect that. "Got it, Richie."

"I'll shoot you if you call me Richie one more time, too."

27

"Ah, now that I don't believe. But out of deference to your mother and her provenance over your nickname, I'll restrain myself."

He actually looked a little amused now. "Deference to my mom, but not to me?"

"Mothers are special. You should always be nice to people's mothers." The cab pulled to a stop and I got out as soon as I could. "You got cash?"

"Nope, just cards."

"Shit. We'll have to move fast, then." If the Feds knew Rich had me, then they'd already be monitoring his credit card transactions. "C'mon. Pay the man and let's go."

The nicest thing about Walmart was that, even undeniably bloodstained and bedraggled as we were, we didn't really attract any special attention there. You had to look exceptionally shitty to get a second glance in a place like this, but I still kept my hood up as we headed for menswear. "Casual clothes," I murmured.

"All they carry are casual clothes." Rich glanced at me. "You need anything?"

"Nah, I'm fine in these." And if I could clear a path to one of *my* safehouses, I'd have more than enough supplies on hand once we got there.

He grabbed some T-shirts, a hoodie pretty similar to mine, and a pair of jeans.

"How about a ball cap? Or a…whatever the fuck this thing is," I suggested, picking up a dank-ugly, pseudo-camouflaged thingamajig. Jesus Christ, people put these on their heads? Why, to draw attention away from their faces?

He took it away from me. "Next?"

Next up was a ten-dollar toolkit, which I hoped would be robust enough for what I needed, then a cheapo burner phone that was *exactly* what I needed. A few sandwich fixings and bags of jerky later, and we were ready to check out. Rich got a couple hundred dollars from an ATM, and we headed into the parking lot.

I scanned the parked cars, looking for a gem. I needed something mid-nineties or older, preferably a Civic, I was good with those, but I'd take—

"The Camry," I said, heading for the back of the lot. It looked like a '95, which was practically ideal. There weren't a lot of people this far back to watch us break in, and lucky me—the windows were partially rolled down. Getting in was a breeze. Actually jumping it…

Shockingly, it wasn't as simple as just jamming a flathead into the ignition and turning. That was a good way to break cheap tools, and I had the feeling that our time here was limited. I took off the cover of the steering column and threw it in the backseat, then pulled out the battery wires. I connected the ignition wire, then very carefully stripped the starter wire and sparked it against the others. The engine turned over, and I revved it with a sense of satisfaction. "Yesss."

"Nice," Rich commented. He'd partially changed while I was working—it was kind of weird not seeing him in his dark, crisp suit jacket. "Now move over."

"What?"

"I'm driving."

"I started the car!"

"And I'm the one that's going to drive it, so move over or get in the backseat."

We didn't really have time to argue, and the backseat smelled like someone had left a small mammal to die back there. "Fine." I slid over into the passenger side and glanced out the open window. What I saw had my hand clenching on the door handle. "We've got company."

To Rich's credit, he said "Where?" instead of wasting time asking if I was sure.

"Turning in on the west side of the parking lot." It was a G-man car if I'd ever seen one, a dark, bland SUV with tinted windows. It came to a stop right in front of the store, and two men in suits got out and ran inside, their hands on their holstered guns. Okay. We hadn't been made out here, at least, but *damn*, we'd only been inside for ten minutes. "We need to leave."

Rich's hands tightened on the worn steering wheel. "I know one of those guys."

"Know him or not, we can't *trust* him!" I needed to keep Rich focused, remind him why agreeing with me was the smart thing to do. "If that man isn't your brother—or hell, even if he *is*—we just don't know enough yet to make a smart decision. We can't reach out yet, not until we have more information." *Listen to me, believe me,* trust *me.* "That guy didn't end up bleeding beside you in that hotel hallway, Rich. Unless he's one of the people who did, we can't make any assumptions about his loyalty. The Grimaldi family has a lot of reach, and a lot of experience at figuring out where to push to make people help them. Just—please. Leave it for a little longer."

Finally he nodded, and I relaxed enough to breathe again. "All right." He pulled slowly out of the parking lot and into traffic. The guy behind the wheel of the SUV didn't even glance our way.

"We have to get away from the traffic cameras. Find some no-name motel that lets you pay by the hour and comes with WiFi." My bomb's timer was tick-tick-ticking away, and I needed to handle that before anything else.

And after that...well, we'd see how reasonable Mr. Marshal was feeling by then.

Chapter Three
Rich

Something had died in this car, and my reluctance to join it was the only thing that kept me from ditching the battered old Camry and trying for another vehicle. Regardless of the festering smell, Leo was right. We had to keep moving.

Windows down, air conditioner blasting, I casually cruised along the freeway in the thickening afternoon commute. The plan had been to move Leo to a long term safehouse before rush hour had a chance to box us in. Had everything gone smoothly, we'd have been out of Chicago before most of the normal law-abiding citizens had broken out of their daytime jail cells.

Now that everything had gone to shit, we were down to forty miles an hour in a car that smelled like death, and my passenger was getting increasingly squirrely as more traffic poured onto the clogging interstate. If there was a wreck and we had to slow down or stop, he'd probably have a coronary.

I didn't think I'd be far behind, especially as our forty mile-an-hour crawl slowed to thirty, then twenty, and finally that irritating trudge where it felt like we were speeding if the needle crept above fifteen. If only to keep from agitating him further, I concentrated hard on not fidgeting and not tapping my thumbs on the wheel. I even managed to avoid murmuring "come on, come on, *move*" at the SUV in front of us that seemed to think it was possible to maintain a safe following distance in the middle of gridlock.

Under the surface, I was an anxiety-riddled mess. I'd been to combat before. I knew what it was like to be shot at. I knew what it was like to watch a friend get dropped by a bullet right in front of me. Having to make snap decisions that could kill myself and my brothers? Been there, done that, had the undiagnosed PTSD I didn't tell anyone about because my dad had said it might disqualify me from this job that I suddenly wasn't so sure I wanted after all.

The part I didn't know how to deal with was taking fire from guys who were supposed to be on my side. Accidental friendly fire was one thing. Having your own men turn on you? What the fuck?

I told myself the assailants might just be Grimaldi operatives. I didn't want to accept the alternative, but the more I thought about it, the higher the bile rose in my throat and the faster my heart pounded. This had to be at least partially an inside job. I didn't want to believe it, but there was no way around it. Marshals were tight. We knew each other. We trusted each other. It was impossible for some slippery-ass Mafioso to casually slide into the ranks and be a part of the kind of high security detail we'd been on today. There sure as shit wasn't any way multiple Mafiosos could infiltrate an op like this, least of all in the time since Leo had turned state's evidence. At some level, marshals *had* to be involved.

Fuck. This was bad. Real bad. Like *how the fuck do I get us out of this* bad. This was worse than being pinned down and outgunned by insurgents in a desert firefight with three wounded Marines and no way to radio for help because this time I couldn't be sure one of my fellow Marines wouldn't turn his gun on us and—

"Hey, you want to take it easy?" The sarcasm almost covered the borderline hysteria in Leo's voice, and snapped me back into the present.

I eased off the gas, backing down from the SUV's bumper as the driver flipped me off. I loosened my grip on the sweat-slicked steering wheel and squirmed in my damp shirt as I took a few slow breaths to bring my heart rate down. The tunnel vision gradually widened until I had enough peripheral vision to see my passenger white-knuckling the armrest.

He cleared his throat. "Uh, you okay?"

"Yeah. Sorry." I wiped one hand on my pant leg. Then the other. They were shaking. Hopefully he didn't notice.

Leo was quiet for a long moment, but I could feel him watching me. The scrutiny did nothing to help me bring myself back down. Finally, he said, "There's a McDonald's coming up off the next exit. Maybe we stop there?"

I glanced at him. "You hungry?" The thought of food made me want to gag.

"Yes, actually. The 'B' in FBI is apparently for 'breakfast only', because they sure as shit didn't give me anything else."

"Then eat some of the stuff we got at Walmart."

He huffed like I was the biggest moron on the planet. "*Also* I can use their WiFi to tag in and keep my server from unloading everything."

"Fair enough." I started making my way across four lanes to the right so I could take the upcoming exit. Admittedly, it wasn't a bad idea. Maybe an ice-cold drink would help me pull myself together. Some of my buddies had said it helped them focus when they felt a flashback coming on. In fact, that was how one sergeant wound up becoming an alcoholic—he'd grab an ice-cold beer to keep himself in the present, and then he'd drink it just because it was there. Didn't take long before he came to the conclusion that just having a cold beer in hand all the time would help keep the demons away.

I shook myself and focused on the road. The ramp was coming up. In fact, if I went off on the shoulder and gunned the engine, I could whizz past the last four or five cars and be off this fucking freeway.

Except it would be just my luck that a cop would see me do it. Or one of the cars would decide to block my progress and maybe even hit me. No, I'd wait until the crawl got us close enough to actually take the ramp like a civilized driver. Even if it killed me.

A solid ten minutes later, I pulled into the parking lot beneath the Golden Arches. I didn't like the looks of the place. The parking lot had an entrance and an exit, either of which could be blocked without much effort. The restaurant itself was like a little island of colorful lights and plastic—visible from any number of spots that could be used as sniper perches. Some of those potential perches were so ironic they were almost funny. Just what I needed—the official report to show that I'd been picked off at a McDonald's from the Burger King across the street.

The building had two entrances that I could see, and likely one in the back. From the counter where we waited to order, I could keep an eye on those two entrances, but I couldn't see past the kitchen or around to the other side of the restaurant where there might be one more. I could also only see half of the parking lot. The entrance to the lot and drive-thru weren't visible.

My neck prickled. Maybe we should've used the drive-thru. Except no! That was Evasive Driving 101. Drive-thru lanes were one of the quickest places we could get boxed in, and I didn't trust that rickety Camry to get us over the curb if we needed to make an escape. Assuming we even had that much room to maneuver. One of those big SUVs right up next to us would keep us pinned down.

We should've kept driving. Shouldn't have stopped. The gridlock was only going to get worse, and every minute we were down here was sixty new opportunities for a wreck to happen and stop traffic for hours on end. But Leo needed the WiFi. And we did need to eat. And we'd been alone long enough—

Long enough we should've maintained our lead instead of giving anyone a chance to catch up with us, which we'd now handed them on a silver platter. Or at least a plastic McDonald's tray. What were we thinking? What were we doing? How the fuck were we going to get out of this restaurant and out of this town and then where the fuck did we go an—

My stomach lurched and my mouth watered in that telltale way that sent panic through me. Without a second thought, I darted out of line and straight for the men's room.

When nothing more would come up, I stayed still. On my knees on the dirty tile, I closed my eyes and rode out the dry heaves. Fuck. What was happening to me? I was *trained* for this.

Yeah, because boot camp absolutely told us how to handle it when your own goddamned men turned their guns on you.

Still. I knew what I was doing. WITSEC was nothing new. On the other hand, WITSEC during a massive episode of the PTSD no one knew about? Not something I was accustomed to.

When my stomach had settled down as much as it was going to, I spat one last time, flushed the toilet, and staggered out of the stall.

Leo leaned against the wall by the sinks, arms folded across his chest and legs crossed at the ankles like he was trying to look relaxed and maybe a bit bored. All he managed to pull off was annoyed. "You all right?"

I nodded, but my gut damn near found a second wind as I realized I'd *abandoned my witness* and left him out in the open. He could've been killed. Picked up by hostiles. Hell, he could've run.

At the sink, I cupped my hands under the water and rinsed the acid out of my mouth.

"If I'd known McDonald's bothered you this much," he mused flatly, "we could've gone to BK instead."

"Duly noted," I croaked without looking up.

"You going to be all right?"

Maybe if I stop fucking up at every turn.

"Yeah." I swished some more water in my mouth before spitting it into the sink. "We should get moving."

"We should. But before we do, you want to tell me what the fuck this is all about?"

"Not particularly." I splashed some water on my face, then turned off the faucet and reached for the paper towels.

Leo's reflection glared at me as I dried my face and hands. "Let me rephrase that—what the fuck is this all about?"

"Let's save story time until we're someplace safe." I tossed the paper towel in the trash and headed for the door. "We need to get out of—"

He grabbed my arm, stopping me dead. His grip was painfully tight, fingers digging in and finding bruises that hadn't been there this morning. "No. I have to rely on you, and I need to know I *can* rely on you. Which means I need to know you're not going to have another fucking breakdown out there on—"

"It wasn't a breakdown." I wrenched my arm loose and got right up in his face. "And in case you haven't noticed, there's only one way out of this bathroom, so unless you'd like to up the odds of someone cornering our asses in here, I would suggest we go. *Now.*"

His lips thinned. "Fine. But once we're settled in somewhere, you're gonna tell me what's wrong up here." He tapped his temple. "Got it?"

"Fine."

I opened the door enough to check our surroundings. So far it was all clear, but the restrooms were tucked in a little alcove at the back of the restaurant with almost zero visibility of everything else. We stepped into the alcove, and I swept the restaurant. All clear as far as I could tell. Nothing seemed out of sorts in the parking lot either.

There was, as I'd suspected, another door back here near the bathrooms, so we took that one. "Did you get anything to eat?" I asked as we strode toward the car.

"It can wait. I logged into my server. That was the important thing."

"Good."

Just before we reached the car, he stepped in front of me. "*I'm* driving."

"What? You don't—"

"I don't have fucking panic attacks while I'm driving. Now get in the passenger seat and let's go."

I wanted to argue, but I didn't like how exposed we were and how few escape routes we had. We needed to get moving before anyone caught up with us.

So I got in on the passenger side and tried not to let the smell of dead whatever make me throw up again.

After almost forty-five minutes of stop-and-go, traffic broke up enough for Leo to get the speedometer to fifty-five. The signs said we could go seventy, but it was still too congested for that.

Still, just being able to move faster settled some of my nerves. Minute by minute, the city faded behind us. The sun was getting lower too, and in another hour or so, we'd be able to move under cover of darkness.

The panic from earlier was gone. I was still terrified and had no idea how we'd ultimately get out of this, but my head wasn't so scattered. Training was beginning to push trauma aside, and my marshal brain kicked in, overpowering the war-battered Marine brain.

I cleared my throat, which had finally stopped burning. "We need to grab another car, then find a place to hunker down for the night."

Leo nodded. "We're far enough ahead we should have time to swap plates too."

"Good idea." I chewed the inside of my cheek. "There's a junction coming up. Take the eastbound highway. We'll stop at an ATM, get as much cash as we can, then take a car and head west. That should throw them off our trail."

"Maybe two ATMs." He glanced at me. "Your bank have a withdrawal limit?"

"Yeah, but I have multiple accounts." I paused. "So we stop at the first ATM we find, then at the next one down the highway. That should tell anyone who's watching that we're heading east. Double back and go west in a different car, and we should be able to find some place to sleep."

He nodded again, but didn't speak.

Some of the tightness in my chest eased. I was thinking again. I felt less brittle and more like a competent U.S. Marshal.

Leo followed the intersecting highway east, and after three exits, took an off ramp. At a local credit union's walk-up ATM, I took the biggest cash advance I could from a credit card, and left the receipt hanging from the dispenser. Then we got back on the highway, and two miles down, pulled off again.

There were a couple of banks and several stores that probably had ATMs, but he kept driving toward a cluster of hotels. They were chain hotels—a Howard Johnson, a Comfort Inn, and a La Quinta—surrounded by fast food joints and a couple of convenience stores.

"I have an idea," he said. "But we'll have to split up for a few minutes."

I shot him a sidelong look. As much as I didn't like the idea of separating, he was obviously intelligent and didn't seem inclined to take off. "Okay?"

He put on his signal, and as he turned into the 7-Eleven's parking lot, he said, "Go to that hotel across the street and book us a room. Use your real name, your real credit card, the works."

I watched him dubiously.

Leo huffed. "Look, as far as anyone knows, you still think your guys are on the up and up. Anyone would take off and lay low until the bullets stop flying, but they have no way of knowing if you're actually on the run, or just keeping your head down. If they see you using your real info, that'll send the message that you're *not* going off grid."

"So they'll think I haven't caught on that they're dirty."

"Exactly."

"Assuming they don't think you're holding me hostage and forcing me to use my accounts."

Leo shrugged. "Either way, it won't tip them off that you know something's up."

I was still uneasy, but didn't argue. Though I wasn't convinced this was a good idea, I didn't exactly have any *better* ones to offer. U.S. Marshal training was woefully lacking on how to elude the U.S. goddamned Marshals.

Parked alongside the 7-Eleven, he killed the engine. "There's an ATM inside, so I'll go in and get cash from one of my accounts."

"Aren't your cards frozen? And didn't you surrender them when we took you into WITSEC?"

He smirked. "Not all of them."

Damn. He was good at this. "Does, um, anyone know about that shit you have to tag in with? The information that will be released if you don't check in?"

The smirk faltered. "Uh. Yeah. They, um." He cleared his throat, shifting his gaze to the dashboard. "I might have threatened a few people with that before everything went to shit."

"Of course you did," I muttered. "All right. So, hotel and 7-Eleven. And when the cavalry comes…?"

"We'll be long gone in another car, heading westbound like you said."

"You think we'll find another car that's old enough to hotwire?"

"Nope." He grinned. "We're going to rent one."

I blinked. "You're joking."

"I'm not."

I shook my head. "Most rental cars have LoJack trackers. And—"

"Rich." His expression turned serious. "You trust me?"

"I don't know you from Adam, but we don't have a choice except to trust each other."

"Exactly. So." He nodded toward the hotel. "Go in. Rent a room. Chat with the desk clerk and drop details about where we're going. Look agitated and ask at least two or three times about the best way to get to the airport or something." He paused, probably seeing the disbelief in my expression. "Trust me. It'll work."

I studied him, then shook my head and laughed. "I think between the two of us, the wrong guy is working in WITSEC."

"Pretty sure they wouldn't hire me with my rap sheet." He unbuckled his seatbelt. "Now let's get moving."

My pride wanted to be a bit bruised over the fact that my witness was taking charge and seemed to have a better plan than I'd thought up. There'd be time to stroke my ego later, though. We still needed to get the hell out of town.

While he went into the 7-Eleven, I walked across the street to the Comfort Inn. Acting agitated didn't take much "acting;" I just didn't fight the jittery anxiety still hanging on from earlier. Shifting my weight. Wiping my sweaty palms on my sleeves and pant legs. Glancing over my shoulder. Checking my watch.

The clerk noticed, too. She watched me warily in between checking in a middle-aged couple surrounded by suitcases. When they were through, I stepped up to the counter, and she still managed to look uneasy even as she smiled. "Can I help you, sir?"

"Yeah, I, uh…" I glanced over my shoulder for effect, and then lowered my voice. "I need a room for the night."

"One person?"

I swallowed. "Two." I took out my wallet, praying like hell Leo really did have a solid plan, and handed her my driver's license and credit card. As she entered my information, I dropped my voice even further. "By the way, how long does it take to get from here to Indiana?" Screw the airport—I wanted to give the impression we were heading *way* the hell out of here.

"Couple, maybe three hours depending on traffic."

I fidgeted. "Any shortcuts? Faster ways in case there *is* traffic?"

She glanced up at me, eyes narrow like she was buying my act. "Not really, no."

"Fine. Fine." I waved a hand. "Do you know if it makes more sense to take I-90 or I-30 if I'm heading on to Ohio?"

She pursed her lips and seemed to give it some thought. "Either way, I guess."

"And where's the nearest place to rent a car?"

She gestured at the road outside, and pointed to the left. "There's an Avis about half a mile that way. You can't miss it."

"Perfect. Thanks."

She continued processing everything. Just as I'd hoped, she even photocopied my driver's license.

Once we were finished, she gave me the room keys, and I headed outside to meet Leo. He was already on his way back from the 7-Eleven, a plastic bag in hand.

"How'd it go?" he asked.

I held up the room keys. "How about on your end?"

"Without a hitch. And the guy told me there's an Avis—"

"Half a mile up the road."

He blinked, then grinned. "Good. You asked too." He nodded toward the road. "Isn't too far to walk, is it?"

"Not at all." We grabbed our things out of the Camry, and as we started walking, I nodded toward the 7-Eleven bag. "What's in the bag?"

"Duct tape and a pack of Red Vines."

I eyed him. "Do I even want to know what they're for?"

He shrugged. "I was hungry."

"The duct tape, Leo."

"You'll see."

At the Avis, we went through the same motions I had at the hotel. Real names, real credit cards, real everything, plus some comments about the best way to get to Ohio via Indiana. If anyone wanted to find where we'd been, they wouldn't have to look hard. The plan was imperfect, and acting anxious turned out to be much easier when I was getting seriously anxious for real. Depending on how closely our cards were being monitored, the Marshals or the Grimaldis could descend on us in no time. We needed to be burning rubber toward Iowa—or anywhere other than Indiana or Ohio—like *now*.

But Leo wasn't done yet. As we got into the rental car—a newer model silver Volkswagen that was generic enough not to stand out *and* didn't smell like an overheated corpse—he told me to drive over to the movie theater we'd passed on our walk to the Avis.

Impatience and anxiety both conspired to make my heart thunder and my stomach try to lurch. "For *what?*"

"License plates." He started working at the barcode sticker on the passenger window.

"What's the point? The rental agency will tell the cops what car to be looking for, and—"

"And there's eleventy billion of these on the road. The cops won't pull over every single generic gray VW—they'll just compare the plates, and when they do, they'll move along because it won't be the droid they're looking for." He paused, shooting me a look. "Come on. We need to get going."

I swore under my breath and drove over to the theater. The theater parking lot was packed with cars, and there was what appeared to be spillover parking in front of an abandoned box store next door. While the theater lot was brightly lit, this one was dark, and when I parked and killed the lights, the whole place seemed eerily devoid of life.

"I checked the movie times while I was in the 7-Eleven." He craned his neck to look at the theater. "Five screens just started, and two showings get out in the next twenty minutes. That's our window." He handed me a screwdriver from the toolkit, which he'd grabbed from the Camry. "Swap out plates. You know the drill."

I scanned the lot. It was dark enough and there was no one around, it wouldn't take much to grab a couple of plates without being seen. I turned back to Leo. "All right. You going to help?"

"No." He took out a smaller screwdriver, and then fished around in the 7-Eleven bag for the duct tape. "I'm going to get the LoJack out of this car so they don't chase us down after we fail to turn in the car tomorrow."

We both worked fast. Criminal or not, I had to admit I was impressed at how deftly he relived the Volkswagen of its LoJack tracker and duct-taped it under the bumper of a nearby Jeep. And he did it in the time it took me to swap plates with a nearby sedan. Long before one of those two showings ended, we were on our way out of the parking lot with a couple of Nebraska plates, and a few minutes later, we were heading west while our paper trail—and strategically placed witnesses—very emphatically pointed east.

It wasn't a great plan. Hell, it wasn't much of one at all. But it would buy us a little time, confuse the people on our tail, and let us put some distance between us and whoever they were. Hopefully it gave us enough time and distance to stop, catch our breath, and come up with an actual strategy, but for the moment, I'd take what I could get. I didn't know what we were up against, how close behind us—or worse, how far ahead of us—they might actually be. I didn't know what the fuck kind of plan we needed, never mind could pull off without getting ourselves killed. This was so far out of my wheelhouse, it wasn't even funny.

Where was this *shit in all those training simulations?*

"All right." Leo tore into the bag of Red Vines. "So what's our next move?"

I exhaled, drumming my thumbs on the wheel. "We find a shitty little motel and stop for the night."

He offered me a Red Vine. I waved it away. My stomach was still questionable.

He bit off a piece of the candy. "What do we do tomorrow?"

I shook my head. "Don't know. I haven't gotten that far yet."

"We'll think of something."

Silently, I nodded. And I hoped like hell he was right.

Chapter Four
Leo

There was nothing worse than being presented with an opportunity and not knowing what to do with it.

The difference between dreamers and dealmakers, Tony had liked to say, was that dreamers only *thought* about what they'd do if the chance of a lifetime dropped into their lap. Dealmakers took that chance, stitched it into their souls and fucking *ran* with it. Things might backfire, but the more willing you were to take a chance, the more opportunities came your way.

Tony had been good with people in a way I'd never managed. He'd been raised in the court of public opinion, presenting himself as a reformed Mafioso's prize child to everyone outside the family, and as a badass operator more than happy to mete out old-school justice to everyone else. He'd walked that line like a boss, and I'd been in awe of his skills.

I'd told him that once, in a rare moment of pure honesty, and Tony had laughed and ruffled my hair.

"Don't worry, kid," he'd said with a grin. "You stick with me and you'll learn it all."

So much for that.

The thing was, it was clear that Rich had issues. Possibly he had very bad, very intense issues that might end up having fatal consequences for me, and fatality was to be avoided at all costs. I wasn't really afraid to die—being taken out to an abandoned parking lot at the age of fourteen, put in a bulletproof vest, and shot over and over until my torso was the color of an eggplant had cured me of that intrinsic fear. Fear of not accomplishing my goals, though, that was real. Revenge was the most important thing left in my life, and failure wasn't an option. To avoid failure, I had to survive. The question was, would I be better off with Rich at this point, or without him?

I was pretty sure he wasn't going to turn on me. That was good, a point in his favor. He was a marshal, a law-enforcement officer, and like it or not I'd have to deal with those *stronzos* if I wanted to put the Grimaldis away for good. Why get rid of my only reliable key back into that world, especially when he was at least partially inclined to listen to me and take my advice?

Because he might be batshit crazy, that was why. I knew PTSD when I saw it—plenty of the old guard made a regular practice of self-medicating with drugs and booze, and the longer you stuck with the trade, and the more you saw, the more that made sense. What was the old saying? There were old mafiosos and bold mafiosos, and the bold ones ended up becoming nightmare fodder for the old ones. Or something like that.

The unspoken rule was, unless you were particular friends with the person suffering, you didn't bring it up. Didn't say shit, didn't do shit, let them handle themselves until they put you in danger. If that happened, then you blessed them with a bullet to the back of the head and took all their troubles away. Nobody got through the life without developing issues, and it was hypocritical of me to pretend otherwise, but this—I needed a guy who could drive down the fucking highway without freaking out, and judging from what I'd seen so far, Rich wasn't that guy.

Ah, well. I'd have to do some digging when we got to the motel. Rich talked a big game about shooting me and pulling out the cuffs, but I was willing to bet I could slip him fairly easily. Then it would be just me and whatever I could pull off on my own before I went back to the Feds and…and walked into another fucking inside job, this time without having any idea of who was on my side or not? Did I take the chance to get away from Rich while he was still kind of fucked up from his episode, or did I stick with him and take my chances on his sanity holding long enough to be of use to me?

God fucking damn it. See? Opportunity knocked, and I didn't know whether to open the door or fire a bullet through the peephole.

I snapped out of my contemplations as the engine abruptly shut off. "We're here."

"Here" was a roadside motel with half the fluorescent lighting in the sign burnt out, turning what would have been *Come On Inn* into *Com In*. I was just juvenile enough to snicker at that. "Nice."

"It looks like the kind of place that won't ask for ID if you're willing to pay double."

"Even better. I'll get our stuff together if you get a room."

"All two bags of stuff."

I stuffed the last Red Vine in my mouth. "Nah, we're down to one now."

Rich looked at me with a slight twist to his lips, like he was trying to keep from vomiting again. "How can you finish all those things after everything else you've eaten in the past few hours?"

I shrugged. "I have a high metabolism, and probably a third of my teeth are fake at this point. The sugar's not gonna make them any worse." That was what happened when you *literally* got your teeth kicked in by someone farther up the food chain. One of the mob's selling points—they knew some damn good dentists. "Go get us a room. I still promise not to run." And damn it, I meant it. Fine. If that was the direction I was going, then we really *were* going to have to talk, because there was shit I needed to know about Rich if this was going to work.

We both got out of the car and he headed inside to the office while I leaned against the hood and checked for coverage. That was the problem with burner phones— shitty access. The sooner I could get someplace that had some decent equipment stashed, the better. But where to go? Each of my spots had their selling points, but they weren't without weaknesses either. Some we'd have to go back into the city to get access to, or end up taking a long and risky trip around on highways that were almost certainly going to be chock full of cops and cameras. Maybe it was better if we—

A key on a long wooden fob suddenly dangled in front of my face, jolting me. "Number Thirteen," Rich said.

I grimaced and hoisted the shopping bag full of our gear off the ground. "Lucky number thirteen. Great." I followed as he led the way to the very end of the row of rooms, where the bulb flickered over the dingy numbers. "This feels so teenage slasher fic."

"Stay out from under beds and inside closets and you should be fine," Rich said with an almost-smile, which made him look unfairly handsome. The lifestyle I'd grown up in kicked most of the pretty out of people by the time they hit thirty, but Rich still had it in spades, even if he'd gone through a rough patch. A surge of unwanted attraction made my hands clench, and I fought it down. That was the *last* thing I needed to deal with right now.

He opened the door and stood aside. I went in and, shit, the smell of bleach was almost overwhelming. On the other hand, I'd much rather smell bleach than any of the myriad filthy scents a place like this might have on offer. It had two beds, a fan, and a bulky television that looked like it came straight from the 90s. "Home sweet home."

"It could be worse."

"It so could." I took the bed farthest from the door, and watched Rich relax minutely. He felt better in a position where he could see and react faster, then. One tiny mystery down, a million yet to go. I waited for him to get comfortable—as comfortable as locking the door, ensuring the window was locked, and checking the bathroom could make him—before springing my first question on him. "Tell me what set you off on the highway."

Bam, the frown was back. "Nothing specific."

"Not good enough."

"It'll have to be."

I threw my hands up in the air. "I'm trying to make this easier for you! If you tell me what some of your triggers are, then I can work to avoid them, but I gotta know first. You say it's driving, then I will happily get behind the wheel. Enclosed spaces—fine, we'll keep the windows down. If it's—"

"It's nothing like that."

"Bullshit. People don't just lose it for nothing, Rich." I needed to get him off the defensive. Ease, familiarity—using his name might help. Or it might wind him even tighter, but no guts, no glory. "I help you, you help me. That's how this works."

Rich laughed. It sounded uglier than I'd expected, harsh and more than a little broken. "You? Help? You're a goddamn career criminal, a soldier for the Grimaldis. How in the world are you going to help me with anything?"

Fine, he wanted to play it that way? "Other than getting us cars and supplies? Other than keeping you from driving up some SUV's ass during rush hour? Other than not running the other way screaming when I found you puking your burger out in a fast food toilet stall?"

"It won't happen again."

"You don't *know* that."

"And you don't know that it will, so let it go."

I sighed and flopped back on the bed. Jesus fucking Christ, save me from strong and silent types. "I genuinely don't give a fuck what's going on in your head or why," I said, and it was almost true. Part of me—a small part—did want to know more, know some of the details of why and how this incredibly dedicated guy had ended up with shadows in his head. I could ignore that part of me for the greater good, though. "You don't want to give me details, that's fine. Just tell me what I can do to make our chances of success go up, because after all the shit I'm going through before trial has even *started*, I think I deserve to know."

"Why are you doing it?"

It was my turn to frown. "Doing what?"

"Going through all this shit." Rich sat down on the bed across from me and untucked his T-shirt, but didn't go any farther. Too bad—I'd pay money to see his bare chest. "Why turn on the Grimaldis in the first place?"

I chuckled. "You didn't get the full file on me, huh?"

"I had a file, but it didn't include all the whys, just the how."

Great. I was feeling so much better about the professionalism of our federal justice system. "I'd gone as far as I could in the organization, and for some people that was too far."

"But you were making them a lot of money."

Ah, so he had more than just the bare bones after all. "Yeah, but not in a way they liked. Computers and algorithms and online gambling, it was all a little too removed for the mob's delicate sensibilities. They like having a heavier, more localized hand."

Rich shook his head. "I don't buy it. Plenty of people run overseas gambling schemes, and shutting them down is a jurisdictional nightmare. That's not what the Grimaldis had a problem with."

50

Oh, fuck him. "It is, it really is." That and my ideas for how to invest their money once it was made, hoo-boy. They hadn't liked those one bit. "Not a lot of technological innovators in the Mafia."

"You're still not telling the truth."

"Pot, meet kettle." Still, trust went both ways. Maybe he'd give a little if I made it look like I was caving. Besides, nothing I intended to tell him was something he couldn't find online. "Look, I was never going to be family. My dad was a made man, but I'm half Albanian, and Dad's been in solitary confinement in a federal penitentiary for years now. I've never gotten much support from the don, and the one person who had my back was murdered by his own brother, so…yeah. Seemed like as good a time as any to make a fresh start."

"Who was murdered?"

I steeled myself internally. It didn't matter if he knew. "Antonio Grimaldi, the don's oldest son."

There was a bit of a reaction, a widening of eyes and slight drop in his jaw. If you knew about the family at all, you knew Antonio. He had been the public face, the gem, the turnaround story. He'd been too good to be true, but that had been part of his appeal. "Why would the don okay a hit on his own son? *Between* his children?"

"I don't know if he approved it or not, but Matteo didn't suffer any consequences for going after Antonio." The hatred that seethed like tar in my heart, thick and consuming, threatened to overwhelm me, but I beat it back and locked it down tight. "I was stuck there. No way to get any farther without a sponsor, and plenty of people who were suspicious enough of me that it wouldn't take much for them to convince the don to order a hit on me. I'm trash, compared to Tony. If they could get rid of him, then I didn't stand a chance."

"So you ran."

"So I made a deal," I corrected, because fuck him, if I'd wanted to run nobody would have ever found me again. "A deal that has the potential to take out the entire Grimaldi operation, and will, as long as we can find someone to trust on your side."

"About that." He took a deep breath, and I steeled myself. "I think I should call in."

"Absolutely not."

"There are people I *know* aren't a part of this that I can turn to."

"There's no such person."

Rich scowled at me. "My father is a marshal, I'm pretty damn sure I can trust *him*."

Red alert, red alert, tread carefully. "Maybe," I conceded, "but you have no idea who's with him right now. If I wanted to figure out where you'd gone, the first thing I'd do is get your dad under surveillance. You contact him, and whether he's on your side or not, any info you give him is immediately suspect."

"We can't just do nothing."

"We won't. I've got three different safehouses set up within a hundred miles, and they all have copies of my equipment. We get to one of those and I can do some digging."

"You have a way of spying on federal agents?" Huh, there was less anger and more interest than I'd expected in his tone.

"No, but I've got my fingers in every corner of the Grimaldis' finances. I haven't pulled any triggers yet because the D.A. told me my access was evidence, but I can track their financials without alerting anyone. We can see if they've made any suspicious payments to federal employees or their families."

"What makes you think your safehouses are going to be secure?"

"They might not all be, but I can check on their security before we move." I sighed. "I swear, I'm not fucking with you. I just want to give us the best chance possible of surviving this shit show."

Rich's eyes met mine, and I felt pinned to the bed by their conflicted intensity. He wanted to reach out to his team, I could see that, reach out to the people he relied on. He was *used* to being part of a team, probably had no reason to watch his back or sleep with one eye open, the way I'd grown up. I was asking him to betray all his sensibilities by going along with me on this.

"We'll see how it looks in the morning."

I exhaled softly, full of relief. "Okay. Okay, great, I'll check it then and if things look good, we'll move on. If they don't, we'll regroup. Yeah?"

"Something like that." He nodded toward the bathroom. "You can have the first shower."

"Thanks." I hightailed it to the tiny bathroom and locked the door behind me. Not because I thought Rich would try to get in, but because...I needed the distance right now. The *symbolic* distance, at least. I needed to be alone, to remember that I *was* alone in this, no matter how useful the marshal might be to me. He could turn into a liability just as fast as he'd become an asset, and I couldn't afford to forget that. I'd stick with him, for now. Trust him as far as I could throw him, which wasn't far. If he kept being amenable, then we might be able to pull this off.

If he lost his shit again...well, hopefully I'd have more chances to put some distance between us, if that was the case.

The water was clear and eventually hot, and the stall even had a little round sliver of soap left in the dish. I scrubbed up fast, then grabbed a scratchy grey towel and wiped myself down. An old nine-millimeter wound on my thigh, a peppery smatter of scars from a shotgun on my left shoulder, the thick ropey tissue on the top of my right index finger where Matteo had pressed his knife down to the bone...my body was a map of reasons to hate the Grimaldis. I didn't need to go into any more detail with Rich, not with all these marks speaking for me.

The truth about Tony wasn't for anyone else.

I put my T-shirt and boxers back on and headed back to the bedroom. Rich had turned the TV on and was watching the evening news. "Anything on us?"

"Not so far."

"They're keeping it quiet for a reason, then."

"Probably." He glanced at me. I felt the weight of his gaze roaming over my skinny, battered body like his hands—brisk, efficient, and unemotional. "You should sleep."

"That's the plan." Fuck, I was tired, too. Was it really just this morning that I'd been getting ready for my meeting with the D.A.? It felt like a week had passed between then and now. "You could go shower too," I offered as I slid between the stiff sheets. "You have to believe I'm not going to run away at this point."

"Maybe."

I didn't know what he was saying maybe to, and by now I was too tired to analyze it. My head hit the pillow and my body didn't care that the light was still on, the TV was still droning, and I'd almost gotten shot a few hours earlier. I was unconscious almost too fast to be surprised by how easily I was falling asleep in the company of a stranger.

Fuck it. I'd worry about it tomorrow.

Chapter Five
Rich

Sand. Sun. Screaming. Blood. Gunfire. Explosion.

A hallway.

A *hallway?*

Where the fuck was I? Corners. Too many—which way? Fuck. Where was the…why was I in full battle rattle in a hotel?

Gunfire. Take cover. Where? There *was* no cover. There was nowhere to—

Strong hands suddenly pinned me to the wall.

Fists. Feet. No way in hell were they taking me. Not again. Fighting like hell, I—

"Fuck!" A sharp pain in my shoulder made my eyes fly open. Something coarse burned against my chin, pulling my focus back into the present.

In light spilling in from outside, I could just barely make out the texture of cheap carpet. My chin stung. So did my cheekbone, though I didn't remember it hitting the floor.

CARI Z & L.A. WITT

Because I was on a floor. Facedown. Pinned with an arm twisted behind my back and a heavy weight on top of me. My bare torso felt like it was being eaten by ants thanks to being ground into the carpet.

No more sand. No more hotel.

Wait. It *was* a hotel. Not a hallway, but…

"You done?" A familiar voice growled in my ear.

I closed my eyes and tried to remember where I was and who I was with.

Leo.

I was still disoriented, my body still jittery with cold, electric panic coursing through me, but no one was shooting. All the breath left my lungs, and I nodded, forehead scraping the carpet.

The weight on my back eased up. A second later, the grip on my arm loosened. My wrist, elbow, and shoulder hurt like a motherfucker as I gingerly straightened them. Slowly, we both sat up. I leaned against one of the beds. He sat on the edge of the other, looking down at me. I assumed he was looking down at me, anyway. He was completely backlit, all of his features obscured by shadows. We were both breathing hard. I wondered if he was shaking, or if that was just me.

The clock between the beds showed 4:59. I almost wanted to laugh because of course it was 0500. My time in the Marine Corps had permanently set my body clock to snap me awake at 0500. The only variable was whether I woke up like a normal person, or jolted out of a nightmare into a cold sweat and a disoriented panic with old scars throbbing like the wounds were fresh. It was only by the grace of God I'd made it through my training for the Marshals without losing my shit like this. Then again, training had been a completely controlled environment. Everything had been scheduled and safe. Even the most hellish simulations, the ones that had felt utterly real, had been safe enough because I'd been pretty sure our instructors didn't actually want to kill us.

Turn me loose in the real world, though, with unknown variables and weapons firing live rounds, and…shit.

After a long silent moment, Leo leaned to the side, and I closed my eyes a second before he switched on the light. Then, slowly, I opened them again.

And that was when I noticed the blood trickling from his nose and one corner of his mouth. Fresh panic shot through me. "Oh shit. Your face. What did—"

"Yours doesn't look much better, compadre."

I dabbed at my mouth and nose, which were surprisingly tender. Sure enough, my fingers came away bloody. "Fuck." I started to get up, but he stopped me with a hand on my shoulder.

"Sit tight." He stood. "I'll grab us some towels."

He walked past me, and I rubbed my forehead with the heel of my hand. Christ, I was a wreck. How the hell was I supposed to keep my head in the game and get us out of our predicament when my past demons insisted that now was a good time for a brain party?

Leo reappeared a moment later, bare feet scuffing on the hard carpet, and dropped a towel in my lap. He took his seat on the bed again.

"What the hell happened?" And why was my throat raw? I swallowed, but it didn't help.

"You were freaking out," he said. "I tried to wake you up, and you came at me."

"Oh." Heat bloomed in my cheeks. I hated it when someone saw me during a nightmare. I should've warned him. Should've known the day we'd had would trigger something during the night. But then he'd have asked questions I was too embarrassed to answer, and I would have been too stupid to just suck it up and tell him. And I figured those questions were coming now anyway.

Neither of us said anything for a while, but it was only a matter of time. After we'd both mopped up some of the blood, and the bleeding had mostly stopped, he stared down at me with those intense eyes. "So now can we have a conversation about what the fuck happened to you?"

I focused on the angry red bloodstain on the towel in my hand. I didn't talk about this crap enough to have stock answers. None that wouldn't send me back down that gunpowder-scented rabbit hole.

Leo shifted, and the ancient bedsprings creaked under him. "When was your tour?"

My head snapped up. "What?"

"Had a hunch you'd been to combat." He gestured at my left arm. "And that's kind of a dead giveaway too."

I ran a hand over my ink as if that might wipe it away and kill the conversation. No, it wasn't subtle. The Globe and Anchor really *was* a dead giveaway. The SEMPER FI across the top…yeah. The five names, each with a pair of dates, were pretty obvious too. I supposed if I hadn't wanted this conversation, I should've worn a shirt to bed.

I swallowed, pretending my mouth didn't feel parched and sandy. "I did four tours."

Leo made a choked noise. "*Four*?"

Without looking at him, I nodded. "Couple into Iraq. One in Afghanistan. The fourth…" I laughed dryly. "I'd tell you, but then…" My humor faded as I trailed off. It was a joke I'd made a few times, and it was usually funny. Not now.

"But then you'd have to kill me," he finished, not sounding very amused.

I wiped my hand over my face. "Sorry."

"So you have PTSD this bad, and they let you work as a marshal?" His tone was unreadable. I couldn't tell if he was disgusted with the Marshals, felt sorry for me, or what.

I let my head fall back against the edge of the mattress. "The Marshals don't know about it."

"How could they not know about it? Don't they…" He flailed a hand. "*Screen* you assholes?"

Sighing, I nodded. "Turns out if you know how to answer their questions just right, you can fly under the radar." His eyebrow arched, and I shrugged. "What? It isn't like they can draw blood and say you tested positive for PTSD."

Leo rolled his eyes. "But why would you lie about it? If it would keep you from getting this job, maybe you shouldn't have the job?"

I glared at him. "Want me to call in my resignation now? Let them send someone else to stay with you?"

His teeth snapped shut and he returned my glare. "You know what I mean."

"Yeah, and I also know that the only one who had your back and survived is the combat-fucked-up deputy marshal who squeaked through the psych evals. Don't look a gift horse in the mouth."

"Maybe that gift horse could try not to clock *me* in the mouth, yeah?"

I winced. "How'd you learn to fight like that, anyway?"

Leo snorted. "You were asleep."

"Yeah, and I've tackled sleeping Marines in the middle of nightmares. That shit's for real."

Sobering, he watched himself playing with the bloody towel in his hands. "I was born into the Mafia. You don't stay alive if you don't know how to fight. Especially not when you're a half-breed."

Neither of us said anything for a while. I wasn't sure what there was to say at that point.

Then Leo pulled in a deep breath as he looked at the alarm clock. "We're already awake. Maybe we should hit the road."

Awake. Driving. Running. Fuck, the thought exhausted me all over again. The adrenaline crash from yesterday had been the only reason I'd slept at all, and now the adrenaline from my nightmare was crashing too.

"Fair warning," I said. "These, uh, flashbacks take a lot out of me."

His eyebrow arched. "How much?"

"Enough that I can function, but I'll be sluggish. Hungover, I guess. Unless I get a few more hours of sleep, but that's not going to happen."

"Okay. I'll drive."

A shower helped me feel closer to human and somewhere in the ballpark of awake. The strange clothes screwed with my equilibrium—I didn't feel like myself, and the farther I was from myself, the farther I was from getting my shit together.

It would have to do.

Oddly enough, the familiar weight of my shoulder and ankle holsters helped. That was a step closer to *me*. To Deputy Marshal Rich Cody, the guy I'd been twenty-four hours ago. I needed to be that guy now. Otherwise Leo and I would wind up like my friend and mentor, dead on the dirty floor of a hotel hallway in—

No. Don't think about that now.

I took a few deep breaths and sat down to put on my shoes. I could do this. I just wouldn't think about any of it. The only thing to think about was our next move, and right now, that was simply *move*. The longer we stayed in one place, the more danger we were in. We'd come up with a destination later. For now, just *go*.

I dropped the key off at the front desk while Leo put the bloody towels in the trash bin outside. They probably wouldn't have raised any eyebrows, but we'd agreed not to risk a maid getting alarmed and calling the cops. The rust-colored carpet masked any blood that had landed during our scuffle, and we'd somehow managed to keep any droplets from hitting the sheets or blankets.

With the evidence discarded and the key returned, we got into the rental, made a quick stop for coffee, and hit the road before daylight.

We were clear of the city now. It was mostly farm country out here, with occasional clusters of cookie-cutter suburbs. It was flat. Way too flat. Too open and exposed. I itched for mountains and their winding curves and nearly invisible side roads. If we could get to Wyoming or Colorado, and even into the foothills of the Rockies, I'd be able to breathe easier.

For now, it was just cornfields, wheat fields, and the occasional roadside motel where we'd stop and steal another car. By the time the sun came up, we were three cars and God knew how many miles into Iowa.

Most morning commuters probably hadn't even rolled out of bed yet, so aside from some scattered eighteen-wheelers and a handful of cars, we had the long strip of blacktop to ourselves. Leo set the cruise control at seventy-five, just five over the speed limit, and drove like anyone else on the road. Middle or right lane. Only getting into the left lane to pass someone who was going below the speed limit. Nothing aggressive. Always using his blinker. We went by two speed traps—bored-looking state patrols tucked into the bushes in the median—and they probably didn't even notice us.

As my heart rate settled down after the second speed trap, and I kept an eye on the Crown Vic in the side mirror, Leo turned on the radio. He flipped a couple of stations, then stopped on one that was probably a Top 40 station, but who the fuck knew because the deejays wouldn't shut up. Morning deejay banter made my teeth grind. I was tempted to tell him to turn it off, especially while one of the men droned on about some insanely boring story about something that happened while he was making his coffee.

I was about to reach for the button myself when the woman announced it was time for the news, and Leo's posture tensed almost imperceptibly. I watched him from the corner of my eye as she read the headlines. It was mostly the usual shit. Some celebrity scandal. The latest nonsense in Washington. Updates about some road construction that promised to snarl traffic for a while.

"In local news," she continued, "authorities say three members of the notorious Grimaldi clan may walk after a star witness was gunned down in a Chicago hotel yesterday afternoon along with several officers. The identity of the witness hasn't been released, but police have identified the gunman as Leotrim Nicolosi, the son of Pagolo Nicolosi, who is currently serving six consecutive life sentences for his work as a hitman."

My throat was suddenly too tight for air. Leo's knuckles whitened on the wheel. His lips pulled into a bleached line, and he glared at the road like he could threaten it into staying straight, flat, and clear until we were a thousand miles from here.

The reporter went on. "Nicolosi is said to be armed and dangerous, and traveling with an unknown man who may be an accomplice or a hostage. Anyone who knows of his whereabouts is advised to contact authorities, but do not approach. Photos of both men are available on our website. If you—"

Leo switched off the radio, which should have filled the car with merciless banter-free silence. Instead, the air was taut, thrumming with *oh shit* from both of us.

His voice was little more than a croak as he said, "They'll shoot me on sight."

"You're still too valuable to the case." It sounded lame. As if his role as key witness would operate like a bulletproof vest, and he'd be on his own without it.

Leo shook his head. "Look at me, Rich. You show a cop a picture of a guy who can pass for an Arab, and tell them he's a cop killer..." He swallowed hard. Then again. As if he were on the verge of hurling his coffee onto the steering wheel.

"You said yourself the Grimaldis know about the information you're threatening to leak," I said quietly. "If they're as deep into the Marshals as we think they are, they have to have a standing order to leave you alive."

"Maybe." Leo turned to me. "But we can't assume they've infiltrated the police forces. Especially not in every state we might pass through. If the Grimaldis or the Marshals catch up with me first? They'll make me shut down that account, and then they'll shoot me. If a cop catches me…" He trailed off. There was no need to spell it out.

And the shitty part was I didn't have anything to say that would make him feel better because I had a feeling he was right. His Italian and Albanian blood did give him a somewhat Middle Eastern appearance. A non-white cop killer? From a family of criminals? Who potentially had a federal agent as a hostage? That was a *"shoot first and ask questions later"* scenario.

Fuck. This was bad. Everyone at the D.A.'s office— not to mention marshals who were still clean—had to be shitting themselves over this, but the damage was done. Someone had told the media to look for someone matching Leo's description, and now Leo would be shot on sight if anyone caught up with us.

"What do we do?" He glanced at me, and the desperation in his eyes made him look almost childlike. He'd been scared before. Now he was creeping toward full-on panic.

I moistened my lips. "Do you trust me?"

Facing the road, he chewed his lip. Then, slowly, he nodded. "I don't have a choice."

"Okay. Look, I know it's risky, but we need to reach out."

"To who?" He was barely whispering.

I stared at the road like it might offer up an answer. He was right that my dad was probably under fifty layers of surveillance. My partner and mentor was dead. A badge didn't necessarily make someone trustworthy—not after yesterday—and cops were gunning for Leo's head now anyway.

And for that matter, if the Grimaldis truly had infiltrated the Marshals, there was no telling how many of them were in or how high up their tentacles reached. There were thousands of marshals, but I had no way of knowing who was and wasn't compromised—either in Grimaldi pockets or under Grimaldi surveillance. Of those who were compromised, it was impossible to guess if they'd been blackmailed, if lies had been spread about Leo, or if the family had been quietly worming their way up the ranks for years so they'd be in a position to track and eliminate witnesses. Literally all I knew was that I knew nothing.

So yeah, Rich—reach out to who?

Fuck. That…complicated things. I drummed my fingers on the armrest. There was no guarantee about anyone, but there were some people I'd trusted with my life before. If I couldn't trust them now, then we were fucked anyway, so what the hell? And maybe I couldn't make contact with anyone inside the Marshals, but there were people outside the department. People who I could safely bet were neither compromised nor monitored.

"Stop at the next gas station," I said. "I've got a friend who's off-grid and might be able to help."

Leo didn't protest.

The next gas station was twelve miles up, but it felt like a hundred before we finally pulled in under the yellow and red Shell sign. Leo stayed in the car, a baseball cap and sunglasses shielding him from anyone who might have checked the radio station's website for his photo and description. I topped off the tank, then went inside.

"Excuse me," I said to the girl at the counter. She couldn't have been older than twenty. "Is there a payphone somewhere?"

She blinked. "A what?"

I pursed my lips. *Really?* "A phone I can use. My battery's dead." I held up my cell, grimacing pitifully. "I just need to make a call."

She snapped her gum and pulled a portable handset out from under the counter. "This work?"

"Perfect. Thanks." I gave her a quick smile, then took the phone and stepped away. While I pretended to be interested in a display of sodas, I kept my back to the security camera in the corner and dialed the number from memory.

It rang four times, and I was about to start cursing when a gruff voice answered. "Yeah?"

"Oh thank God. Smitty, it's—"

"Chainsmoker? Holy shit, is that you?"

I almost smiled at the nickname I hadn't heard in ages. Almost. "Yeah, it's me. I need help."

Something moved in the background, like he was tensing or sitting up. "What's up?"

"It's a really long story. I'm working in WITSEC now, and my witness and I…" I glanced around in case anyone had wandered into the shop and might overhear me. "It's just a really long story. But we need to hunker down somewhere and lay low until we figure out who's trying to kill us."

"Whoa. That's some heavy shit. Where are you?"

"I think we're about two days from you. Maybe a day and a half if we gun it."

"You need me to meet you somewhere? Need backup?"

I closed my eyes and sighed, relieved that the only questions he was asking were about how he could help. "No, we'll get there. We'll be fine."

"You need anything? Ammo? Beer?"

I chuckled. "Ammo's good, and I could probably use something stronger than beer."

"What're you carrying?"

"Forty-five and a thirty-eight."

"Roger. Now get moving so nobody catches up with your ass."

"I will." I paused. "Look, man, I'm not gonna lie. I have no idea what I'm bringing to your door if these guys catch up with us."

He laughed. "Unless they've got the gear to nuke us from orbit, we'll be fine. Get your ass over here."

I smiled. "Thanks. I owe you."

"See you soon, brother." Then he hung up.

I gave myself two seconds for a relieved sigh before I took the phone, a couple of Cokes, and a pack of Red Vines up to the counter. After I'd paid, I headed back to the car.

"You good to keep driving?" I asked as I got in and held out the Red Vines.

Leo didn't notice them. He barely seemed to notice me. His attention was fixed on the side mirror.

My neck prickled. "What's up?"

"There's an SUV by the air compressor. Hasn't moved in a few minutes."

I subtly looked in my own side mirror. Sure enough, a battered old Explorer sat beside the air and water station. The windows weren't tinted in that blatantly obvious secret agent kind of way, but they were dark enough to obscure features. Two silhouettes were visible. "They put any air in their tires?"

"No. They haven't gotten out of the car."

My stomach curdled.

"How the fuck did they find us?" he whispered as if they might hear us.

"They don't call it a manhunt for nothing," I muttered. "They're probably focusing on where we used our credit cards, but they'll be fanning out anyway just in case." It was like department store security guards breaking up a fistfight. Enough would move in to defuse the situation, but the rest would fan out in search of the shoplifters who were in cahoots with the brawlers. Still, most of the resources would probably be concentrated around the hotels and the arterials between there and Indiana, so unless these guys had made us for sure and called in backup, we had fewer vehicles to elude.

Leo started the car. "They teach you that fancy driving in your training?"

"Yep."

We looked at each other.

Then, without a word, I got out and went around the car while Leo hoisted himself across the console, and I heard the Explorer's engine rev before I got back in. I threw the car in drive, hit the gas, and peeled out of the station, not even bothering to put my seatbelt on until we were already screaming up the ramp.

The Explorer fell in behind us. They knew they'd been made because they came right up on the bumper, not even bothering to hide that they were following us.

Gripping the wheel in both hands, I accelerated. When they tried to pass on my left, I drifted left until they had no shoulder. When they tried on the right, I drifted right.

"They get ahead of us," I ground out, "they're going to try to knock us into the median."

Leo muttered something that might've been Italian. It might've even been a prayer. Then, "Uh, we might have bigger problems."

Just as he said it, an eighteen-wheeler changed lanes up ahead. He moved left until he was straddling the line between the passing and center lanes. The truck to his right straddled the line between the right and center. Then they started slowing down.

A moving roadblock.

Shit.

I gritted my teeth. "Hang on."

Leo grabbed the *oh shit* handle. I stole a glance to make sure he had on his seatbelt. He did.

I accelerated until I was on the ass of the truck on the right, and let myself ease toward the shoulder. The

Explorer was still on my bumper, but I could see around it enough to do a quick sweep and make sure there weren't any other cars nearby.

"Hang on!" I jerked the wheel hard to the left, sending us careening—almost drifting—across the lanes and into the median. As the tires left the pavement, the wheel rattled in my hands, but I held tight. The dirt in the median was loose, and I fought to keep the car straight. Once I'd straightened out, I accelerated, spraying grass and gravel in all directions. For a few seconds, the world was nothing but yellow dust and rocks clattering into glass, and then we were on solid ground again. Other cars scattered around us. Horns blared and tires squealed. I didn't have time to see if anyone had crashed, but I hadn't heard any smacks or crunches, so maybe we were good.

The trucks were behind us. So was the Explorer. A vehicle like that was too top heavy for a stunt like mine, but the trucks were parting now to let it through.

The speedometer needle was creeping up on a hundred now. One speed trap or actual roadblock, and we were fucked. We needed—

There.

An off ramp. The road looked like it wound into some low hills. Perfect.

I took the ramp as fast as I dared, easing off the gas and braking just enough to take the turn at the end without flipping. A couple of tires got some air before coming down hard, but she held the road, and I tore past the twenty-five mile-an-hour sign.

"Watch for anything I might hit," I said through my teeth. "Cars, kids, whatever."

Leo said nothing, but I thought I sensed him nodding. He was holding that *oh shit* handle with both hands now, practically hanging from it as I took a twenty-mile-an-hour curve at a hair over sixty. The car slid, inching dangerously close to the sharp edge of the pavement. The whine of the engine and the roar of road noise drowned out my pounding heart and Leo's muttered cursing. I took a left. Then a right. Both way too fast.

The Explorer wasn't up my ass, but it was on us, and when we hit a straightaway between a couple of rotting cornfields, the driver took advantage. The way he was coming up on us now, I fully expected him to ram us if he got close enough, so I floored the gas.

Up ahead, a tractor took up most of the road. He was…definitely not going eighty-five.

"Rich." The *oh shit* handle creaked under Leo's weight. "Rich, you don't have room. You're not going—"

The Explorer smacked into our ass end.

"Fuck!" we both shouted.

I accelerated. Leo didn't protest any further.

The farmer looked over his shoulder, and his eyes widened with fear. He steered to the right, giving me a little more room, but it wasn't enough to make it past without going onto the shoulder. What little shoulder there was.

I could have kissed my driving instructors right then— partly on the shoulder, partly on the rough pavement, I sailed past the tractor.

The Explorer tried to do the same.

Wobbled.

Overcorrected.

And rolled.

I hit the brakes hard, kicking up more dust, and when I'd slowed enough, I turned around.

"What are you doing?" Leo asked. "We need to get the fuck out of here!"

"I want to know who's following us." I slowed to a stop where the Explorer had gone off the road. "Stay here."

He muttered something that was probably insulting.

I got out of the car, drawing my forty-five as I did.

"What in tarnation are you boys doing?" the farmer was screaming at me as he jogged stiffly from his tractor. "You're going to—" He saw my gun, and halted.

"Stay there, sir." Weapon poised, I crept toward the place where the Explorer had come to rest. It had torn a path through the wilting cornrows before landing on its top, carcass tilted at a weird angle in the soft earth while two wheels continued spinning. It must've rolled two or three times at least.

One of the occupants had been flung free of the vehicle. The angle of his neck said he was no longer a threat to me or anyone else.

I kept my gun trained on the vehicle as I moved closer. No one moved or made a sound. A bloody arm protruded from the mangled driver side window, bent at an unnatural angle, fingers twitching in the dirt. I crouched low. The airbag had deployed, but the driver was definitely dead. Getting there, anyway. There was someone else in what used to be the backseat. I got close enough to carefully reach in and feel for a pulse. None.

Exhaling, I stood and holstered my weapon.

I moved to the man who'd been thrown from the car and checked his pockets. To my horror—but not really surprise—I found a U.S. Marshals badge on him. My heart sank.

Leo materialized beside me.

I didn't look at him. "Thought I said to stay in the car."

He ignored me. His gaze was fixed on the unblinking eyes of the marshal, who was staring skyward. Slowly, Leo crouched beside him.

"He's a marshal," I said, trying not to throw up. "Deputy Marshal Rosario."

"No, he's not." Leo's voice was low. Hollow. Haunted. "That's Damiano Caruso." He looked up at me, his expression echoing his tone. "He's one of Grimaldi's men."

I glanced back and forth from him to the corpse.

So the Grimaldis *had* infiltrated the Marshals, and probably not just recently.

We were so fucked.

.

Chapter Six
Leo

Damiano Caruso. Fuck my life, but I should have seen this coming.

The thing is, I hadn't seen Damiano for almost seven years. One day he was there, a mink among the foxes, a little sleeker and more stylish than a lot of the other guys who worked for the Grimaldis, and the next he was gone. None of us were encouraged to ask questions about it, and I'd figured he'd gotten on the wrong side of the don and been banished to the Nevada operation, or maybe somewhere a little deeper and more permanent. Instead, he'd been ghosted. Of fucking course.

I had laid eyes on the entire Grimaldi financial network, and there were a few things about it that still gave me pause. Not the loan sharking or the money laundering or the gambling—hell no, that was my comfort zone. It was *where* the money went sometimes that made me stop and think. Weird LLCs with nothing but a PayPal account listed in connection to them, getting one thousand, two thousand, even ten thousand dollars a month from the family coffers.

I'd brought it up with Tony once, but he'd brushed it off, told me not to worry about it. "That's the price of keeping our hand in," he'd said vaguely, before distracting me with his own hand. Well, apparently "keeping your hand in" translated to "supplementing the incomes of the people we have working in law enforcement."

I should have dug deeper. I should have worked harder. I should have seen farther, and now it was more serious than the Grimaldis paying cops and agents to look the other way while they sent their hitmen after me. It was even more serious than them paying the Feds to come after me directly. This was *infiltration*, this was cleaning a guy's background like a pro and putting the wolf in with the sheep, to wait until they were needed and take advantage when they could. This…was fucked up.

"God motherfucking damn it." It wouldn't do me any good to punch a corpse in the face, but I was sorely tempted right now. Damiano Caruso. Who else was undercover? How many?

I needed to know more, which meant I needed to get somewhere safe with the access I needed, pronto. "We have to go."

For a second I was afraid my escort was going to freeze up again, but Rich just shook his head and stood. "Yeah. Let's get going." He walked purposefully to the farmer, who was looking on with wide eyes, his gnarled hands trembling.

"What the…how in the hell…"

"Sir." Rich put a hand on his arm and guided him back toward his tractor. "What you need to do now is sit down and call 911. Tell them there's been an accident, tell them where, and wait for them to show up." I was surprised we weren't hearing sirens already, honestly.

"And what about…what about you and—"

"Sir, I'm on official federal business and need to vacate the premises immediately. You stay here, tell the police what you saw, and wait for instructions. All right?"

"Uh-huh." The man nodded his head in time with Rich, who was still holding onto his arm. "I…I can do that. But you two boys, don't you need to—"

"Thank you for your cooperation." He let go of the man, who stumbled a little, and headed straight for our car. I followed him and got in as fast as I could.

"We need a new car," Rich said as he pulled back onto the road. And we did, for more than one reason; the alignment on this poor thing had been screwed to high heaven.

"Something fast."

"Something that can make it through mountains."

"Yeah, *quickly*. It's not winter, we're not going to get bogged down in snow." Although considering my luck lately, maybe that wasn't an absolute given. "But not mountains, no. We need to go back to the city, there's a safehouse where we can—"

"Nope."

"What do you mean, *nope*?"

"There's no way we're going back to the city right now. Are you crazy? If they can track us out here, it'll be a hundred times easier there."

"It's in a suburb," I argued. "Traffic cameras are few and far between, we could do it."

"Absolutely not."

"Fine." Maybe he had a point. "I've got another place fifty miles farther out. The amenities aren't as good, but I can make it work."

"I think it's safer to assume that every place you think might be secure is actually compromised," Rich said bluntly. "You're probably not the only computer genius the mob employs. They've had time to work on you, time to backtrack and figure out where you've been spending

CARI Z & L.A. WITT

your time and who with. I wouldn't be surprised if they know each and every one of your safehouses at this point."

That stung. "I've been careful."

"Obviously not careful enough."

That stung even *worse*, because he was right. Tony and I had taken precautions—we'd had to—but Matteo had found us, and Matteo was, frankly, as thick as a mile of pig shit. Either Tony had let something slip, or Matteo had help that I didn't know about.

But I fucking would, before this was over. And once I was done with him, Matteo and his little helper would be missing more than their trigger fingers and their pride.

"I've already set up a place for us to go," Rich said. "Completely off the books. Nobody will think to look for you there."

Easy to say, less easy to guarantee. "Where is it?"

"About fourteen hundred miles west of here."

"Fourteen hundred—Jesus Christ!" I'd never been further west than Chicago, and that was how I liked it. "You think we're going to make it that far with this kind of heat following us around?"

"I do if you're as smart as you say." He stretched his neck from side to side, grimacing for a second. "We need another car."

Yeah, we did. "Head for the nearest town and find a mall."

We drove for another twenty minutes in silence before we reached the next decent-sized town, with a convenient outlet mall right beside the highway. "Stay near the back of the lot," I said, automatically running cars through my head even as I tried to comprehend the fact that we were about to drive for—fuck, all day and all night? Two days? Anyway, he wanted to take our chances on the road so that we could hit up someplace that I had no assurances about, other than Rich basically telling me to trust him. *Ha*. We'd fight that out in a minute, though. "There—the silver Scion, park next to that."

"A sports car?"

"An older sports car," I said, shaking the nerves out of my hands and trying to relax some. I could do this. I had been boosting cars for years, one little Scion no easy. "Twelve years old, and this model is pretty easy to start up as long as you can get into it." I glanced in the window of the car, did a double-take, and started to laugh.

"What?"

It took me a moment to get myself under control—it felt good to laugh after so much dire shit lately. "*Ahhh*-ha, m'kay, it's just…" I reached out and pulled on the handle, and the driver side door swung open. The smell of stale corn chips and Axe body spray drifted out. "Oh, man. Bullseye."

Rich looked at me like he was afraid I was going to fall over. *Not yet, G-man.* "What the hell?"

"This car," I gestured grandly at the Scion tC, which— now I looked at it, caught the ding on the side panel and the slight crumpling on the back bumper which were oh-so telling, "belongs to a teenager. A teenager who left it unlocked."

Rich's mouth dropped open. "No. We're not that lucky."

"Sometimes one man's luck is just other people's stupid." I passed him a screwdriver. "Get us a new license plate, I'll get her going."

Four minutes later, we were back on the road in slightly more style, and I was spoiling for a fight. "So, why are you okay right now?"

Rich frowned. "What do you mean?"

"Because, after—*that*, after a fucking car chase and a mobile roadblock and way more shit that we were expecting, you're not…you seem…" How did I say *surprisingly not crazypants* without sounding like a douche?

"No gunfire."

I blinked. "No gunfire. Really? That's all it takes?"

"Not always, but the gunfire is the worst."

"You can look a dead marshal straight in the eye and not blink, because he died on impact instead of getting shot?"

Rich's frown became a scowl. "It helps to know he was a Mafia piece of shit, but yeah."

I shook my head. "I don't get you, man."

"I'm not that complicated."

"I beg to differ. Where are we going?"

"I told you, somewhere safe."

I sighed. "Elaborate on safe."

"The place belongs to a buddy of mine—" And that was as far as he went, because I had to stop him there.

"God damn it, you have no buddies now! Remember? Every single person you've ever worked with in the Marshals is a suspect!" How relentlessly optimistic was this fool?

"He's not a friend from the Marshals. He's from before."

"What, a Marine?" I scoffed. "Like that's any better."

"It is, actually."

I was going to have to get the hand puppets out at this rate. "Rich. They know you're with me. You're being actively searched for. You think your superiors aren't combing through every inch of your past, trying to get a handle on what you'll do next? Every buddy you've ever had is going to be watched!"

"Not this one."

"How do you know that?"

"Because he's a paranoid son of a bitch who built himself a bunker in the middle of nowhere as soon as he was discharged," Rich said matter-of-factly. "Smitty probably trusts the government even less than you do. He's not getting under anyone's surveillance without knowing it, and I'll contact him once we get close to make sure his place is still safe. It's going to be fine."

"*Porca puttana troia lurida.*" Whatever god there was, save me from "the bonds of brotherhood" or whatever

Rich thought was operating here, but I couldn't honestly say I had a better idea. My face hurt from where he'd hit me, my body was *still* trembling a little in the aftermath of that fucking car chase, and I was close to hitting a wall. "Fine. Wake me up if we're about to die."

"I doubt you'll need me to." The bastard had the gall to sound amused. I scrunched down in the passenger seat, laid my head against the window, and prepared to get absolutely no sleep at all.

When I woke up, Rich was shaking my shoulder, and the sky had gone from morning blue to evening twilight. "Where are we?" I muttered as I shook my head, trying to clear the cotton from my brain. My neck ached from the awkward position and my bladder was killing me, but apart from that I felt almost...refreshed.

"Somewhere with WiFi." Sure enough, the pizzeria in front of us had a little sign advertising free WiFi. "I'm going to go in and order us some food, you keep your secrets from spilling all over the internet."

"I...yeah." I was lucky he'd remembered. Shit, *I* should have remembered, should have set an alarm to ensure I got up in time to keep things in order. I hadn't expected to sleep for so long. "I'll do that." Rich got out of the car, and I shamelessly watched him walk into the pizzeria before turning my attention to my phone. Fuck it, anybody would have watched, Tony included. When he wasn't on the verge of a breakdown, Rich moved like a fucking tiger.

I logged in, entered the right passcode on the right site, and reset the clock for another twenty-four hours. I really needed to spend some quality time with my data, see if I could track down more ghosts who might be coming after us, but the speed here was too slow for that. I checked the news instead. Celebrity drama...escalating international conflicts...presidential bullshit...nothing on us so far, which was nice. I skimmed the articles, letting my eyes fly over headlines interspersed with

advertisements for skin cream and life insurance—ha—
before something caught my eye.

Local bad boy makes good in brother's name. It was an
innocuous enough headline, but the picture beneath it was
of Matteo.

Bull. Fucking. Shit. I tapped on the article and started
to read. The introduction was nothing I hadn't read
before—Mafia ties, infamous partier, low level criminal,
that sort of thing. The kind of bad press that got around
when your daddy told you not to be a fuckup and you
couldn't quite manage it, but at least you weren't in jail.
Then I saw a line that stopped me in my tracks.

*In the wake of his brother's violent death, Matteo Grimaldi has
pledged to make a fresh start in the community, beginning with a
generous charitable donation to the local youth center. "I always knew
I'd never be able to live up to Tony's expectations," he told me. "It
made me more than a little bitter, to be honest. I figured, why even
try? But since Tony's death, I realized that I have to try, even if I'm
not gonna be as great as he was." He gestured at the building behind
us. "Tony spent a lot of time here working with the kids. It's where
he met Leo, you know? He mentored that punk through the roughest
times in his life, and then Leo repaid him for it with a bullet to the
head. Things aren't gonna get better by ignoring these kids' needs,
though."*

*Leotrim Nicolosi is the prime suspect in an incident that
resulted in the deaths of seven federal officials yesterday. Apparently,
the recent death of Antonio Grimaldi can also be laid at his feet.
When I asked Matteo Grimaldo about Mr. Nicolosi's connections
with his family, he replied, "Leo was never a part of the family, not
after what his father did. Blood tells in the end, you know? Tony gave
him a chance, and Tony paid for it. I wish he'd never set eyes on Leo,
but it's too late for wishin'."*

I shut the phone off and set it carefully on the
dashboard. I should have been angry—hell, I knew I was,
somewhere inside. Maybe it was residual fatigue, maybe it
was being too disconnected from it all to give a damn, but
all I really felt in that moment was cold and sick. Like it

wasn't bad enough I was being blamed for killing a bunch of federal agents, now they'd gone and pinned Tony's death on me too? Just the thought of laying a violent hand on the man who'd been my lover made me feel ill. It hadn't been that way between us, never. He'd been the only good, gentle thing in my life, and now people would think…

Nobody who cares will believe that story. But that was just the problem. Nobody cared at all. I hadn't had a letter from Papa in months, I couldn't risk reaching out to Gianna, and Uncle Angelus had warned me against contacting him. Nobody gave a shit, and therefore in the eyes of the world, I had murdered Tony Grimaldi. Fucking fantastic.

I got out of the car, slammed the door shut and stalked off toward the trees fifty feet away. I needed to piss, and a chance to get myself under control before Rich came back and wondered whether *I* was on the verge of a fucking breakdown.

Chapter Seven
Rich

I was halfway back to the car when my blood turned cold.

Leo was gone.

What the fuck?

I looked around, the bags of food and soda nearly tumbling out of my hands. Where the fuck had—

There.

He was over by the trees, hands jammed in his pockets and gaze fixed on the ground. I wanted to be livid with him for scaring me like that, but I was too relieved to see him. No one had grabbed him. He hadn't taken off. Maybe he'd just needed to stretch his legs or something. Crisis averted.

"Hey," I called out. "You ready to go?"

He turned my way, and he looked…not good. Scared? Angry? Even from here, I could practically feel him vibrating with something.

Shit.

My heart was thudding hard as we returned to the car. Leo didn't make eye contact or say a word, but the way he slammed the door spoke volumes.

Uneasy, I slid in behind the wheel. The bags of sodas and food in my hand were cumbersome, but I didn't give them to him yet because I didn't want them unloaded back into my lap.

"Hey." I cocked my head. "What's wrong?"

Leo didn't jump. His lips were pressed tightly together, his jaw moving like he was grinding his teeth. I legitimately couldn't tell if he was about to explode with rage or break down crying. Both, maybe?

"Leo?"

He closed his eyes and exhaled. Pressing an elbow into the door, he rubbed his forehead with a hand that I suddenly realized was shaking. Before I could prod again, he murmured, "I checked the news. Matteo Grimaldi is playing the reformed Mafioso. Acting like some goddamned saint for the media. And he's…" Leo moved his hand lower and rubbed his eyes. His Adam's apple bobbed. "I'm the prime fucking suspect in murdering Tony."

"I know."

Leo's hand dropped, and he glared at me.

I showed my palms defensively, nearly dumping the food into both our laps. "Hey. It's not news to anyone familiar with your case, all right?"

That eased some of the sudden hostility, but not much. Leo pulled his gaze away and stared out the windshield. "They're going to kill me. Once they catch us and shut down my…" He sighed, waving a hand. "They're going to fucking kill me."

"I'm not going to let that happen."

"Yeah?" he barked, the word oozing sarcasm. "You sure about that?"

"You're still alive, aren't you?"

He opened his mouth like he was going to speak, but seemed to think better of it. He slouched against the seat, and I took advantage of him being subdued for a moment.

"Here." I put the bag of drinks in his lap. "We need to hit the road."

Leo didn't protest. While I pulled out of the parking lot, he arranged the soda bottles in the cup holders. Then he started poking around in the bag of food.

"I wasn't sure what you liked," I said as I rolled through a yellow light. "And I didn't think we had time for them to make pizzas or anything, so I just grabbed a couple of sandwiches."

"Sandwiches are fine." Foil crinkled. "Which one is yours?"

"They're both the same."

And that was the end of the conversation for a while. We ate our sandwiches. I drove. White stripes flew past. Other cars came and went. None of them seemed interested in us. Leo didn't speak. I didn't speak. The silence wasn't comfortable, but I didn't expect anything to be comfortable any time soon.

Fifty-some-odd miles after the pizzeria, Leo spoke.

"I didn't kill Tony."

He didn't sound defensive or angry. His voice was soft, the words flat and almost reluctant, as if he'd just spent all that time trying to decide if he should say them at all, and still wasn't entirely convinced.

I glanced at him. He was staring out the windshield, expression neutral but eyes focused hard on something in the distance. As I faced the road again, I asked, "His brother did?"

"Yeah. And they…" He fell silent again, but only for a minute or so. Then he pulled in one of those long, deep breaths like he was about to say something really big. I held the wheel tighter as if whatever it was might startle me into swerving.

"I knew before I turned state's evidence that they were going to pin it on me," he said. "The don and Matteo both thought Tony was being corrupted. In a way they couldn't tolerate. And they blamed it on me." He exhaled. "More than that, they want me dead because they don't want anyone to know *why* they had to have him killed. Because it would leave a stain on the Grimaldi name. They…want us both dead."

Corrupted…

Blaming it on…

Stain on the Grimaldi name…

The pieces wanted to fall together in my head, but I refused to assume. I needed to hear him say it. I glanced at him again. "This wasn't business, was it?"

"No." The whispered word barely carried over the subtle road noise. He didn't speak. I didn't speak. More white stripes whipped by.

Something crinkled. I looked over, and Leo was picking at the plastic bag he'd been using to catch lettuce and bread crumbs from his sandwich. After a moment, he said, "As soon as they realized Matteo hadn't taken me down too, he and his father started spreading rumors that I was stealing from the family. That I was skimming, writing the code for the gambling programs so I'd take hundreds of thousands right out of Grimaldi pockets." He pressed his arm below the window again and rubbed his head like it hurt. "They've convinced everyone in the business that I'm a liar. My word isn't worth shit anymore. And if they've got people in the Marshals, then those rumors are getting through your ranks too. The Marshals have to know by now that I'm blackmailing the family. I guarantee every attorney involved in the case has heard I'm a pathological liar and a thief, and they've probably poisoned a few jurors too."

I swallowed. Fuck. And he wasn't going to say it, was he? I got the feeling he was trying desperately to say it. Like he needed someone in the world to know, and maybe to believe him, before the family caught up with him and put a bullet in his head.

Stomach twisting, I hoped to God I wasn't wrong. "How long were you with him?"

Leo stiffened. He was so still, so quiet, I genuinely wondered if he was remembering to breathe. When I turned to him briefly, our eyes locked, but I couldn't hold his gaze long enough to parse what I found there. Some shock, yes, but more? Maybe. I couldn't say for sure.

My gut churned harder. I'd overstepped, hadn't I? Made an assumption? Yanked a card away from his vest and slammed it down on the table before he was ready to play it. Christ. Now things were going to get—

"Three years."

My head snapped toward him just long enough for a split second of eye contact.

He blew out a breath. "We were together three years."

Now it was my turn to go quiet because I had no idea what to say to that. What was there to say to someone being accused of killing the man he'd been with for three years?

Leo had apparently found his voice, though. "We did everything we could to fly under the radar. He knew if anyone ever caught us, we were dead. Literally dead." He shifted a bit, almost like he was trying to burrow backwards into his seat. "Gianna—his sister—is the only reason I'm still alive. She tipped Tony off that someone knew about us. He…" Leo pushed out another breath. Then he sniffed. "I tried to save him too, but…" Another sharp sniff.

I didn't know what to say, but maybe steering the conversation away from Tony's death would be a good place to start. "What was he like?"

"Huh?"

"Tony." I glanced over, catching sight of a faint shimmer in Leo's eyes. "What was he like?" Now I was regretting the question. The guy was grieving. He probably didn't want to talk about—

"He was amazing," Leo whispered. "Being a part of that family, he should've been a hard-assed bastard who thought killing people over business was totally normal. He should've been just like his brother, you know? But he was…" Leo paused, then laughed softly. "You want to know something that was really hard about keeping our relationship a secret? One of those things I didn't expect?"

My throat tightened. I shook my head.

There was a smile in his voice as he said, "I was a soldier for the family, so I went to stuff. Weddings and funerals and that kind of shit. We just couldn't, you know, go together. But I'd see him there." He laughed again, the sound barely audible. "God, seeing him with his nieces and nephews was the most adorable thing. He just…he *loved* kids. I always had to work really hard not to stare at him when they were playing. I don't think I ever loved him more than I did when I saw him with those kids. And I couldn't—" He cleared his throat. "I couldn't tell anyone."

I swallowed. I was tempted to ask if he and Tony had ever thought about a family of their own, but that would just be battery acid in an open wound. They had to have known a happy ending was never in their future.

And that thought damn near broke my heart. I'd had boyfriends, and I'd been devastated over breakups, but I couldn't imagine how much Leo and Tony must've loved each other. How devoted did you have to be to someone to stay with them when you knew it would earn you a bullet to the head? And then when that bullet eventually came for your lover? And you were still alive while he was dead for no other reason than loving you?

The road blurred in front of me, and I wiped my eyes as subtly as I could. Holy fuck, was I almost crying over someone else's relationship?

Oh hell, why not? I was raw from watching my mentor get gunned down in front of me and being betrayed by the men I was supposed to trust, and yeah, I *was* getting choked the fuck up from hearing Leo tell me about what it was like to love someone who'd taken a bullet for loving him back.

I didn't think Leo noticed, though. He was gazing out the passenger side window, probably staring into a past with someone whose death had been as devastating as it was inevitable.

How do you come back from losing someone like that?

Beside me, Leo sniffed again. He swiped at his eyes, hand shaking.

"You okay?" I asked.

He pushed out a ragged breath. "I think it's all just…it's sinking in." His voice had been pretty even, but now it was unsteady. On the verge of breaking. "My family's gone. The Grimaldis want me dead. I can't even trust the fucking Feds. And Tony…God…" He rubbed a hand over his face. "All I have left is the means to destroy the Grimaldis. After they're gone…I've got…" His hand went to his mouth, and he sort of muffled what sounded distinctly like a quiet sob.

When I looked over, he'd squeezed his eyes shut, and a tear slipped down to his finger. His shoulders were so tense I could *feel* it. He was at his breaking point, and he seemed to be fighting a losing battle against passing that point.

Without any other ideas about what to do, I reached across the console and wrapped an arm around him. "Hey. Come here."

I half expected his pride or distrust to make him stiffen and jerk away, but…no. He sank against me, and he stopped fighting. He barely made a sound, but the trembling was heartbreaking. Was this really the cocky little shit who'd been led into that hotel room where I'd been dying of boredom? How much pain had he been hiding in that moment when I'd wanted to slap the smirk right off his face?

We didn't know each other. We didn't particularly like each other. But right now, all we *had* was each other. So I offered him my shoulder, and he took it. I kept one hand on the wheel and the other arm around him, and as the interstate took us deeper into the west, I let him fall apart while I drove us toward—I hoped—safety.

He's all I have now. I'm all he has now.
Please, God, let that be enough.

Chapter Eight
Leo

Some fucking tough guy I was.

None of this shit surprised me, *none* of it. I knew I was going to be blamed for Tony's death, so why did it hurt when the reality of it slapped me across the face? Probably because it came couched in Matteo's smug-as-fuck fake remorse, cementing his prodigal son status by coming back to the fold and publicly revering his dead brother. The brother *he'd* killed, that bastard. Matteo didn't know what love was beyond loving himself—he barely had enough imagination to understand emotions like love, or fear, except when it came down from the don. I gave him a month, tops, before he gave up the good-boy routine and went back to hookers and heroin.

Except I wasn't going to give him a month. Not if I survived whatever Rich had in store for us.

Speaking of…I'd backed out from under his arm five minutes ago, and he hadn't said a thing. Didn't point out to me how much of a whiner I was being, didn't mutter "thank God" under his breath, didn't look at me with

CARI Z & L.A. WITT

disgust… I didn't know what to make of it. If being a Marine and going on to become a marshal contained anything even close to the layers of bullshit masculinity that came with working for a family, he *should* have been disgusted. Should at least have acted a little more long-suffering before giving me a chance to get my stupid self under control. But he hadn't. Was it the PTSD? Or maybe—

Come to think of it, he hadn't even blinked when he found out I was gay. Sure, that might have been in my file too, at least the suspicion of it, but nothing? Not even a little blip? Not even a moment of hesitation before offering a little comfort, the way any all-American straight boy would have?

Maybe he was just more enlightened than your average jarheaded, badge-toting jock, or maybe…Maybe he had a personal reason for being a little more accepting.

Rich's tense voice cut through my musings like a knife. "We're being followed."

"Who?" I craned my neck to look back at the traffic behind us. It had picked up in the past five minutes, probably a crowd's mass exodus after the end of the game at the nearby university's arena. Our speed had dropped a little, and Rich wasn't trying to pick it back up.

"Right behind us, the Honda CRV. It pulled up after the last exit and hasn't moved since." As I watched, the vehicle swerved a little, like it was going to try and go around us but the driver couldn't quite muster the nerve to do it.

"You sure they don't just want to pass?"

"I've given them three opportunities in the past five minutes, and they haven't taken any of them. They just stay on our bumper and menace."

"Spotters?" I offered, my blood going a little cold at the thought. If the car was being tracked by helicopter, it was going to take more than Rich's fancy driving to get us to safety.

"Maybe. I can't see anything up high yet, but that doesn't mean there's nothing up there."

"Damn it." Just what we needed. "Well, we ca—shit, they're making their move!" The CRV swerved hard into the left lane, closing the gap between us fast. "Give me your gun!"

"I can't just—"

"You're driving, I'm not, now give me your fucking gun and let me handle them!" I could take out the tires if I was careful. Rich grimaced but handed over his gun. I made sure it was ready to fire, then slowly rolled down the back driver side window and took aim. I could do this. They were fishtailing a little, but not so much that I couldn't blow out that front right tire and hopefully send them careening into the guard rail. I took a breath, exhaled slowly and—

"Wait!"

Rich's hand on my shoulder startled me so bad I almost took the shot anyway. "Jesus Christ, what?" I snapped. Only now, as they pulled up alongside us, I could see it. The passenger side window rolled down, and instead of looking into the barrel of a gun, we were treated to— painted ass cheeks? I blinked, just to make sure I was actually seeing this. Yep, we were being mooned, and on the pale, flabby flesh was written the words VIKINGS SUCK.

A second later the butt disappeared, and a face wreathed in red and black grinned out at us. "Your team sucks, motherfuckers! Eat Devil Dog ass!" A chorus of hoots and shouts echoed from inside the car, and a moment later the CRV pulled ahead of us and vanished into the traffic.

I stared for a second, dumbfounded. "I think—I think I just almost killed a bunch of frat boys."

"Fuck." Rich squinted like he wanted to shut his eyes, but couldn't as long as he was driving. "Yeah. They must have seen a decal or something on the back of the car."

I glanced back and checked. I couldn't make out more than the outline, but sure enough, there was a decal of a head topped with a horned helmet on the back windshield. We'd stolen a car belonging to someone who supported those idiots' rival team. "Holy shit."

"Pretty much."

"And they have no clue how close they came to dying just now."

"Which is good. We don't need the collateral damage or the attention it could bring us."

He had a point. On the other hand…"They were really fucking annoying though, huh?"

Rich's mouth curved a little. "Yeah they were."

"I doubt the world would be a much darker place without those few random idiots. I'm not advocating killing them!" I added as he frowned at me. "I'm just saying, it's not like that was a car full of nuns and orphans or anything, just a bunch of drunk morons who like to finger paint on each other's asses." It totally figured that the first bare ass I'd seen in weeks would belong to the Pillsbury Dough Boy.

Rich didn't even crack a smile. "I shouldn't have tagged them as following us. It's obvious in retrospect, they weren't even trying to be subtle."

And now he was punishing himself for not being clairvoyant. "Rich. Come on. The last guys weren't being subtle either, and you nailed them just fine. Let's—" *buy a liquor store and drown our sorrows* "—find somewhere to pull in, okay? I think we could both use some sleep." I sure as hell could. Jesus, had it been just this morning that I'd woken up to Rich's nightmare and a fist in the face when I'd tried to calm him down? It felt like a million hours had passed since then.

Rich looked like he wanted to argue for a moment, but finally sighed. "Yeah, you're probably right."

I leaned in closer to him, close enough that I could smell the faintest remnants of deodorant and sweat and a little of the grinder he'd had for dinner. It shouldn't have worked for him, but goddamn, did it ever. "I'll let you in on a secret. Me? I'm almost always right. If everyone around me did exactly what I said, this world would be running a lot more smoothly."

"The world is a mess, and you just need to rule it?" he replied, a little smile on his face. He was being cute, which meant it was probably a quote, what was it—oh. A Whedon fan.

"Exactly. I'm like Dr. Horrible, except with way more game."

"Not enough game to keep you out of this mess."

"God himself couldn't have kept me out of this mess," I said, and I believed it, too. I didn't put much faith in a benevolent God, but I kept my hand in with the devil out of necessity. Any higher power out there had made its move, and the fact that I still had Rich on my side—hell, the fact that I was still breathing at all—meant that there was a chance for my own admittedly-twisted sense of justice to prevail. A chance, that was all I needed.

That and Rich, apparently. And some sleep.

A few exits later, Rich pulled us into another run-down roadside motel. He checked us in while I gathered up the trash from dinner and threw it away—we'd need another new car soon, but there was no reason to treat this one like a pigsty in the meantime. By the time he came out with a set of keys, I had our plastic sacks of equipment ready to go. Backpack, I should have bought a backpack when we were at Wal-Mart. Next time.

The room he led us to was on the second floor, right in the middle. I didn't like the placement—it would turn into a perfect place to box us in if we were found—but beggars couldn't be choosers. This room was just as bland as the last one, except the walls were peach instead of white, and the bedspreads looked like cotton instead of polyester. Fancy.

I flopped down on the bed farthest from the door and shut my eyes. "I feel like I could sleep for a week."

"Adrenaline dump finally getting to you?" I heard the rustle of Rich's plastic bag, but didn't look up. "Or do you even feel it much anymore?"

"Oh yeah." I knew the type he was talking about, though, the men—and sometimes, women—who'd gone through so much and seen so much and *done* so much that they were numb to it all. People who couldn't be reached except through drugs or a particular vice, people who didn't remember how to duck because it felt too much like cringing. Those people usually weren't careful enough to last long. "I feel it, man. Of course I do, you know that, I was a fucking wreck today. But if the family teaches you anything, it teaches you to take a shot and keep on firing."

I turned my head in his direction. "But if I'm the one who wakes you up with nightmares tonight, you have to—" And that was as far as I got before my tongue caught in my throat, because Rich had stripped off his shirt and thrown it aside. He had one of the plain black T-shirts he'd bought yesterday in his hand, but not *on* him yet, and the sight was…distracting. Really fucking distracting.

"Have to what?"

I shook my head a little. "Um. Have to go easy on me." Which, shit, sounded like innuendo, and I didn't want him to take it that way because I wasn't sure I *meant* it that way, but goddamn, he had a nice body. Broad chest, flat, ripply abdomen, the kind of arms that I could lift weights for ten years trying for but still never achieve…just, nice. Really, really…

Rich grinned and stepped past me. "I'll try not to hit you again, if that's what you mean. And I won't let you clock me either." He shut the bathroom door behind him, and I rolled onto my stomach, pushed my face into the pillow, and groaned. Fuck. Since when had I had such a thing for tattoos?

There was something about the way he moved that reminded me of Tony, something leonine and assured, at least when Rich was feeling good. I liked that confidence, I liked the way it made me feel safe. Stupid, idiotic, but there you go.

I briefly wondered what Rich's ass looked like, then pinched my side hard. I hadn't been dropped into the middle of some fucking fairytale here. I wasn't a damsel in distress and Rich wasn't Prince Charming, any more than Tony had been. Keeping me alive was his job, and I needed to let him do it and not get distracted.

I sighed and pulled out my phone. Time to keep my secrets for another day.

Chapter Nine
Rich

The shower felt good, and it was clearing away the day's grossness, but it didn't do a damn thing about my head. From the moment those elevators had opened and the whole world had exploded, my head had been a wreck. I'd given up on thinking that was going to change any time soon. Good thing all my combat training had taught me to keep going, keep aiming, and keep shooting even while there were demons screaming in my ears.

"*When it's all over,*" a gunny had shouted over a transport jet's engines en route to Kandahar, "*you can drink, scream, cry, hit something. Whatever you need. But you save that shit till you're home, or I will shoot you before Haji does.*"

I'd taken the advice to heart. It had gotten me through my combat tours, and yeah, as soon as I'd gotten home, I'd drunk, screamed, cried, and hit something. Still had the scar between my knuckles from when my fist had found a stud instead of going through the drywall.

Eyes closed, I let the tepid water stream over my stiff body. I would get through this without losing my head.

Leo's life and mine depended on it. All I had to do was get us to safety—even temporary safety—and then I could break. Nightmares. Flashbacks. That near catatonic paralysis when everything came crashing down too fast and hard to process. Just had to get to Smitty's in one piece, and I could crumble. Just hold on until then.

I didn't know how useful it was to try to bargain with the demons in my head, but that didn't stop me from trying.

The water was getting uncomfortably cool, so I turned it off and stepped out. As I dried off, my mind shifted to that little exchange before I'd gone into the bathroom. The way Leo had stopped mid-sentence and conspicuously raked his eyes over me. Goose bumps prickled my neck and back. It didn't help that I knew he was gay, and that he may have actually been *looking* at me. Like *that*.

Fuck. That was something I could hold onto. Even if I was just imagining it, the thought of Leo being attracted to me was a pleasant distraction from everything else. Stupid, maybe, but I'd take whatever I could get to keep my head together until this was over.

Assuming it didn't distract me too much. Which it wouldn't. I could handle this.

I actually made myself believe that right up until I stepped out of the bathroom. Leo was lounging across the bed in nothing but a pair of jeans. He had one leg bent and canted to the side with the remote lying on his inner thigh, and the light from the TV was playing across his bare abs and sharp features. Holy shit.

And he was watching me.

His dark eyebrows rose. "What?"

"Sorry." I cleared my throat and busied myself with scrubbing my hair dry with the thin towel. "Just, uh…"

His chuckle was low and devilish, but he didn't say anything. He probably didn't need to. We both knew I'd been checking him out.

There was a quiet voice deep in my head trying to persuade me to act on it. The stress relief alone would be worth it, and maybe we'd both sleep better. Nothing wrong with casual sex in a foxhole, right? Okay, so it hadn't been an actual foxhole when I'd hooked up with Valentine in between convoys, but a shipping container in hundred-degree heat wasn't much better. And it had been the stress relief we'd both desperately needed.

It had also made it that much more devastating when I'd watched a rocket take out Valentine's Humvee two weeks later.

I shuddered, tamping down the memory right along with my attraction to Leo. Maybe screwing would be some temporary relief, but at the end of the day, Leo was a witness and I was a marshal. I was responsible for his safety, not his orgasms.

An image flickered through my mind of Leo in the throes of a powerful climax, and I actually gasped.

"What's wrong?" There was a grin in Leo's voice.

"Nothing." I turned and tossed the towel into the bathroom. It landed on the edge of the bathtub, then slithered down and pooled on the floor. Meh. Whatever. I stepped out into the main room and tried like hell not to look at Leo. "I need to go find a payphone."

"Wait, what?" The humor was gone, and the bed creaked with movement. The remote clattered to the floor. "Who the fuck are you calling?"

"My dad."

Leo growled something that didn't sound English or Italian. Albanian, maybe? Probably cursing, anyway. He huffed sharply as he stood. "We've been through this. You can't—"

"He won't know where we're going." I faced Leo. "But I need to reach out to someone. And it's better to do it now while we're in the middle of nowhere than when we're hunkered down at my buddy's place."

Leo's lips thinned. "How do you know we can trust him?"

"I don't," I said simply. "But we've got the fucking Mafia after us, and they've infiltrated the Marshals. We need all the allies we can get."

He exhaled and rolled his eyes. "We've *talked* about this, Rich."

"I know. But if I use a payphone here in Bumfuck, Nowhere, and then we hit the road—"

"Then at least wait until tomorrow morning." He set his jaw. "Tell him we're heading south, and as soon as you're off the phone, we continue west."

Damn it. So much for an easy way out of the room for twenty minutes.

I sighed. "Fine. Okay. First thing in the morning."

Leo nodded, and he relaxed as he went back to the bed and sat down. I took a seat on the other one and tried to figure out what to do with my hands, my eyes, my mind—

"So this guy we're meeting," Leo said. "What's he like?"

I shifted uneasily. "He's good people. A little crazy, but the Marines will do that to you."

"I always heard Marines were crazy going in."

With a quiet laugh, I shrugged. "There's probably some truth to that too."

"Can't think of any other reason why someone would enlist." A smirk played at his lips. "Besides the uniforms."

"The uniforms are a plus." I sat back against the headboard, trying to look more relaxed than I was. "Most of the guys I knew in boot camp were either trying to prove something or didn't have any other options."

"Which one were you?"

"A little bit of both." I laced my hands behind my head and stared up at the ceiling. There was a tiny cobweb behind the light fixture, twitching intermittently in the subtle breeze from the humming air conditioner, and I focused on that.

"So what were you trying to prove?"

I didn't answer right away. The memories were painful, and I'd never been able to share them with many people. I supposed if anyone understood, maybe it would be him. Still concentrating on the twitchy cobweb, I took a breath. "I played sports in high school, but never the *right* sports. I played tennis and ran track. Hated football. Sucked at baseball. My younger brother was a football and basketball star, and everyone in the family bragged about him at every turn." I swallowed. "Senior year, I took three state titles in track and was almost undefeated in tennis. At my graduation party, everyone was talking about my brother getting a full-ride football scholarship."

I didn't look, but I could feel Leo watching me.

"They offer you any scholarships?"

I nodded. "A few. I just didn't want to play anymore. You want to talk a kid out of doing something, just ignore him long enough and he won't have any reason to keep going." I finally turned to Leo. "What's the point of working that hard and playing that well if your parents only show up so they can brag about their other kid?"

He winced. "But if you enjoyed it…"

Shaking my head, I looked up at the cobweb again. "I get that. Eighteen-year-old me didn't. Mom and Dad didn't care, so why should I?"

"Kids can't see the forest for the trees." He paused. "What does that have to do with the Marines, though?"

I closed my eyes and let out a long breath. "There were people in my family who gave me shit for a long time about sissy sports. About *being* a sissy. The one time I ever got into a fight in junior high, I had my ass handed to me and never heard the end of it from my uncle or my grandfather. I…wasn't a tough kid. Never was."

"You were trying to prove you were a man." It wasn't a question.

My cheeks burned as I nodded.

"Did it work?"

I looked at him again. "What?"

"Did it work?" he repeated. "Did they think you were a man after you enlisted?"

I laughed bitterly. "Turned out the people who actually mattered already did, and the rest…well, Grandpa's dead and nobody in the family talks to that uncle anymore."

"Why not?"

I moistened my lips. After the conversation we'd had in the car, and the way we'd both been looking at each other tonight, I was hesitant to go there, but hell, why not? "He lost his shit at Thanksgiving one year." I gulped. "Because he didn't think it was appropriate for me to bring my boyfriend to dinner."

The room was suddenly so quiet, I could almost *hear* the cobweb somersaulting above the light. In the back of my mind, my dad and uncle's shouts still echoed from the fight that had started at the table, spilled out into the hallway and the front yard, and finally ended with the slamming of a car door.

I could barely speak above a whisper as I said to the light fixture, "That was the same night Dad and I made peace over everything that had made me think the Marines were my only option. He apologized for making me feel I wasn't enough of a man for him. It was a rough night, but…looking back, I'm glad it happened."

More silence. More cobweb twitching.

Fabric rustled and bed creaked softly as Leo moved around. He settled, and then spoke almost as quietly as I had. "Are you and your dad close?"

"After that?" I nodded. "Yeah. We weren't when I was a kid, but ever since that night? You better believe it." I realized after a moment what Leo had been thinking, and I turned to him again. "My dad had my back when his own brother came at me. That's why I know he'll have our backs now."

Leo swallowed like it took some work. "It's not him I don't trust. It's everyone who's probably listening to him."

"I know. But he's got people in the Marshals. He knows people all the way up the chain." I sat up, swung my legs over the bed, and looked him in the eye. "If things go to shit at Smitty's, Dad might—"

"If things go to shit?" His eyes widened. "I thought you trusted this guy!"

"I do. And his place is in the middle of nowhere. If there's a place on this planet we're safe, it's there. But anything could happen, and we need contingencies, and my dad's got people."

He pursed his lips. Finally, he dropped his gaze and nodded. "All right. But I'm sticking with what I said—we hit the road as soon as you're off the phone."

"Absolutely."

He met my eyes again. We stared at each other in silence. Tense, loaded silence. Was he waiting for me to say something? Was he supposed to say something?

Abruptly, he stood. "My turn for a shower. Then I suggest we get some sleep."

"Right." I cleared my throat and sat back. "Good idea."

And I definitely did not watch his firm, jean-clad ass as he walked to the bathroom.

Not surprisingly, the night was a long one. On the bright side, I didn't wake up screaming or flailing. On the not-so-bright side, that was because waking up screaming required going to sleep in the first place.

I dozed enough to be coherent in the morning, but for the most part, my mind had been spinning in too many directions on too many axes to really, truly relax. Would we make it to Smitty's? Would we be safe there? Did anyone know where we were? Should I trust Leo's gut and not call my dad after all?

I'd tossed and turned, and even contemplated jerking off a time or two. Not because I was horny—I wasn't, not even with Leo stretched out on the other bed—but just to knock me out. I'd thought better of it, though. Leo wasn't the heaviest sleeper in the world, and I had a feeling if he woke up to me rubbing one out, it would be even more awkward than after he'd had to tackle me mid-nightmare. Especially when it was just hours after we'd both come out to each other.

So I'd left well enough alone.

Now it was 0500, so I didn't bother trying to sleep any longer. I got up, fumbled with the ancient coffeepot, and poured myself some of the worst coffee I'd had since I'd been in a warzone.

The taste was weak, but the smell must have been strong because some grumbling and stirring came from the other bed. "Coffee?" he muttered.

"Yeah, but it sucks." I poured what was left in my cup down the bathroom sink. "I think I saw a fast food place up the road."

He growled something. Then he sat up. His black hair was a mess of curls, and his jaw was dark with stubble. Sweet Jesus…

I turned away before I got busted staring again.

Neither of us said much while we got ready to go. We dressed, checked weapons, spent a few minutes watching the news in case we were mentioned, and by 0600, we were on our way out the door.

The fast food restaurant up the road wasn't one I'd heard of. Maybe an independent place, or maybe we'd driven far enough to be in another region. Like when the Carl's Juniors disappeared and were replaced by Jack in the

Box, or when you'd driven far enough south to start seeing Waffle Houses every twenty feet.

Well, whatever. Their coffee was fantastic, especially compared to the motel room swill.

And as a bonus—there was a dusty payphone outside the entrance.

Leo leaned against it while I fished some change out of my pocket. He didn't say anything, but he didn't have to. The crevices between his eyebrows said it all—he didn't like this.

I dropped the coins in the slot and punched in my parents' landline. The phone rang twice on the other end before my mom's sleepy voice said, "Hello?"

"Mom, it's me."

"Richie?" She gasped. "Honey, where are you?"

"I need to—"

"Rich?" My dad had taken the phone. "What's going on?" His voice was calm. Conversational, even.

"I'm buying tickets for a game. You want to come?"

Leo's eyebrows quirked.

Without missing a beat, Dad asked, "Who's playing?"

"Depends. I can get Cowboys or Bears."

"Hmm." He was quiet for a minute. "Cardinals have a better lineup this year."

I frowned. "What's wrong with the Cowboys?"

He laughed. "Everything, son. Everything. Bigger crowd, for one thing."

My blood turned cold. "You think they'll have that big of a turnout?"

"Sounds like it's gonna sell out."

I barely bit back a curse. "So…Cardinals, then."

"Cardinals." He paused. "Fifty-yard line, if you can get them."

"Fifty-yard line. Got it." I suppressed a shudder. That wasn't good. "Can you buy beer this time?"

"You bet. Call me when you have the tickets."

"Will do."

"Sounds good. Love you, son."

"Love you too."

When I hung up, Leo cocked his head. "So, we're going to Phoenix?"

"No." I started toward the car. "We have to move. *Now.*"

Leo jogged after me. As we got in the car, he said, "Not Phoenix, then?"

"No." I smirked and started the car. "Come on, we're not *that* on the nose with our codes."

"So…" He made a *go on* gesture.

I drove us out onto the interstate, gunned the engine, and blazed down the strip of asphalt toward the distant mountains. "'The Falcons are playing' means some shit's gone down and I'm hitting the road. 'I can get Cowboys or Bears' means I need to know if he's heard anything. When he mentioned the Cardinals, that means he knows what's happening. And a sellout crowd means we've got company coming." I shifted uncomfortably, gripping the wheel tight as white lines flew past. "Asking him to buy the beer is telling him I need him to keep an ear to the ground and fill me in when I call back."

"Wait, you're calling back?"

I nodded.

He huffed impatiently. "Rich, for fuck's sake. We—"

"Relax. We'll hole up at Smitty's for a few days, and then I'll take off to make the call."

"Take off *where?*"

"Wherever I need to go to make sure nobody tracks us to Smitty's."

He grumbled something. "So what was the deal with the fifty-yard line?"

"That's how he tells me how bad shit's getting. Fifty-yard means we're in deep shit."

Leo squirmed beside me. "How deep?"

"Deep enough we're not stopping until we get to Smitty's."

"That's…over a thousand miles."

I didn't speak. I just pressed the accelerator.

After a minute of silence, Leo asked, "Why do you and your dad have a code like that? I thought you both trusted the Marshals."

"We do. Well…did." I let my head fall back against the seat. "But the nature of our jobs sometimes means we can't disclose where we are. When I was a kid, he and I came up with a code so if he ever needed us to bug out, he could tell us without tipping anyone off. You work with mobsters and shit, anything can happen, you know?"

Leo nodded silently.

"So he worked out a code with my mom, and he taught it to us when we got older. We kept it going when I was in the military too."

"Did you ever have to use it?"

I shook my head. "Not until now. He drilled it into our heads and quizzed us constantly about it to make sure we didn't forget." I tapped my thumbs on the wheel. "Annoyed the shit out of me back then, but I'm glad he did it."

"Yeah," Leo said dryly. "Me too." He paused. "If I'd known you guys had some elaborate code, I'd have said okay to you calling him sooner."

"No, it's best like this. We couldn't risk staying in one place or being traced. Even if no one knew what we were saying, they'd still figure out where I was." I sighed. "Code or not, you were right that it was a risk."

"But if you'd called sooner, he could've started listening to the grapevine."

"He probably started listening as soon as he found out what happened." I sighed. "And from the way my mom sounded all panicked when she picked up, they know what happened. Or at least, they know something happened. But anyway, he's going to look into it, and I'll call and get an update when I think it's safe. For now"—I gestured up ahead—"we get our asses to Smitty's and go underground."

A day and a half, two more vehicles, and three bags of disgusting fast food later, I drove a battered Chevy pickup down a tree-covered and gravel driveway.

"Tell me we're here," Leo grumbled.

"We're here." I carefully maneuvered across the leaf-littered gravel. It didn't look icy, but we'd already slid a couple of times on the winding mountain roads, and I wasn't about to roll the stolen truck when we were so close to our destination.

Leo leaned forward, staring out the windshield, and his breath hitched. "You have *got* to be kidding me."

Despite being tired and cranky, I couldn't help chuckling. "Don't worry. That's not the main house."

He eyed me dubiously.

I understood his concern. The log cabin looked like it was barely big enough for one person. Like one of those tiny houses that had been all the rage for a while—two hundred square feet at the most. I was pretty sure I'd crapped in outhouses bigger than that.

Beside the building was a truck that didn't look to be in much better shape than the one we were driving. It was coated in mud from the bedrails down, and the rear window was covered in stickers. Knowing Smitty, the slogans and pictures ran the gamut from vulgar jokes to equally vulgar political commentary. I didn't bother reading them. My eyes were about to cross anyway, and Smitty and I didn't exactly vote along the same lines. I just wanted sleep, not a fight.

As we got out of the truck, the cabin's front door opened. Smitty stepped out, and I wasn't surprised to see him in a pair of camouflage pants and combat boots with a black USMC T-shirt. Some guys wore cammies to look all tough and badass, but Smitty knew what I did—they were fucking comfortable. I lounged around in them myself sometimes.

His red hair was long and curly now, and he had a full mountain man beard, which covered some of the scars on the right side of his face. He still wore the black eyepatch. Always said he liked looking like a pirate, but I think he just hated the way glass eyes felt.

Even though he didn't have the flat abs from his Corps days, his arms and shoulders said he wasn't slacking when it came to PT. The guy looked good.

"Chainsmoker!" Smitty bellowed. "Man, it's been a minute, hasn't it?"

I laughed as I came toward him. "Yeah, it has. How you been?"

"Getting by." He pulled me into one of his famous bear hugs and squeezed. "Good to see you, buddy."

"Yeah, you too," I sputtered. When he let me go, I gestured at Leo. "Leo, this is Smitty. Smitty, Leo."

Leo extended his hand, but Smitty held out his left one. It only took Leo half a beat to figure out why—the two-pronged metal hook extending from under Smitty's right sleeve caught the light. He switched hands and shook Smitty's left. "Nice to meet you. And, uh, thanks. For putting us up." His eyes flicked toward the house like he still wasn't convinced.

"You got any gear?" Smitty motioned toward the truck with his prosthetic. "I can help you haul it inside."

"We don't have much," I said. "We, uh, kinda had to hit the road in a hurry."

His eyebrow arched over his good eye. "You're gonna tell me that story, you know." Jutting the hook toward Leo, he added, "I've seen his face on TV."

Leo and I exchanged uneasy glances.

"I'm on your side, brother." Smitty clapped my shoulder. "But you better be straight with me, all right?"

111

At least he didn't add his usual crack about "...*as straight as you'll ever be*." He'd bust my chops, but he'd never out me to someone.

"I will."

We took what gear we had into the tiny cabin. Then Smitty lifted a large panel in the floor, revealing a brightly lit staircase underneath.

"I still think you need to add the music to that," I said. "It just doesn't have the same effect without."

Smitty rolled his eye. "I'm not playing any Legend of Zelda music, you punk. Now get down there."

I chuckled and started down the steps. Leo followed, and Smitty's heavy boots thunked after us. The panel over our heads closed with a thud, and I heard Leo's breath hitch.

I glanced back at him and smiled. "It's okay. The hallway's a little claustrophobic, but the rest is pretty open."

"What the fuck is this place?" Leo asked. "A missile silo?"

Smitty barked a laugh. "You're smarter than you look, man."

"Huh?"

I chuckled. "It is a missile silo. Or, well, it was."

"Nah, it still is," Smitty argued. "Just...no missile in it anymore. Aside from the one in my drawers."

Groaning, I threw up my hands. "Oh my God, Smitty. We are so not measuring dicks this time, all right?"

"This time?" There was a note of amusement in Leo's voice. "Is that a thing you guys do?"

"We do a lot of weird shit." I glanced back again and shrugged. "Get a bunch of Marines drunk in a missile silo, and you never know what might happen."

"Yeah." Smitty sniffed. "I'm still finding pieces of paintballs around the place, you know that?"

I laughed, the sound echoing down the long, cramped hallway.

"I'm not even going to ask," Leo said.

"You won't have to." I chuckled. "Get a couple of beers in us, and I guarantee you'll hear the whole story."

The hallway ended at a set of steel double doors. I leaned into the push bar, then gestured for Leo to go ahead.

He did, and as soon as he was clear of the door, he just stopped and stared. I didn't blame him. I'd done the same damn thing the first time I'd come here.

The place reminded me of one of those atrium-style hotels—open in the center with ring-shaped floors all the way down. The top was thick, dirty glass that let in some daylight, though I didn't know if it could still be opened, and the middle went down far enough that I couldn't lean over the railing without getting vertigo. Stairwells connected each floor to the one below it, and the previous owner had installed a couple of bridges four and eight floors down, one going east-west and one going north-south. I didn't know if all silos were this big, or if this one had housed an exceptionally big missile, but I'd never asked. Kinda didn't want to know.

The balconies were gunmetal gray and utilitarian, but rooms were surprisingly spacious and homey. I couldn't wait to show Leo Smitty's man cave, especially if he'd finally gotten around to putting in a pool table.

Smitty locked the double doors behind us, then led us down a few levels.

Leo gestured at one of the bridges. "Why do I feel like you guys have had Star Wars reenactments on these?"

Smitty and I both snorted.

"Guilty," I said.

Leo chuckled, shaking his head as he rolled his eyes. "Yeah. I was right—Marines are fucking crazy."

"Damn right." Smitty beamed. "Now come on. I'll show you the guest rooms."

Chapter Ten
Leo

Of course Rich's friend lived in a missile silo. Naturally. Because God forbid he knew any normal people. On the other hand, depending on normal people would probably get us both killed, so I was more appreciative of Smitty and his bizarre living arrangements than I would have been before everything went to hell.

My room was more like a suite, and way nicer than any hotel we'd stayed in over the past few days. The bedding was soft, the shower looked mildew-free, and it was right next to Rich's, which…should have been close enough, but when he shut the door felt like miles away. My gut clenched when I lost sight of him, and that reaction disturbed me. I was willing to admit I relied on Rich. I was even willing to admit I liked him at this point, but the idea that I was becoming dependent on him for more than purely utilitarian reasons bothered me. I had learned my lesson when it came to relying on other people. I needed to get over myself.

I decided to do that by getting to know Smitty better. It was clear that he and Rich were close, and equally clear that this guy was bugfuck paranoid. I could probably learn a thing or two from him, and it wouldn't hurt to pick his brain a little bit when it came to Rich, either.

I found Smitty in his kitchen, sitting at the table with a book and drinking a cup of coffee. I checked the title of the novel, then did a double-take. "*The Princess Bride*?"

"Best revenge story ever," Smitty said, casually turning a page with his prosthesis.

"You're an Inigo Montoya fanboy?"

"The guy doesn't know when to quit. Doesn't even know *how*." Smitty's smile was sharp, and so was the look in his eye when he met my gaze. "He would have made a good Marine."

"If you say so."

"I do. Room suit you?"

"It's great, yeah. Thanks."

Smitty put the book down and crossed his arms. "I've gotta say, you're the politest mobster I've ever met."

I wanted to snark *Oh, and you've met so many, have you*, but I held back. Rich had to deal with me—Smitty didn't. I needed this guy to like me. "You catch more flies with honey, and all that."

"That would be a good metaphor, if I were a fly."

"Yeah, you're more of a hornet," I agreed, and that got me another smile. "Look, I'm not going to be a dick to you in your own house. You didn't have to agree to help us out, and I appreciate it. I have the feeling Rich and I were about at the end of our rope, otherwise."

"Right. Just how badly have you fucked things up for Chainsmoker, anyway?"

"Why do you call him that?" My question was met with stolid silence. I took the point and continued. "Pretty badly, but I want to make it clear that *I* was only incidental in fucking things up. Did he tell you at all about what's going on with the Marshals?"

"Some," Smitty allowed. "It's rough, when your own people turn on you. You're a high-value target, if dirty marshals are risking their identities to come after you."

"Think of it less like 'Rich's own people are turning on him' and more like 'criminal infiltrators are being unmasked in an effort to stop us,'" I said.

"Undercover mafiosos can't explain everything, though."

I remembered the cluster fuck at the hotel and nodded reluctantly. "No, they can't. Rich has been careful about reaching out to anyone in the bureau. He's had one conversation with his dad, and that's it."

Smitty scoffed. "Careful? Rich?"

I shrugged. "Okay, I've kind of *made* him be careful. He's an obscenely trusting guy, you know that? Good in a car fight, though."

"He is trusting," Smitty agreed. "Too trusting, a lot of the time. You'd think he'd have had that wrung out of him by now like the rest of us, but he's just gotta be the Boy Scout about some things. Me, though? Trust isn't an issue for me."

"Because you trust no one?"

"Because I can count the people in this world I can trust on the one hand I have left, and Rich is one of them. You don't even come close." Well. It was good to have that out in the open, at least. I had to know where I was starting from to get anywhere else. "And hang on there, *car fight*? Not a bar fight?"

"No, it was literally a car fight."

"What the fuck were you two doing with cars?"

"Being chased, mostly. Rich did some fancy driving and got some bad people off our tails."

"Lost them in traffic?"

"More like lost them to being unable to control their vehicle. Dead." I drew a finger across my throat, curving it like a smile. "As doornails."

"Huh."

I'd had enough sparring on his terms. It was time to change the mood. "You got a pack of cards?"

"Sure."

"Want to play a few rounds of poker?"

He set his book aside. "Maybe. We don't have much in the way of stakes, though." *You don't have shit*, he was polite enough not to say out loud, but I was an expert at translating a whole dictionary of expressions at this point.

"We can play for whatever you've got around. Potato chips, candy, some other easily portable vice. Or information," I added, and I could see I had his attention with that one. "The loser of each hand has to answer the winner's question, as long as it's not too personal."

"Who decides if it's too personal?"

"The loser, of course." I grinned at him. "Come on, I'm not strapping you to a chair and bringing out a cattle prod or anything—this is purely for fun, not an interrogation. Unclench your jaw, relax a while."

After a moment, Smitty got up from the table, completely silent. I thought maybe he was leaving, maybe I'd lost him, but he only went as far as the counter, opened a drawer and pulled a battered pack of cards out. He tossed them to me. "You shuffle."

I pulled the cards out and ran them through my hands appreciatively. There was something about a well-loved deck that called to me, reminded me of the old gambling rooms the Grimaldis used to run back when my father was still around. He'd work security, or sometimes play himself, and I'd be there in the corner, smelling the cigar smoke and listening to the clink of ice in glasses and low, easy-going threats between friends as games played out.

The older men had called me his little shadow, kinder to me than the younger, hungrier ones who only played to win a buck. They'd been happy to let me watch the games, and they'd taught me how to bluff and when to fold, when to call and when to raise. Some of the most pleasant times of my childhood had taken place in those dark back rooms, too warm and so smoky that it stung my eyes, but enjoyable despite all that.

I shuffled the deck a few times, getting my hands used to the feel of the cards, then raised one eyebrow at Smitty. "How about Texas Hold 'Em? No need for blinds or burning cards, since it's just the two of us and we already know the stakes."

"Blinding and burning. Sounds like just the card game for a mobster."

"Thanks, you're too kind." That got a reluctant smile, and I dealt us each two cards before he had time to reflect any longer. Three cards face up went into the center of the table, and I put the deck aside and glanced at my hand, but spent more time looking at Smitty's face as he looked at his own cards. The guy was pretty relaxed about it—easier to read than a stoic, but less fun. Still…

"You don't like your hand."

He glanced up at me. "I like it fine."

"No, you don't. I bet you've got…hmm, low number cards, different suites. Couple that with no face cards in the flop, I think you're looking at a lot of nothing right now."

He shrugged. "There are still two more rounds to be dealt, although why bother waiting to deal them, since we're not betting as we go?"

I smiled. "For the sake of conversation. Getting to know each other."

"Everything I really need to know about you, Rich will tell me."

"But you can ask about things that Rich doesn't know."

"Like what?"

"I don't know. Make a side bet."

"Fine." He squinted at me. "If I win, you forfeit the right to refuse to answer."

"I'll see that." I dealt the fourth card into the middle, the turn. My hand wasn't looking good, but Smitty didn't need to know that. "If I win this hand, you have to get me a beer before the next one."

"I'd have gotten you a beer anyway."

"Yeah, but now you'll *have* to."

"*If* you win."

"Right." I nodded. "If."

"Fine."

I laid out the fifth and final card on the board. Still no face cards, but there was a pair of nines showing. "Oh, nice."

"Do you always talk this much when you play poker?"

"Only when I know I'm going to win." The corner of Smitty's lips curled up, and I knew I had him then. He was a confident guy, fun with his friends, that much was obvious from how he and Rich had treated each other when we walked in the door. He was cooler with me, but I had his number now. "Show me what you've got."

He turned his cards over. "Three of a kind."

"Not bad, not bad." I showed him my own. "Two pair, nines and Jacks."

"Son of a bitch." He shook his head but got up and headed to the fridge. "Here." He tossed me a can of— what was this stuff? I couldn't even tell—the label was in German. "What's your question?"

"Oh, it's a big, dark, heavy one, are you ready for this?" I leaned forward and murmured, "For fuck's sake, why do you call Rich Chainsmoker?"

Smitty actually laughed this time, and I knew I'd played it right. Keep it light, keep it relaxed, and the real work would come easier farther down the line. "He got sick off a single cigarette once, only time I ever saw him try to smoke. Of course, it was a shitty cig to begin with, smelled disgusting, but we were in the middle of the ass end of nowhere and it wasn't like there were a lot of options. Chucked his cookies five feet." He pushed his cards back toward me. "Deal again."

I did as the man said, and we worked through another dozen hands over the next half hour. It took longer than normal because of the side bets, which ended up being the best part of the game. At one point he made me do a handstand, which just about landed me on my ass in the middle of his kitchen. I retaliated by making him speak for the next round in a pirate voice. As for the questions themselves…well, they could have been worse. The first round that I let him win, he asked how many people I'd killed.

"Three," I said immediately.

"You're that sure?"

"It's not the kind of thing you forget. I didn't live in a war zone, spraying bullets everywhere and hoping for maximum casualties. I was given a target, I went after the target. All fellow mobsters, just in case you're thinking otherwise." I could see by the slight relaxing of his posture that he had been.

His second question was easier in a way, but also harder. I didn't mind talking about myself, but I didn't like talking about my family. So of course, he asked me, "Is your dad really a hitman?"

"No more than anyone working for the family."

"That's not an answer."

"True, it's not." Well, this was the last hand *he* was winning for a while. "No, my father isn't a hitman. He was loyal to the Grimaldis and he did some dirty work for them, but he was never a professional killer. Didn't have the stomach for it, or so he said. My uncle, on the other hand?" Smitty blinked in apparent surprise, and *ha*, yes, I saw where he was going with this line of questioning. Someone had had time to Google me. Better I tell him now than drag the process out over another round of poker. "Yeah, he's a hitman. Was, at least, before he retired. He worked for the Albanian mob though, not the Italians." I snorted. "The Italians *wish* they had someone with my uncle's reputation in their employ. They tried to poach him several times, tried to kill him at least twice. He always came out ahead, though." I looked over at Smitty and grinned, wide and fake. "New hand."

By the fifth win in a row for me, Smitty was getting frustrated. Not angry, as I'd figured, but frustrated. "How are you doing this?" he muttered as I laid down a straight flush. "Counting cards?"

"I can count cards," I admitted, shuffling the deck again. I spun them from one hand to the other, arcing through the air between my fingers. It was the kind of dumb parlor trick that would have gotten me slapped across the head back home, but Smitty just looked reluctantly impressed. "I'm good with numbers, and it's not actually all that hard to count a single deck. But in this case?" I reached into my lap and pulled up the three cards I'd cached last round. "I'm just using good, old-fashioned sleight of hand."

Smitty stared at me. I stared back, waiting to see if he was going to get mad. When he burst out laughing, I sighed with relief—quietly, so he didn't notice it, but it was there nonetheless. "You son of a bitch," he chuckled after a moment.

"Why's Leo a son of a bitch?" Rich asked as he joined us in the kitchen. I froze as he walked past me toward the fridge, briefly transfixed by his fresh, clean scent. He'd had a shower and changed, and he looked genuinely relaxed for the first time I'd seen. The lack of frown lines made him look years younger.

"He cheats at cards."

I rolled my eyes. "I cheat at *life*, this shouldn't be a surprise to you. Another hand?" I smirked at Smitty. "Double or nothing? I promise to play it straight. I've already gotten more information out of you that I'd hoped for when we started."

Rich sat down at the table with his own beer and looked between us a bit suspiciously. "What kind of information?"

"Mostly about you," I said cheekily. "I now know your mom's name is Marie, your dad is less than a year away from retirement and bitter about it, and your younger brother played pro ball for the Seahawks for two years before injury took him out of it for good." And now was doing a whole lot of nothing, from the way Smitty described it, apart from buying flashy sports cars and having flings with ladder-climbing women. Sounded like he was handling retirement about as well as Rich's father expected to.

"You could just have asked me all of this, I would have told you."

"Yeah, but it's more fun to pry it out of Smitty here."

"One more hand," Smitty agreed. "Double or nothing, and Rich gets to watch you and make sure you don't cheat again."

I pressed one hand to my heart. "Are you accusing me of being a liar? Honey, sweetheart, love muffin, I thought we were past that!"

"You just admitted you've been cheating this whole time!"

"Yeah, but that's not *lying*. You cheat with your body, but you lie with your mind. Lying is blatantly rude, whereas cheating is just something you get away with when the other person isn't paying close enough attention." I could feel Rich's gaze on me, more serious than it should have been, but I did my best to ignore it. Thank God I had a complexion that didn't show a blush. "Come on. One more hand, and the winner gets to ask two questions, whatever they want, no evasion allowed."

"Fine, but Rich deals."

"Sounds fair." Our fingers brushed as I handed Rich the cards, and the hairs on my arm stood up. I was seriously touch-deprived if a little thing like that was enough to give me goosebumps. I grinned and sat back. "Go ahead."

I got a good start with my hole cards, a queen and a jack, but as Rich laid the cards out in the middle of the table, I could see that the board was against me. Two seconds with that deck and I could have given myself a damn royal flush, but I had promised to be good this time. Fine. "Pair of queens."

Smitty laid his cards out. "Straight flush."

"What the hell?" It was the best hand he'd had yet. I looked from the perfect row of spades to him, and then to Rich. "Did *you* cheat this time?"

"It's probably just karma," Rich said. *Jackass.*

Smitty smiled evilly. "My turn at last. First question—is the prospect of getting revenge worth everything you're going through now?"

What the fuck kind of question is that? He was apparently done with throwing me slow, easygoing pitches. I gritted my teeth for a second and bit back my initial reaction of *fuck you.* "If it pays off in the end, I'd go through a lot more."

"Fair enough." All of the levity had gone out of his expression. The game had definitely changed from lighthearted to professional interrogator level. "Second question—what are you going to do if you get your revenge? Do you go out in a blaze of glory and take everyone out around you as well, or do you have a long game in mind?"

I stared at him for a moment. "I'm not suicidal."

"Not what I asked."

"I'll do what I have to do to get even."

"Still not an answer."

Rich shook his head. "Smitty…"

"It's not that hard a question, man." He hadn't looked away from me yet. "Pretty simple, really, and pretty fucking important. So what have you got, Leo?"

Past a certain point, the future hadn't been weighing very heavily on my mind. I couldn't even consider what I might do once I got what I needed, because it loomed so large over everything. "I don't know," I said at last. "Does that make you happy, me telling you I don't know? Because I'm not giving up Rich either way, and I don't think you're gonna be able to convince him to ditch me." I shrugged. "Not your style in the Marines, leaving a man behind, right?"

"You're not a Marine."

"Nope. I'm worse." I leaned a little closer. "I'm his *responsibility*." I pushed my cards over to Rich and stood up. "My turn for a shower, I think." I walked out and tried not to read too much into the complete silence I left behind me.

Chapter Eleven
Rich

Smitty watched Leo leave. I watched Smitty.

An odd apprehension curled in my stomach. I assumed Smitty was waiting until he was sure Leo was out of earshot before saying anything, which meant he probably didn't like him. That or this was just stunned silence, which would shock the hell out of me because I didn't imagine there was much left in the world that could render my old war buddy mute.

Finally, Smitty took a swallow of his drink, shook his head, and looked at me. "Fifty bucks says you wind up fucking him."

I sputtered, almost choking even though I hadn't been taking a drink myself. "Come again?"

"Oh come on." He tapped his hook emphatically on the table beside the cards they'd been playing. "I *know* you, Smoker."

"Yeah? And?" I gestured toward the door. "He's my witness, man. People are trying to kill us."

"Yep. He is. And they are. And you're here." He waved the hook at our surroundings. "If the way he's looking at you means what I think it does…" Smitty paused, then smirked. "For the record, there's condoms and lube under the sink in his bathroom."

I stared at him, jaw slack. "There's…he's…" I had to shake myself as all the thoughts tumbled over the top of each other. "First, why do you keep condoms and lube in the guest bathroom? And second, what the fuck do you mean 'the way he's looking at' me?"

"Because you're not the only one who stays at my place," he said. "And you ain't the only Marine who plays for your team."

I kind of wanted to ask who else in our platoon had been queer, or if it was just someone else he'd known from the Corps, but that didn't seem as important right now. "Okay, and how's he's looking at me? What's that all about?"

Smitty chuckled, patting my arm with his hand. "Like I said, I know you. And that guy?" He poked his hook toward the door. "He's into you."

I shook my head. "Dude, it's nothing like that. Trust me—if he had half a chance, he'd hitch his wagon to someone a lot more competent so he can stay alive."

"Doubt that."

"He's not into me—he just doesn't want to die, and I'm the only one he can trust right now."

Smitty pursed his lips, the motion deepening some of the scars on his face. "So it's just my imagination that whenever you're not looking, he's undressing you with his eyes?"

"Yes!" I rolled my eyes. *Don't get my hopes up, asshole.*
Wait, what?

I tamped that thought down in a hurry. "Okay, you know what? It doesn't even matter. Yeah, he's hot. And maybe he's into me. I don't know. But it isn't like we can act on it."

"Why not?" He shrugged.

"For the same reasons Valentine and I never acted on it while we were out on a mission? Christ, Smitty."

Smitty snorted. "Uh-huh. And when you and Valentine were back at base camp and we weren't out getting shot at?"

Heat rushed into my cheeks. "Uh…"

"What? You guys didn't think you were exactly subtle, did you?"

"Um…" I cleared my throat. "Well, I mean…look, the point is that we never did anything when we were out on a mission."

"Right. But right now, you and Leo are basically back at base camp. You're away from the action. You've got some downtime." He shrugged again. "Why not?"

I stared incredulously at him. "Why are you practically shoving me into bed with him?"

"Because I get fifty bucks if you two fuck."

"Hey, I didn't agree to that wager."

"No, but you will if you aren't a pussy."

I scowled. That had always been the foolproof way to get another Marine in on a bet. Either take the bet and risk losing, or listen to everyone's shit about you being too much of a coward to make a simple bet.

"Son of a bitch," I muttered.

"So, you're in?"

Rolling my eyes, I nodded. "You're going to lose, though. He's my *witness*."

"And Valentine was your supervisor. Didn't stop you then, and I don't think it's going to stop you now."

I flipped him the bird. "I guess I don't need to ask you what you think of him now."

"You still can." He reached for his drink. "I have opinions about him besides whether or not I think you guys want to gargle each other's balls."

A laugh burst out of me. "Well now I'm really curious." I planted my elbows on the table and put my chin on my hands. "*Do* tell."

His expression turned a little serious, though there was still some mischief in the twist of his lips. Even that faded after a moment, and he sat up a bit. "He's not stupid, that's for damn sure."

"Tell me something I don't know. The guy's so smart it's scary."

Smitty nodded slowly. "No kidding. And he's…" Smitty's good eye lost focus, and he was silent long enough to make me fidget. "I like the guy. Didn't think I would after what you told me about him being a crook and all, but…" He exhaled slowly as he sat back against his chair. "The kid's scared out of his mind."

I straightened. I definitely hadn't expected that.

"He was digging for intel," Smitty went on, "like he wanted to make sure he had all his bases covered. Knew what he was getting into by staying with you."

I swallowed. "So he doesn't trust me?"

"That wasn't the vibe I got. The opposite, actually."

"What do you mean?"

"I mean…" Smitty chewed his lip. "It was almost like he was second-guessing himself. Like he doesn't trust how much he trusts you."

My lips parted.

"He's already committed, you know?" Smitty went on. "It's you and him against the world until this thing is over, and he wants to make sure he's not being an idiot by trusting you to stick with him."

It was my turn to sit back, and I didn't even know what to say. I could barely breathe. Leo had been rightfully suspicious of me from the start. We'd had to trust each other out of sheer necessity, but I'd never gotten the impression he *wanted* to trust me. Least of all enough to cheat an ex-Marine at poker in the name of getting enough information.

Smitty cleared his throat and glanced at his watch. "Listen, there's still a few hours of daylight left. I can run into town and get anything you boys need. There's food and beer around, but I can pick up some more."

"That might not be a bad idea. Especially if we need to hit the road—it would be good to have something to take with us."

"Can do," he said with a sharp nod.

"Thanks." I dug out my wallet and handed him some cash. "Let me know if it's enough." I paused. "And if there's a place to get a burner phone…"

"There's a cell phone kiosk at the mall two towns over." He slid the money into his back pocket. "Long as you can wait a couple of hours."

"I've got nothing but time," I said dryly.

"Well…" He cracked open his soda. "Soon as I'm done with this, I'll head out and pick up everything."

"Thanks." I clinked my can against his.

We hung around for a bit and drank to the buddies we'd lost in the desert. Then he went into town for supplies and a phone.

And in the silence, I wondered for the millionth time how Leo and I were getting out of this one.

While Smitty went into town, I wandered around the missile silo with my thoughts.

It was weird, feeling claustrophobic in a place like this. If anything, it should've had the opposite effect. The silo was deep and cavernous, enough that leaning over the railing could mean some serious vertigo. I'd learned that the hard way during some shitfaced paintball a while back.

It felt even bigger today because, for the moment, I was alone. My footfalls echoed off the metal grates, emphasizing how much space was above and below and around me.

And still, I couldn't catch my breath. The cylindrical walls were closing in around me. The bottom of the silo, which I couldn't even see, was crawling upward. Thank God the top was clear. The Open Skies Act required a transparent top so the Russians could look in and see that there was no missile, and it meant I could see daylight outside and maybe not feel quite so much like the place was moments away from crashing down on my head.

There's no way out.

I couldn't escape that thought any more than I could escape this place on a moment's notice.

There's no way out.

"They're trying to cave in the entrance!"

"Fuck 'em up, Smoker. They collapse that shit, we're not getting out of here."

"Incoming!"

I shuddered, cold sweat trickling down between my shoulder blades. I was not going to have a flashback. Not here. Not now.

Leaning on the railing, gripping the steel bar with both hands, I closed my eyes and took some slow, deep breaths as I pointedly ignored how the whole silo was tilting to the left, then the right, then back again. This was not the same as that cave in the wilds of Afghanistan. The insurgents we'd been fighting had known those complex tunnels and switchbacks better than we ever could have. No one knew Leo and I were here. Even if they found us, Smitty had an endless supply of weapons, booby traps, and plenty of things that could be *used* as weapons.

But if they did find us, there was no way out.

That was the part that kept making me want to hurl my guts over the railing. If someone found us, if they found the cabin, if they found the door, if they made it through the tunnel…they'd have our backs to the wall. They'd have reinforcements, too. We just had us, our wits, and a finite supply of ammunition, explosives, water, food…

"We either stay in here and let them box us in, or we go out in the open and get shot."

"At least out there we've got somewhere to go."

"Yeah, but in here, we can still—"

"Guys, we need to make a call. Wolf's not going to last in here or *out there."*

"Fuck," I whispered shakily. My hands were slick on the railing. Wolf hadn't lasted. Neither had Sully—we'd gone out in the open and a sniper had taken him out. We'd been fucked either way. In the cave. Out of it.

Just like now. We were cornered. Pinned down. No way to—

"Rich?" Leo's voice spun me around.

"Leo. Shit." I took a breath to steady myself. "You scared me."

"Sorry." He sounded sincere, and he was studying me as he came closer. "You all right?"

"Yeah. Yeah, I'm just…" I looked up to avoid his gaze, and that was a mistake. Was the roof always that low? I could see out, thanks to the thick, dirty glass, but it still seemed like it could cave in at any moment and—

"Hey."

I jumped again, partly because he'd again pulled me out of a semi-panicked thought, but also because he was *right there*. Right in front of me. An arm's length away. Close enough that when I pulled in a deep breath through my nose, I caught a faint hint of…aftershave? Shower gel? Something spicy and masculine. Something that dug a whole new breed of *oh shit* from the depths of my fucked-up head.

You're not just a witness anymore. You're my responsibility, but you're also…

God, Leo. How do I make sure nothing happens to you?

"What's going on?" Had he ever spoken this gently to me before? "You're shaking."

I looked down. Yeah. Oh yeah. I was shaking. Hands. Knees. Voice.

Sagging against the railing, I sighed and ran an unsteady hand through my hair. I couldn't tell if my hair was damp because my hand was sweating or my scalp was. Maybe both. Christ, I was a wreck.

"I'm just…" I pushed out a ragged breath. "Overthinking everything, I think."

Leo tilted his head. "What do you mean?"

"I mean, I'm…" I swallowed the nausea burning its way up my throat. There was no point in trying to be cagey. I couldn't think clearly enough to bullshit anyway. "I'm not going to lie—I'm scared."

Without missing a beat, Leo said, "I fucking hope you are."

I eyed him, not sure how to respond.

"We've got the Grimaldis on our tail, and they've got people in with the Marshals, the FBI—hell, they've probably got people in with fucking Santa Claus." Leo exhaled hard, revealing his own nerves for the first time. "If you weren't scared, I'd say there's something seriously wrong with you."

Well, there was that. But still, could he even imagine the depths of my fear right now?

In my mind, I saw myself sprinting to the McDonald's restroom to heave when my PTSD had caught up with me. I saw myself waking up with Leo pinning me down after I'd clocked him in my sleep. He'd been blindsided by my past and my fear enough times. Maybe now was the time for some serious honesty. Get it out on the table while the bullets weren't flying.

"Look." I met his dark eyes and forced back my nerves. "I don't know what we're up against. All I do know is that we're two guys who want the same thing—to make it out the other side of this. We're in it together, you know?"

Leo nodded.

"And I'm not going to pretend that I know how we're going to get through this," I went on, struggling just to keep my voice audible. "But I will do everything in my power to make sure we do. Both of us."

He nodded again and inched a little closer. "I know you will. And so will I."

I searched his eyes, not sure how to read him.

He put his hand on my forearm. "We'll figure it out. And quite frankly, there isn't anyone I'd want on my side more than you."

I blinked. "Really?"

"Yeah." His fingers twitched a little, like he wanted to squeeze or maybe even caress, but was forcing himself not to. "I'd rather be doing this with someone who has the balls to admit when he's in over his head and doesn't have all the intel than someone who thinks he's got a handle on everything. You're willing to listen to me and my ideas. You're willing to accept that you might be wrong instead of charging ahead, tripping over your own dick, and getting us both killed."

"Oh. I…hadn't looked at it that way."

"I have. Believe me. Yeah, I was worried I was stuck with a clueless rookie and we were both fucked, but man…" Whistling, he shook his head. "You've got this, Rich. And I've got your back."

I stared at him, struggling to make sense of what he'd said. "You're…you're not supposed to have my back. I'm supposed—"

"We're not witness and marshal anymore." He shook his head again, and this time he did squeeze my arm. "We're two guys in a warzone. If you've got my back, I've got yours."

I swallowed hard, then put my hand over the top of his. "I've definitely got yours."

"I know you do." His smile was so genuine and heartfelt, it made my fear for his safety burrow that much deeper, and it also kind of made me want to cry. I couldn't think of a better ally either. If the bombs started dropping, we had this. We could do this.

As long as we could get out of the missile silo.

The walls started closing in again, and I squeezed my eyes shut as panic tried to surge through me.

Leo's hand slid up to my elbow. I focused hard on that contact. So hard I almost didn't hear him whisper, "Talk to me, Rich."

I opened my eyes, and…

No. I didn't want to talk to him. I didn't want to think about the missile silo constricting around us, or the roof caving in, or the cavalry on our tail.

Hand still shakier than I would've liked, I reached for his face. Leo's eyes flicked toward my hand, but then met mine again in the same instant my fingertips brushed his face. I touched him tentatively at first. He didn't pull away. If anything, those near-black eyes dared me to do more.

That all you got?

I wondered for a second if it was, but somehow tapped into some deep well of courage and touched him more fully—palm against his cheek, fingers drifting across stubble that wasn't quite five o'clock shadow yet.

Under my hand, his cheek rose slightly as a grin came to life on those full lips.

He stepped closer, letting his shoe brush mine.

I'll see your hand and raise you…

His fingers caught on my shirt just above my waistband, tugging just a little, before coming to rest on my side. Warm. Heavy. Firm. *There.*

Then his eyebrows rose.

Your move.

I gulped. How the hell was it—when an army of criminals were trying to find and kill us—that I could reserve any fear or nerves for what we were doing right now? I supposed it didn't matter. I could. Leo wasn't just some guy I'd met in a bar with a few bottles of liquid courage in my veins. If I fucked this up, it wasn't like I could bow out, leave, and never see him again. We still had to have each other's backs even if we made things awkward.

I didn't have a chance to fuck it up, though. Leo must've gotten impatient, or maybe he'd caught on that I was paralyzed by nerves, because he grabbed the back of my neck with his free hand, pulled himself across that last sliver of space between us, and kissed me.

Oh my God. I'm about to owe Smitty fifty bucks, aren't I?

Chapter Twelve
Leo

The kiss started off gentle.

Not the kind of gentle that I'd had with Tony, the sort that just happened when you'd been with the same person long enough to know what they liked. Those kisses had been familiar, sweet, a pleasant prelude to what was to come. When gentleness was a rare commodity, you hoarded it like gold with whoever could give it to you, and Tony had always gone easy with me. No, this was nothing like that kind of gentle.

This kiss felt like holding a hand grenade and wondering whether it was going to go off, like handling a knife by the blade and trying not to get cut. This kiss was brilliant and stupid and completely necessary, for me at least. I was so tired of wanting him and hiding it. I was so tired of watching Rich struggle and not being able to do anything about it other than talk, talk, talk. It was ridiculous, because I *knew* this was a bad idea, getting involved with a marshal, but I wanted it anyway. Rich was all I had now. I *needed* him, in as many ways as I could get him. If that was mercenary, then so be it.

I gripped the back of his neck harder and turned his head, getting a better angle on his mouth. He opened his lips and I plunged my tongue inside, tasting his heat and the faint sour tinge of beer. I half expected him to try and pull away, but he didn't. He traced his hands down my arms, and then slid them around my waist, pulling me in tighter. He was getting hard, but I wanted him desperate, I wanted him so hard and ready that he *hurt*. I wanted him to want me as badly as I wanted him. I straddled one of his thighs and ground against him, pushing him against the railing as I fought for more contact, more heat.

"*Fuck*." He left my mouth just long enough to swear and tighten his grip on me before coming back harder, as much a bite as a kiss. Not gentle, not even close, and I loved it. This, *this* was what I wanted out of him, need and hunger and more. Nothing like what I had with Tony.

I wanted this experience to be as far from what I'd had with Tony as possible.

I bit his lower lip, and then pulled back. "Are you all talk, or are you gonna make good on that?"

Rich looked a little dazed, the panic that had been trying to burst through the surface of his calm gone like it had never been there. *Good.* "What do you mean?"

"I mean, are you going to fuck me, or just talk about it?" I slid one hand down to his ass and used it to lever him closer, so there was no mistaking just how into this I was. Rich was the type to let questions eat at him if I let them, so it was best to be upfront. "Or maybe you want me to beg."

He snorted. "I'm not going to make you beg."

"I didn't say anything about *making* me beg, Rich. You don't have to *make* me suck your cock until I choke on it either, but I'd be happy to do that too." His hands clenched around my waist, and when he pulled me in for another kiss any sign of his second thoughts were gone, or at least buried under how much he wanted me.

"Bedroom. Now."

I grinned. "You sure you don't want to do it out here? It'd give you one more story to share with your Marine buddies, fucking a mobster in the middle of a missile silo." Shit, it sounded like something out of Cards Against Humanity.

"With my luck, Smitty would walk in at just the wrong moment. Do you really want him getting a front row seat to viewing your naked ass?"

He had a point. "Okay. My room's closer."

"I know." He pulled back but didn't let go, just shifted his grip to one of my hands and tugged me along behind him. I didn't mind—he had a great ass, and I could never mind getting the chance to ogle it, but I wanted my way too. As soon as we got inside the guest room, I kicked the door shut, pushed him up against it and sank down onto my knees. Hitting the concrete stung, but I barely noticed it as I hastily undid his belt and opened up his fly. Rich had gone commando—probably not with this in mind, but I appreciated how quickly it let me get his dick into my mouth.

"Mother*fucker!*"

Some part of me wanted to make a joke, talk about how I'd done a lot of bad things but I wasn't *that* far gone, but I didn't want to pull away long enough to take a breath, much less try to be funny. Holy shit, he tasted good, hot with blood and clean from the shower and just a little sticky at the head. He instinctively thrust forward and I let it happen, let his cock so far in that if I'd still had a gag reflex it would have set me off for sure.

I'd been with a lot of guys before Tony, and I knew all the ways they liked to play, all the power games and bullshit that came from trying to establish who was gonna be the alpha, who topped who, who was the bitch. I might have the skillset of a whore, but I was never going to be

141

anyone's bitch. They pushed me, I swallowed them down and stole their breath. They played it tough, I could be ten times tougher and leave them crying for their fucking mommas by the end of it. I could take whatever Rich wanted to give me—I *wanted* whatever he gave me, even if it was fucking my face so hard his hips bruised my cheekbones.

"Shit, sorry."

Sorry wasn't what I wanted, and I was about to tell Rich that, but instead of pulling away he wound his fingers into my hair, gripping it hard enough to sting my scalp. He tilted my face up so our eyes met, and the wicked expression made my breath catch. "Can't make it too easy for you, right?" he teased. "Since you've got a hard-on for begging." Then he pulled my mouth down to the base of his cock and held me there, not thrusting but so far down my throat anyway it was all I could do to breathe. I loved it.

Rich took over the rhythm and I didn't fight him, just let him move my head over his flesh while I sucked him as hard as I could, working my tongue across the thick vein on the underside of his cock, then swirling it over the head whenever I had the space to. Christ, he was big, bigger than I'd had in a long time. I closed my eyes and fumbled with my own pants, needing the touch like I needed air. Before I could wrap my hand around myself, he pulled my head off his cock.

"No, c'mon, what the hell?" I demanded.

Rich shook his head. "You were about to make me come."

Hello, Marshal Obvious. "That's the point, Rich."

"I don't want to come until I'm fucking you."

"Oh." Well, that was okay then. "Then you better get me on the bed and get busy before Smitty comes back, huh?"

Rich rolled his eyes as he pulled me to my feet. "Don't bring him into this, I'm already going to owe him fifty bucks."

That sounded fishy. "What, he dared you to do this?" I didn't know if the fact that Rich had to be coerced into it made me feel angry or just numb.

"No, but he bet I wouldn't be able to resist you." Rich looked me up and down, his eyes dark and hungry. "He was right."

I'd pay Smitty fifty bucks myself for that ego-boosting information. "Lube. Condoms. Where are they?"

"Bathroom." He was already headed that way. I took advantage of his turned back to shuck my clothes as fast as I could, no thought given to a seductive strip tease. I didn't have the time or patience for something like that right now. Next time, maybe, I could—

I bit off that thought hard and fast. There was no next time. I couldn't see into the future, I didn't know where we'd be tomorrow, much less know if it would be safe enough for something like this. Sex was good, it created a connection, but it was also a distraction. I had the feeling that once we had to give up these thick concrete walls and hit the open road again, giving into distractions would get a lot harder. So there was no next time, there was only now, and right now I wanted Rich's cock inside of me. I wanted him to fuck me so hard I couldn't speak. I wanted him to let go of all his fears and focus every molecule of his being on me.

He came back naked with a condom already on, the bottle of lube open, and I grinned. It looked like I was going to get what I wanted. "Give me that." I reached for the bottle. "I'll do it faster."

"Oh no." I didn't even know he was *capable* of looking like the devil incarnate, but damn. "No, now's the time when I make you want it even more. Get on all fours."

I'd never been good at taking orders. "Make me."

Rich stared at me for a moment, then dropped the bottle and fucking *pounced*. Seriously, it came out of nowhere, and I was fast but I wasn't that fast. He drove me onto the bed on my back, his body hot and heavy between my thighs. He grabbed my wrists and pinned them to the mattress, then kissed me before I could shout at him, rutting his cock against mine and driving me crazy in zero seconds flat.

Fuck, *fuck* yes, this was good, this was what I wanted. This was the need I craved, and right then and there I didn't give a damn whether he used lube or took me dry, I just wanted him inside of me. I hitched my hips up as far as I could, trying to get him closer, to put the thought into his mind. *Fuck me, fuck me, fuck me now.* He was there, he was right there, his thick head pressing against my hole, and all he'd have to do was push and—

He stopped moving. Completely.

"Rich…"

Nothing. He was sweaty, breathing hard, and looking unbelievably smug above me, but he wasn't moving. I smacked him on the shoulder. "Rich, c'mon!"

"No."

"Asshole!"

"That doesn't sound like begging to me."

Oh, that ship had sailed. This was supposed to be about making him need *me*, not the other way around, and I felt an uncomfortable urgency to get him inside of me. "*Fucking* asshole!"

"That sounds more like a command, and still no."

"Why not?"

He didn't reply, just held me down and raised an eyebrow. I could have tried to fight free—probably wouldn't have worked, but it would have made a point—but then I reminded myself that I didn't *have* to fight to have this. I didn't have to push to the breaking point to get what I wanted. It wouldn't be like what I'd had with Tony, but it didn't have to be a battle either. I exhaled heavily in an attempt to get my breathing a little more under control. "Okay. Okay, just let me…"

He kissed me as I trailed off, a little softer than he had before, but finished it with a nip to my lower lip that left my skin hot and swollen. I licked the spot, and now he was the one to swear.

"God*damn*. Yeah, okay." He let go of me and I rolled over, pushing up and back against his hips. He rubbed his cock along my ass, teasing me again, but this time I didn't try to force it.

Not physically, at least. "Fuck, get *on* with it, Rich."

He leaned down and kissed the back of my neck. "Say it nicely, Leo."

Oh, if I ever got the chance to turn the tables on him I was going to be absolutely merciless. "Please get on with it, so you can finally fuck me so hard that we break this bed."

He laughed. "You're so persuasive."

"Wait until you hear me when—*oh.*" Two slick fingers replaced the pressure of his cock, and I groaned with satisfaction as I finally got some part of him inside of me. "Yeah," I breathed. "Yes, fuck, more."

He didn't say anything, just gave me what I wanted, pushing deeper and harder and going right for my prostate, because fuck going slow now. It stung and it ached, it felt amazing and overwhelming, and I couldn't get enough. I forced myself to relax and rocked back onto his hand. Hearing the sound that got out of him, appreciative and *hungry*, was almost as good as coming.

He started in with another finger, but I shook my head. "It's fine, I'm good. Fuck me already." Fingers were nice, but I'd been denied what I really wanted for long enough.

Rich apparently agreed, because the next thing I knew he was spreading my legs farther apart, wide enough for him to really brace himself between them, before he slid inside of me in one long, hard push. His hands gripped my ass like he'd held my head earlier, tight enough to control me, and I didn't mind. He didn't make me wait, just pulled back and thrust inside again, and again, slow and controlled and hard, so hard. It felt incredible, like a wound I'd had for so long I'd simply assimilated the pain of it had suddenly vanished. I hadn't been sure I could really want this again after Tony. It was a glorious relief to know that I did.

"Oh, please." Now I *was* begging, but it felt right. "Rich, faster."

"I won't last as long if I go faster," he admitted between breaths. His palms slid a little on my hips, his control already wavering. "Too fucking good."

"I don't care, I need it." I did, I so did. He must have believed me, because he paused just long enough to push my chest down onto the bed and settle his hands on the mattress beside my shoulders. And then—holy shit, it was like being jackhammered into the ground. How did his hips even *move* like that? I spared a second to appreciate the level of fitness fucking me from a pushup position must take, then happily lost my mind and let myself go.

"Rich, fuck, yes, *ah, ah*, this is—just like that, yes, *figlio di puttana!*" English and Italian blurred together in my mouth to form broken, obscene praise. It took every bit of concentration I had left to fumble a hand beneath my body and grab my cock. I didn't even have to move it, just get a loose grip and let Rich rock my body into overload. I bit the sheet when I finally came, but it wasn't enough to muffle the sounds my orgasm wrung out of me. Those were *nothing* compared to Rich, though.

"Leo." That was all he said as he lost it, all that came out of his mouth as he ground to a halt inside my ass with his release, but it made me shudder with almost shameful pleasure. That was it, *that* was what I craved. Rich was already on my side—he was a good guy, better than I deserved—but now I really had him, and I was going to keep him for as long as it took to get my revenge. If I felt a moment or two of doubt, and alongside that, of *guilt*, well…those weren't emotions I'd be sharing any time soon.

I'd do my best to take care of him along the way. He'd be all right. He just had to get me within sight of the end, and I'd take it from there.

Rich tipped over onto his side and brought me with him, wrapping a shaking arm around my waist and nuzzling his face into the nape of my neck. "Jesus Christ," he muttered.

"Kind of a weird pet name, but…yes?"

He chuckled. "Shut up. You okay?"

"Really fucking okay." And I was, I felt amazing—a little sore, a little sticky, but amazing. I couldn't even compare it to what I'd felt with Tony, it would be like comparing a raging fire to an unstoppable wave. "You?"

"Definitely." He sounded so much better than he'd been just half an hour ago. That was down to me, to *this*, to the pact that we'd made. I might be his responsibility, but in some ways, he was just as much mine.

You can't think that way. Don't get distracted. You set a goal, and you work until you achieve it, or until you're dead. No second thoughts. It's better for both of you.

That was how it had to be. Still…I turned my head and kissed him, quietly now. "Try not to regret this until after you're done with me, okay?"

Rich frowned. "I'm not going to regret anything about this, Leo."

"Good." Hopefully, that would hold true long enough to finish this. I shifted my hips and grimaced. "Shower?"

"Sure."

I held onto his hand as we walked into the bathroom, not quite ready to let go yet. This interlude was almost over, no matter how badly I wished it would last.

God only knew when we'd get another one.

Chapter Thirteen
Rich

"*When it's all over*," the gunny's voice had bellowed over the transport jet's engines, "*you can drink, scream, cry, hit something. Whatever you need. But you save that shit till you're home, or I will shoot you before Haji does.*"

Lying on my back with Leo's head on my shoulder, I wondered what the gunny would've thought of me now. This wasn't over. And I hadn't drunk, screamed, cried, or hit anything. Though maybe in a crude sense I could look at Leo and say I'd hit that. Pretty sure that wasn't what the gunny had meant.

This wasn't over, but there was a pause. A lull in the chaos. With no one shooting at us and no immediate danger, we'd seized an opportunity and blown off some steam. Maybe that meant we'd get through this without losing our sanity. Was that even an option anymore?

"You do realize," Leo mused after a while, "that if someone asks during the trial if I screwed around with my handler, I'm obligated to say yes."

I eyed him, trying to look stern, but the playful sparkle in his eyes made me laugh. "I can't imagine that'll come up during the trial."

"Hey, you never know." He twisted a little, stretched, and propped himself up on his elbow so he could gaze down at me. A few dark curls tumbled into his eyes. "Lawyers ask weird questions sometimes."

"Uh-huh." I brushed his hair out of his face. "And why in the world would they feel the need to ask about this?"

He shrugged. "Discrediting the witness?"

"I think that would do more to discredit me than you, right? Since I'd be the painfully unprofessional U.S. Marshal?"

A sharky grin lit up his face. Trailing a finger down the middle of my chest, he said, "I like it when you're unprofessional."

"So I noticed." I slid my hand along his side and onto his hip, and as I gazed up at him, it was hard not to flash back to every incarnation of Leo I'd seen since the beginning. The smarmy criminal. The scared kid. The needy lover. Everything in between. And as I watched him, guilt trickled through my veins, cooling the warmth my orgasm had left behind.

Leo frowned. "What's wrong?"

I sighed. "This really is unprofessional."

"So?" Another shrug. "I won't tell if you don't."

"It's not that." I pushed myself up, and when I settled, we were both sitting, facing each other with our thighs pressed against each other and the rumpled sheets pooled around us. Without meeting his gaze, I rested my hand on his leg. "I'm supposed to be protecting you. Being objective and…" I shook my head. "Not thinking about how much I want to get you back into bed, you know?"

"Rich." His voice was softer and more soothing than I'd ever heard it. "You're a trained Marine. I'm a criminal who hasn't gotten myself killed yet. We both know when to focus on surviving and not think about getting laid."

I searched his eyes.

"You're overthinking this," he said. "Honestly, I think we're probably in better shape now that we've fucked."

"How do you figure?"

"Well." A playful grin played at his slim lips, and he put his hand over the top of mine. "We're probably less likely to kill each other."

I managed a laugh. "Okay. Fair."

He turned serious and gave my hand a squeeze. "I mean it, okay? We'll be fine. If you don't want to do this again, then we won't, but it's not like getting laid is going to get us killed. I don't know about you, but I could use the break from all the insanity, you know?"

Oh, I knew. I so knew.

Nodding, I whispered, "Yeah, you're probably right. And I'm probably overthinking it."

"You definitely are."

"Shut up." I nudged him playfully.

He chuckled again. "We'll be fine. And…hell, with everything going on? I don't know about you, but I *need* this."

I deflated a bit. Now that he'd said it? Yeah, I needed it too. The release, the contact, the intimacy—I didn't know what all I needed, but I suddenly couldn't imagine us moving forward without doing this. Maybe that was crazy, but what about this situation wasn't?

"Me too." I pulled him a little closer and brushed a kiss across his lips.

He kissed me more firmly, and as he drew back, he whispered, "So what happens now?"

I took a breath. "I'm thinking now's a good time to contact my dad."

Leo swallowed.

"Smitty's getting me a burner phone," I continued. "I'll drive out into the middle of nowhere, make the call, ditch the phone, and come back."

That relaxed him a little, and he silently watched our hands for a moment.

"I'll be careful," I whispered. "I promise."

"You better." He cupped the back of my head and kissed me, demanding access to my mouth. I had no idea if he'd intended for it to go on as long as it did, but it was ages before we came up for air. Minutes at least. Eyes locked on mine, he said, "How much time do you think we have before Smitty gets back?"

"I don't know for sure, but…" I snaked my arm around him. "I think we have enough."

Leo didn't say another word.

I was in the kitchen when Smitty came back.

"Got everything you need." My buddy put a couple of plastic shopping bags on the table. Mostly food and beer, but also a bag from one of the cell phone stores. He handed me the phone and a smaller device. "There's some dead spots out there, so I got you a booster too. It should be enough to get you at least one or two bars even up here."

"Perfect. Thanks." I checked the time. Almost three in the afternoon, so I still had some daylight left. "You mind if I borrow your ride?"

"Long as you don't get it dirty."

I laughed. "God forbid I get any mud on top of the mud."

"Damn right." He paused. "So, when do I get my fifty bucks?"

I blinked. "Huh?"

Smitty rolled his eyes. "Don't even try it, Chainsmoker." He wagged a finger at me. "I can spot your *I just got laid* face from a hundred yards."

My face burned, and I flipped him off. He just laughed.

"I need to go take care of this." I held up the phone. "I might be gone for a few hours. You two can get along, right?"

"I get along with him just fine as long as he's not fucking around at cards."

"Then play…I don't know, Monopoly or something. Just behave, okay?"

He waved me away with his prosthetic. "We're good. Go."

"Thanks, man." I headed out of the kitchen and jogged to Leo's room. When he opened the door, I showed him the phone. "I'm going to go call my dad. I'll probably be a while, but—"

"I know." He stepped closer, touched my hip, and looked right in my eyes. "Be careful out there, yeah?"

"I will." I put my arm around him. "If by chance something happens to me, you can trust Smitty. I promise."

He smiled faintly. "You trust him. That's good enough for me."

I smiled back, though my heart and stomach were doing things they probably shouldn't. "I'll be back as soon as I can."

"I'll be here." A playful smirk came to life, making him look like the confident man I'd met in Chicago. "Probably driving your friend insane."

"Yeah, or robbing him blind at poker."

"Maybe." Leo winked. "Take your time, and maybe I can get him to bet the missile silo. Could be a nice vacation home or something."

I laughed, rolling my eyes. "Behave, Leo."

"Who, me?"

"Yeah, you."

The banter seemed out of place. I needed to get the hell out of here so I could contact my dad. But I was stalling. So was Leo. And if I stood here much longer, I was going to find a way to stall until tomorrow. Or the next day. Or the one after that.

But we didn't have time for stalling. Not if we were going to survive this.

So I sobered and murmured, "I should go." I kissed him lightly. "I'll be back as soon as I can."

"Okay." He swallowed hard as he let me go. "I'm serious—be careful."

"I will."

I left the missile silo and climbed into Smitty's truck. As I fired up the engine, I eyed the tiny cabin in the rearview. It felt weird, leaving Leo behind like this. We'd been virtually joined at the hip since day one, even before we'd been literally joined at the…well, almost hip. I liked the guy, and anyway, the responsibility I had to keep him safe weighed heavily on me. Leaving him felt an awful lot like leaving him exposed, even if he was hidden in the safest place I could imagine outside of Fort Knox.

Still, I put the truck in gear and headed down the long, leaf-littered driveway. Over and over I told myself this was necessary. That I was doing it to keep him safe, not to put him in more danger. I tried to reason that in combat, I'd occasionally had to leave my team to do some recon, and I'd been fine with that.

Except when I'd done recon, I'd had a radio. There'd been contact. Now? Nothing. Sure, I could call Smitty via the burner phone, but that would lead the Grimaldi family right to the missile silo. I'd lose Leo and my best friend in one fell swoop.

So for the time being, I was cut off. Completely severed from the man I was supposed to be protecting.

For his safety. So we could escape this. So we could survive.

I took a deep breath, held the wheel in both hands, and continued down the mountain.

It took almost two hours to get out of the mountains and into the flatlands, and dear God, what a relief when the road leveled out. When we'd left Chicago, I'd deluded myself into thinking I'd feel better driving in the mountains rather than the open countryside. In reality, those winding roads had made my skin crawl. At least this range was heavily forested, so it didn't look like the mountains my team had been in back in the Sandbox. If this were the high desert of California or something, I'd have been fucked. Smitty probably would've been too; no wonder he'd bought a place up here.

The highway took me out into the plains where I could see for miles and miles. Distant rock formations. Even more distant mountains. Canyons. Dry river beds. If I stopped out here, I'd see anyone who came for me well before they were close enough to box me in. The nearest usable sniper perch was easily two or three miles out. If a sniper got me…hell, if he made that shot, he deserved it.

I parked the truck a half mile or so off the road, rolled down the windows, and shut off the engine. I gave my surroundings a sweep.

Certain I was completely isolated, I turned on the burner phone and booster, and muttered "C'mon, c'mon," as I watched it searching for a signal.

One bar. Then two. Then one again.

Good enough.

With my heart in my throat, I dialed my father's number.

"Hello?" My mother's voice.

I pressed my lips together. It killed me not to say something. She was probably worried sick over me right now, and I was desperate to tell her I was all right. But I didn't speak.

"Hello?" she repeated. Then she sighed and called out, "Wendell, I think it's those damn kids again." Into the phone, she growled, "You kids need to knock this nonsense off, or I will call the police!"

Then the line went dead.

I leaned against the truck and stared down at the phone, watching that second bar come and go as the signal wavered.

After about two minutes, the phone came to life with an unknown number.

I put it to my ear. "We still on for the game?" *Is this a secure line?*

"We're good," Dad said.

I released my breath. "Thank God. How is—"

"You need to get someplace safe." The rapid-fire words were laced with a note of panic I'd never heard from him before, and my blood turned cold. "Things are bad. Real bad."

"What's going on?"

"Your brother's getting death threats."

"What? How the—"

"He's amped up his security, but as high profile as he is—"

"That means they know I'm still with Leo," I said. "And that I'm working with him. Question is, are they trying to roll you or me?"

"Hard to say."

"How aggressive are the threats?"

"Escalating." His nerves were definitely coming through now. My dad was scared, and I didn't know how to process that. "It started with some social media posts. Last night, someone put a bullet through Chris's windshield, and when he woke up this morning, the furniture in the living room had been rearranged."

I almost choked. The rearranged furniture could almost seem like a childish prank rather than a threat, but when it was coupled with that bullet, it was much more sinister.

We were here, and you had no idea.
If we made it in this time, we can make it in again.
We can kill you and you'll never see us coming.

I wiped a hand over my face. "Shit…"

"Yeah," Dad breathed. "Whoever's involved in this—and God help me but I don't know who's on whose side right now—I'm…pretty sure they're tightening every noose they can get their hands on."

Something about the way he said that gave me pause. Narrowing my eyes at no one in particular, I said, "What else is going on?"

"The witness's father turned up dead this morning."

My stomach plummeted into my feet. "No."

"Afraid so. And nobody even tried to hide the fact that it was murder."

Squeezing my eyes shut, I swallowed the nausea burning the back of my throat. "So the Grimaldis know I'm helping Leo, and they've got people who can get close to a high-value asset in solitary. Close enough to kill him."

"They didn't just kill him, Rich," Dad said grimly. "They *shot* him. Three times."

The nausea almost won. Someone had gotten close to Leo's father. With a gun. Long enough to shoot him. Three times. And escape. Holy fuck. "We need to get Chris someplace safe. They're going to make good on those threats."

"I'm working on it, but every safehouse and contact I have is compromised. Or I have to assume they are until I know for sure they're not."

I glanced back in the direction I'd come, as if I could pick out which mountain had Smitty's missile silo fortress tucked into a forested slope. "Any way to fake his death?"

"Might not have much choice." My dad sounded like he too was fighting back queasiness. "I'm worried if I make a move, though, someone's going to move in ahead of me."

"Shit," I whispered into the wind.

"Keep your head down," he said. "Wherever the two of you are, stay low and quiet. I'll do what I can for your brother. We don't have an endgame yet, and we won't until we really know what we're up against. Until we have a handle on who's compromised and how far the Grimaldis can reach inside the department, your job is to do exactly what you've been doing from the beginning: keep you and the witness safe and out of sight. Got it?"

"Yes, sir," I said automatically. I never called my father sir, but he was shifting into U.S. Marshal mode and so was I. "When should I contact you again?"

He didn't answer immediately.

"Dad?"

"Oh shit…" He whispered so softly I barely heard him.

Panic surged through me. "What?"

There was sudden movement on the other end. Wind. Footsteps. A whispered curse.

I clamped my hand over my mouth, quelling the simultaneous urges to shout and puke. Calling out to him wouldn't help if something was wrong. He didn't need distraction or something to draw a potential assailant's attention.

The crack of gunfire made my heart stop.

Then there was an impact. Noise I couldn't quite parse.

Something scraped.

And then, a voice.

Not my father's voice.

"Richard Cody?"

I swallowed bile. "Who the fuck is this?"

"I've got a message for Leotrim Nicolosi." With a sadistic chuckle, he added, "I assume you know him?"

Dad. Oh God.

"What do you want?" I croaked.

"Tell him he's got forty-eight hours to meet with Matteo Grimaldi. He doesn't show up? We do to his mom and yours what we just did to your old man."

In the background, a woman screamed. My mother. Oh fuck.

"You got all that, Cody?"

I choked out, "You son of a—"

"Forty-eight hours."

My mom screamed again.

And the line went dead.

Chapter Fourteen
Leo

I knew something was wrong the second Rich walked back into the silo. Smitty and I had been playing cards in the middle of the open room right in front of the entrance to the place, neither of us wanting to admit that we were worried about Rich and hiding it with light conversation and deliberate placement. I'd expected him to come back tense, that would be a given. I'd even kind of anticipated him to come back and tell me to pack up fast, we needed to get going now because we'd been found.

As soon as I saw his face, though, I knew whatever happened had been *bad*. His expression was worse than nervous, worse than serious—worse than he'd looked when he was in the middle of a damn *panic attack*, for fuck's sake. There was a weird sort of blankness about him as he came into view, like some part of him had been turned off. It made my blood run cold just taking him in.

Smitty saw it too, and he reacted to it faster than I did. "Aw, shit," he said, standing up and making his way, slowly and openly, over to Rich. "Who died?"

"I think…" He shook his head a little, like he was trying to clear it. "I think my dad did."

"*Fuck!*" I shot to my feet and headed over to Rich to—hell, I didn't know, how could I imagine I'd be comforting to him when his father was probably dead because of me? He caught my gaze before I could touch him, though, and the bleakness there was enough to stop me in my tracks.

"They got your father too."

"Wait, what?" *No.* "That's not possible, my dad's in solitary. There's no way they could—"

"He was shot three times."

I shook my head. "Whoever told you this, they were lying to you, Rich. Of course they'd lie, those fuckers. They're—"

"Leo." Amazingly, this time I could actually hear the compassion in his voice, and it was for *me*. Wasted on *me*. "My dad's the one who told me, before they—before they broke in and—" He shut his eyes for a moment as he got his voice back. "He wouldn't lie to me about that. He had no reason to. He wanted me—us—to be careful. Your dad's death was a warning, and a threat."

I felt like I'd been plunged underwater. I hadn't seen Papa in so many years, not since I was a little boy, and our contact in between then and now had been scarce, but he—he was the titan of my childhood. He had been my god, and it had taken years for my illusions about him to finally crumble away after he went to prison. He'd been a good soldier for the Grimaldis, better than they deserved. And they had killed him because of me.

Rich looked like he was forcing himself to continue. "They got on the phone with me, right after they broke in and shot my—" He shook his head again. "They have my mom. They say they have your mom too."

The hell they did. "My mother is in Albania."

"Then they went and got her."

"It doesn't—she's not—that doesn't make sense. My dad and I, at least we had *some* contact after he went down, but my mother left at the same time." She'd refused to take me with her. I still remembered the sway of her long blue coat as she'd stood after one last embrace, walking away so fast her heels had blurred. Or maybe that was from the tears. Either way— "I haven't spoken with her in fifteen years."

"Then they don't care. They said they have her, have both of them, and they're giving us forty-eight hours to get back to Chicago to meet with Matteo Grimaldi. Otherwise they'll kill them."

"You have to operate as though they do have her, either way," Smitty put in. "There's no good choice here, just bad and less bad." He had his hand on Rich's shoulder, strong and supportive. I was intensely jealous of him even as I realized I couldn't do what he was doing right now. How could I be there for Rich when this whole fucking thing was my fault anyway? My parents, at least they'd been directly involved in the bloody lifestyle of organized crime. But his? Especially his mom?

One thing was sure. The time for being restrained was over. I was going to bring so much fire and pain down on the Grimaldis, they'd think they were in Pompeii. "I'll pack," I said, turning toward my room. The faster I moved, the less I would think.

"Leo."

"Won't take me a minute." I couldn't look at Rich right now. I fucking couldn't, not if I didn't want to end up throwing myself on the ground and begging his forgiveness. He hadn't signed on for this, not any of this.

"Let him go," Smitty murmured, and I thanked my father's nonexistent God that Smitty was here right now. The guy tolerated me, but Rich was his brother-in-arms. If I could get Smitty on my side, he could help me convince Rich to let me go on alone. I'd get his mom back safe or die trying, and I'd bankrupt the fucking Grimaldis and all their contacts while I did it.

My room was still the mess I'd left it this morning, but at least it didn't smell like sex. That was the last reminder I needed right now, that not even half a day ago I'd been in bed with Rich having some of the best sex of my life. I needed to slash and burn that part of my brain, because whatever we'd had—whatever we'd started to have—was over and done with, no question.

I started shoving things into my bag with no thought of neatness—nobody who saw me was going to care if my clothes were creased. I cleared out the bathroom just as fast and glanced at my phone to make sure my schedule checking in with my account was still being followed. It was, but to be safe—or rather, to keep Smitty and Rich safe, because there was no chance of that for me anymore—I'd ditch this one and get a fresh burner as soon as I got to town. Now that there was no point in being subtle, I needed to make a few calls.

I walked back out into the central room just in time to see Rich cover his face with both his hands. If he hadn't already broken down, he was definitely on the verge. Smitty looked worried, and I didn't blame him. "If you let me borrow your truck, I'll leave it wherever you want once I get to town. You can have it towed back."

Rich dropped his hands, and to my surprise, the tears I'd expected to see weren't there. His eyes were dry, and his expression was hard. "You're not going anywhere without me."

I shook my head. "The time for cooperating with the Marshals is over, Rich. That means you, too. You might still be able to salvage this for yourself if you—"

"No."

"I'm going to find your mom and take care of her, I promise."

"You're not going anywhere without me."

I dropped my bag on the ground so I could gesticulate with both hands. "Jesus Christ, why are you so fucking impossible about this? Look at what being with me has done to you! Done to your family! Your father is *dead.*" Rich flinched, and I felt awful about it, but I pushed my advantage. It was for his own good. "Your mom might be dead. Your friends might be your enemies now, Smitty excluded because he's a damn hermit it a cave in the middle of nowhere, and it's all because of me! I've fucked up your *entire life*, Rich! I'm not gonna be responsible for getting you killed too." I turned back to Smitty. "So, your truck—"

"It's not your call, Leo."

"The hell it isn't!"

"It's *not.*" Rich pointed a finger at me. I wanted to break it. Didn't he get that I was doing this in the safest way possible for him? "You're my responsibility, and I'm not letting you run back to Chicago without me just because it's dangerous. The fact that they got to my family—" he swallowed hard but kept going— "means that I have to stick to you even harder."

"That doesn't make any sense!" Where was this man's sense of self-preservation? "Let me absolve you of any responsibility over me, okay? I'm a fucking adult and I'm officially making myself not your job anymore."

"But you're still my friend."

God *damn* it. Why did he have to say shit like that when I was trying to be mad at him? Smitty stepped into the verbal void before I could get past the lump in my throat.

"Neither of you can ignore this and expect it to go away now. People are gonna hunt you down one way or another. Might as well work together to figure things out." He looked at Rich. "What can I do?"

Some of the tension bled out of Rich's posture. "Can you help Chris? He's been getting death threats, and somebody broke into his house and rearranged his furniture. Dad was thinking about putting him in a safehouse, but he couldn't trust any of his and he didn't have time to set up something else before he was shot." He said it without a quaver, but I could see how much it cost him.

"I can do that. You sure you don't want some more direct help, though?"

"No. You're not getting any more involved in this than you already are."

Smitty looked skeptical. "You're heading into a firefight, Chainsmoker. You're probably gonna need more help in the field."

"I need the rest of my family to be as safe as possible. That includes you."

"I can do more." Smitty gestured at his amputation. "Don't start letting this cloud your thinking."

"I never would. But I really do need you to look after Chris."

Smitty, damn him, backed down in the face of Rich's earnestness. "Fine. I'll figure something out."

"This isn't necessary." I had to try one more time. "Rich, please. Let me look after *you* for once. Stay here, don't get any more involved. I can find your mom." I could, but it wouldn't be pretty. I'd have to make some contacts that were…well, ruthless didn't even start to cover it. "I can get her out safely." Maybe. *If* Angelus turned up some info, and if Gianna helped. "You don't need to come with me."

"I'm coming anyway."

Of course he was. I bit the inside of my cheek to keep from yelling at him while I got myself under control. "Fine. Then we need to go."

"Give me two minutes to pack."

"I'll make sure he doesn't run off without you," Smitty promised.

Fucker.

We didn't talk on our way down the mountain. Neither of us was in a good place for it—Rich was dealing with intense grief that he was holding back by a thread, and I was dealing with a toxic mixture of sadness, fear, and anger that I knew would have me shouting at him again in no time if I opened my mouth.

The silence lasted all the way through arriving in town, me getting out to lift a fresh car and him heading into the store to buy a few more cheap phones. Ten minutes later he met me in the parking lot, where our new, ancient Cadillac idled. "Here." He handed over a phone, and didn't ask me who I was calling as I tapped in the numbers. The time for being Johnny Law was over.

First things first. I called the number I'd sworn not to use except in a true life and death emergency. A perky voice answered on the second ring. "Angel's Carpentry, we do God's work, how can I help you?"

"Yeah, I need to speak to Angelus, please."

Her airy tone went down an octave. "There's no one of that name here."

"Yes, there is. Tell him it's Leotrim, and tell him it's urgent. My house is about to collapse."

"Leotrim?" Now she sounded startled. "I see. One moment please." She disappeared off the line, and a minute later a familiar rumbling bass picked up the conversation.

"Well, if it isn't my little nipper! It's nice to hear from you, but what did I tell you? You better be at death's door, boy."

I actually rolled my eyes. Jesus, nothing turned me into a teenager again faster than speaking with my uncle. He had been a lousy replacement for a parent, but he'd been there, which was more than I could say for my mother. "I

167

get that my continued existence bugs the hell out of you, but give it a rest for a sec. This is about Val."

"Valmira?" He spoke her name with the accent I'd never picked up. "What kind of trouble is my sister in now, and why would she talk to *you* about it?"

That kind of hurt, even though I wasn't about to let on. "She didn't talk to me. It's…this is coming from the Grimaldis."

"Oh, nipper." I could practically see Uncle Angelus shaking his head. "This is what happens when you turn on your own people. If you don't give them loyalty, they won't give it in return. And those Italian bastards have never been as honorable as they like to pretend. If you had just apprenticed to *me* instead of staying with them—"

"Not possible." I was a lot of bad things, but not a cold-blooded assassin with a gift at torture. Not yet, anyway. "They killed my loyalty when they killed my father." It was better not to mention Tony to my uncle. He was as biased about homosexuality as anyone in the Mafia. "And now they say they've kidnapped Val, and they'll kill her in about forty-five hours unless I speak with Matteo Grimaldi."

He hummed thoughtfully. "Who will simply kill you."

"Me and the marshal with me, yes."

"A lawman?" Angelus chuckled. "Ah, Leo. You're better than an episode of *Love and Punishment*. You want to bring a lawman into family business? Are you mad?"

"His mother was also taken. He needs this resolved as much as I do."

"And when our way of *resolution* turns his stomach? Who will keep him from involving his friends then? You're my only nipper, Leo. I'd hate to have to kill someone you like."

"It won't come to that."

"You say that now." He sighed. I could almost see his bulk settling as he did it. Uncle Angelus was a hulking man, tall and broad and gone to fat in the past few years, but he was faster than he looked. "Very well. You want me to pick someone up, then? Spend some quality time with them and see what I can determine about your mother and this other woman before you get here? Where are you coming from?"

"We'll be there in eighteen hours." If we drove straight through, we could do it. "I'll call again when we're close."

"I'll speak to you soon, then." He ended the call, and I stared at the phone in my hand wondering for a moment if I hadn't just made a terrible mistake.

"Your uncle?"

I couldn't look at Rich right now. "Yeah."

"The man who scares the Mafia so bad that even they leave him alone?"

"Yep."

"Good." When I finally glanced his way, his expression was cold. "They killed my dad, Leo. They've got my mom. I can't trust *any* of the other marshals because I have no way of knowing who's compromised. If he's the best way forward when it comes to getting information, then he's the one we've got to take."

"It's going to be messy." I had to put that out there. "Possibly *very* messy, if you know what I mean. But you're going to have to give him the space to work."

"We'll see."

That was probably the best I could hope for right now. "One more call, then we go." It was easier to talk when I was standing still. I dialed a number that I was even more reluctant to use than my uncle's, and wasn't at all surprised to be shunted to an answer service. It was a smart precaution. "Gianna, hey, it's me. I know you're well out of it in New York, but I need you to go back to Chicago. It's a matter of life and death, okay? Text this number when you get there. Thanks."

Rich's hand on my shoulder almost made me start out of my skin. I hadn't even heard him close the distance.

When he looked at me this time, I met his gaze. "Who was that call to?"

"Tony's older sister. Gianna." I had to force myself to speak around the pressure in my throat. "She's a fashion designer in New York City, but she…she knew about the two of us. She tried to help us as best she could, but she's been out of the family business all her adult life. Still…if anyone can exert some influence over the Grimaldi patriarch, it's her. She might be able to temper Matteo a little, maybe find out where our moms are."

"It's worth a try." Rich gently took the Cadillac keys out of my hand. "I'll take the first leg, okay?"

After all the shit that had gone down today, he was still trying to take care of me. And I was weak enough to let him. "Okay."

Chapter Fifteen
Rich

I'd have to sleep eventually, but a cocktail of adrenaline, rage, and fear kept me alert as I flew down I-80. Horrific worst-case scenarios—every one of them involving my mom—kept my foot pressing the accelerator into the floor. Speeding was a huge risk. Getting pulled over at all, never mind for reckless driving, would be a catastrophic delay.

I couldn't justify slowing down, though. This time of night, the interstate was deserted, and I hadn't seen a cop since before we'd crossed into Nebraska.

If someone lights me up, I told myself over and over, *I'll just have to lose them.*

It was becoming all too comfortable, this thinking like a criminal. In combat, we'd had to think like the enemy so we could head them off and take them out before they took us out. Maybe that was why it was so easy now. In a matter of days, I'd gone from a by-the-book deputy marshal to preemptively planning how I'd shake a state trooper off my tail if the need arose. I was kind of afraid to find out how far down the rabbit hole I'd have to go before all this was over. Or if there was any hope of climbing back out.

The sun was starting to warm the horizon as I drove into Lincoln. Early morning commuters meant more traffic to deal with, and potentially more cops with fewer escape routes, so I grudgingly slowed down.

Beside me, Leo stirred. "We stopping?"

"No. Traffic." The loss of speed made the drive feel sluggish, and in turn, made me feel sluggish. Exhaustion started closing in fast, making my eyes itch and the lids heavy. "We should get coffee."

"No, *I* should get coffee." Leo touched my leg. "You should sleep."

"I can keep going for—"

Leo huffed with palpable annoyance. "I am way too tired and way too stressed to get into a pissing contest with you." He gestured up ahead. "Pull into that gas station so we can top off the tank, and then shut up and let me drive."

I glanced at him. "Uh. Okay." I obeyed, and brought the Cadillac to a stop beside one of the gas pumps. "You want anything from inside?"

"Coffee. Maybe a couple of Five Hour Energies or something."

I didn't argue, and went inside. That fatigue was kicking in hard now, and I could barely focus my eyes or brain enough to get food and drinks for the two of us. Paying for it took more work than usual too. Good thing I was using cash and didn't have to worry about which end of a card to put into the reader.

By the time I returned to the stolen Cadillac, Leo had gassed it up and taken the driver side. I slid into the passenger seat and handed him one of the Five Hours.

"Thanks," he muttered, but didn't look up from his phone.

I craned my neck. "What are you doing?"

"Nothing." He shoved the phone into his pocket, and without looking at me, started the car.

"Leo…"

He ignored me and pulled away from the gas station. The phone chirped, the sound muffled by his pocket, and he squirmed a little, cutting his eyes toward me. He didn't speak, though, and didn't take out the phone.

Stress and fatigue coalesced into some hardcore bitchiness, and I growled, "You want to tell me what's going on?"

"No."

I rolled my eyes. "Jesus fuck, Leo. Are we in this together, or—"

"Yeah, we are." His tone was flat and nonnegotiable. "So just trust me that whatever I'm doing is ultimately to help us, all right?"

"Then why don't you tell me what it is you're doing?"

"Because you'd try to stop me." The matter-of-fact tone made me want to choke him. If he hadn't pulling onto the interstate, I might've actually done it. Leo glanced at me, and his obnoxiously stubborn expression eased a little. Facing the road again, he sighed and reached for my hand. "Look, I trusted you when you made contact with your dad, right?"

"Eventually."

"Okay, true." He glanced at me again. "So how about trusting me this time? My ass is on the line just like yours, and my mom is in trouble just like yours is. I'm not going to do anything to sabotage us."

I blew out a breath. As irritating as it was, he did have a point. Leo had nothing to gain by torpedoing what we were doing. And so far, whenever I'd trusted his instincts, he'd been right. In fact, he was pretty much batting a thousand, whereas I'd almost gotten us killed a few times.

"Fine." I sighed. "Is there anything I should be doing?"

"Just have my back when shit goes down."

"And you'll do the same for me?"

"Of course." He gave my hand a squeeze, then put his back on the wheel. "Get some sleep. You'll probably have to pick up around Des Moines."

I didn't argue.

"Damn it, Rich!"

The sharp words and a painful grip on my arm cut through the haze of sand and gun oil, and I blinked my eyes into focus. Bright light made me wince, but I knew instantly it wasn't the Kandahar sun. "Where are we?"

Leo huffed and shoved himself off me. "We just passed through Council Bluffs." Irritation radiated off him. I didn't think I'd ever heard a seatbelt buckle click with more annoyance than it did just then. With a jerk of the wheel and a chirp of tires, he pulled back onto the road—back onto the interstate, I realized now—and accelerated.

I sat up, rubbing my eyes as the disorientation faded. "What the fuck happened?"

Leo clenched his jaw and stared straight ahead. "We're about to go into a warzone," he growled, white-knuckling the Cadillac's wheel. "If you're not up for it, fucking say so now."

The pieces fell together. I vaguely remembered the nightmare—not the dream itself, but the fear—and I must have started thrashing.

"I'm up for it," I said quietly.

"Are you fucking sure?" he snapped. "Because this PTSD of yours seems to rear its ugly head at the worst possible times, and I'd just as soon it didn't take you out while people are shooting at us."

I opened my mouth to respond that I wasn't going to leave him vulnerable, and that I had my shit together. The words died on my tongue, though. With panic still cooling on my twitchy nerve endings, I had to admit that Leo was right to question me. The PTSD didn't rule my life, but it was triggered by me and people I loved being in danger. Which put us in even more danger. Which triggered me even more. And…

"Fuck." I rubbed my eyes.

Leo sighed heavily.

"Look." I turned to him. "We've been through some hell, all right? And you've seen this shit in my head fuck me up. But has it ever happened in the middle of the fray?"

Leo pressed his lips together, flicking his gaze toward me. "What about on the road that first day?"

"Okay, but we weren't exactly being chased right then. Things had quieted down. I was okay when we were actually being chased, right?"

"Yes, but still, how do either of us know you won't fall apart when shit gets bad?" He looked at me for a second. "Give me one good reason to believe I won't have to keep one eye on you while I should be keeping both eyes on everything else."

I thought for a moment, and finally shook my head. "I can't, okay? It's…this isn't going to magically go away. But I've held it together when it's counted before, and I'll do everything I can to hold it together now. That's…really all I can give you."

Leo stared at the interstate for a long, uncomfortably silent moment, working his jaw as his lips turned almost as pale as his knuckles. Finally, he exhaled and sagged back against the seat. "I guess it is what it is. I don't like it, and I think you're fucking stupid for going into a job like this without getting your head worked on, but…" He scowled. "But I want you on my six for this one." He paused, then glanced at me. "I need you in there, Rich."

"I know. I'm not going to let you or our moms down."

I didn't add *I promise* to the end of it, and he didn't ask me to.

He probably knew as well as I did that I couldn't.

We switched off driving and mainlined coffee and energy drinks until we couldn't go any further, and called it quits just outside of Davenport, Iowa. From there, we had about three hours to go to get to Chicago. That was what the GPS said, anyway. I was pretty sure we could do it faster as long as we got moving before traffic got ugly.

In a motel that *generously* called itself The Cozy Inn, Leo sprawled on the queen size bed and covered his eyes with his hand. He'd been driving for the last two hours, and he'd started nodding off thirty miles ago.

I sat on the edge of the bed. "You all right?"

He nodded. "Fucking tired."

"Get some sleep, then. What time do you think we should get on the road?"

"Soon as we can both keep our eyes open." He lowered his hand and looked at me. "How are you holding up?"

I shrugged. "I'll be a lot better when this is over."

"Assuming we're not dead when it's over," he muttered.

"Hey." I took his hand and squeezed it gently. "Don't think like that. You start thinking like you've already lost, you're gonna lose."

Leo closed his eyes and let out a long breath. "It's kind of hard not to think like that, you know? This family is huge. They've got people in the Marshals. They were able to take out my dad in a maximum security facility while he was in solitary. They got my mom from goddamned *Albania*. They figured out you're helping me and got *your* parents." He met my gaze again. "All because they want me dead. It's…hard not to wonder if giving them what they want would stop more people from—"

"Don't even go there, Leo." I shook my head and gripped his hand tighter. "I know it's daunting right now, but don't you dare give up. Because this isn't just about keeping them from getting their hands on you anymore—this is about taking them down so they don't hurt other people. If they're that deep in the Marshals, then they have way too much power. What happens when the next person crosses the Grimaldis and doesn't have your know-how to fight back?"

He watched me silently, and a hint of a smile curled the corner of his mouth. "The know-how or the backup?"

"That too." I rubbed his thumb with mine. "I'm scared too, okay? I'm scared shitless. But we have to just go in and get the job done. We can think about being scared later."

"So, if we don't die, we can stop and be scared later?"

"Basically."

"That's not much of an incentive not to die."

I snorted. "Or we can survive, and then get shitfaced and fuck each other blind until we forget we were scared."

That brightened his expression a little. "Well, damn. Why didn't you say that in the first place?"

I laughed. "Seriously?"

"Yeah, man. If you're gonna give a pep talk, lead with that part."

"I'll keep that in mind for next time."

Leo chuckled. He sat up, sliding his palm over my thigh. I twisted so I was facing him, and rested my hand on the bed beside his leg.

Sobering, he said, "When do we come up with a plan?"

"As soon as we have a goddamned clue what we're up against. The location and all that, I mean." I exhaled. "I don't like flying blind any more than you do, but until I have a handle on, hell, basically *anything*…"

177

CARI Z & L.A. WITT

Leo nodded. "So I guess right now, we just sleep and try not to think about being scared."

"Basically."

He smiled faintly, then cupped my face and kissed me. It was so weird how the world could be falling to pieces all around us, how it could feel like we were literally in the throes of a tornado, and something as simple as a tender, lingering kiss could mute the noise and calm the chaos. It was all still out there, and nothing was fixed, but for just a second, it was still.

I touched my forehead to his. "Whatever it takes, we're coming out of this. Both of us."

"Yeah?"

"Yeah." I caressed his cheek and grinned. "Because I'm way too tired for that part where we fuck each other senseless right now."

Leo laughed, sounding more like himself than he had in a while. "Me too. So...deal. We get out of this alive—"

"And we screw until we can't move."

He laughed again and pulled me into another kiss.

And come hell or high water, we were living long enough to fuck again.

Chapter Sixteen
Leo

When your back's against a wall, you take your satisfaction where you can find it. I was taking mine by methodically stripping the Grimaldis' various accounts of their money. So far I was keeping things just under the reportable limits—I didn't want to tip off the banks yet, and when I went big, I wanted to go *really* big. Specifically big. Big like, say, draining Matteo's personal rainy day fund for whores and coke down to less than he'd need to buy a fucking Big Mac.

Before that happened though, I wanted to be in contact with him. I needed his attention and guarantee that he would listen to me, so his rage didn't get the better of him and end up making things worse for the hostages. Our *mothers*, but I couldn't think about them like that right now or I'd lose my nerve.

I hadn't seen my own mother in so long, I wasn't sure I'd even recognize her. But Rich and his folks had been— no, *were*—close. He needed his mother to be safe, after what had happened to his dad. And I could do that for

CARI Z & L.A. WITT

him, the least of what he deserved, if I played my cards right.

I checked my phone again. The algorithm I used to infiltrate the Grimaldis' financial network was chugging away, siphoning off a bit here and transferring a bit there, nothing they'd notice yet unless it was pointed out. I watched it work with a grim sense of satisfaction. One way or another, I was going to hurt them with this.

"You look pleased," Rich commented from the driver seat. We were on the outskirts of Chicago now, not going into the heart of the city but heading for my uncle's suburb. "Should I be ready for something?"

I checked the time. We still had a day before I was supposed to meet with Matteo, but I was done letting him dictate the terms of our interactions. It was time to go on the offensive. "Just for me to have an uncomfortable conversation with Matteo Grimaldi. I'm going to put it on speaker, but let me do the talking, okay?"

"You sure it's a good idea to be the first to make contact?"

"It's the only way I can be assured he's not going to do something to the hostages before talking to us if he finds out I'm playing Robin Hood on his own."

"You could just wait to go after the money, couldn't you?" *Wouldn't that be safer*, said his subtext, and he had a point.

"I could," I admitted, "but this gives me a chance to reinforce his timing, too. I want him to believe we're going to come to him at exactly the time he set, so he feels like he's got a while to get all his defenses into place. He'll be overconfident. We can use that."

I wasn't sure Rich bought it. Fuck, I wasn't sure *I* bought it, but if things went the way I hoped, we'd be moving in less than ten hours. Rich cleared his throat. "Robin Hood, huh? Does that make me your merry man?"

He was doing his best to stay on an even keel, and I appreciated his efforts even if the joke was lame. "Oh

180

yeah, baby, let me put you in tights and you can be my Little John."

"I don't know that I care for that name."

I shrugged. "It suits you better than Maid Marian." *Okay, time to stop putting this off.* I honed in on Matteo's personal account and used one of my burner phones to dial his cell. I had a knack for memorizing numbers, and I'd thought about calling his a *lot* lately. I waited for him to pick up, my heart hammering in my chest.

"Who the fuck is this?"

All my nervousness suddenly drained away, replaced by pure venom. I was going to make this son of a bitch *suffer*. "Aw Mattie, is that any way to talk to your boo?"

"Leo? What the hell, where are you?" His voice shifted from confused to smug. "I didn't expect you to come crawling in for another day, but if you're determined to get it all over with fast, I guess I'll let you."

"So generous of you."

"It's nice to be the one with all the power, yeah. But then again, you're used to getting fucked by someone in our family, aren't you?"

"Oh yeah, I can take it like a pro." Something about my tone must have clued him in, because when he spoke again, his easy humor was gone.

"What is this? Where the hell are you? Do I need to remind you that I've got your *mother*, Leo? You think I'm afraid to hurt her if you screw with me on this? She's still a looker; it wouldn't be a hardship to fuck her. The marshal's mom, on the other hand, she's not pretty enough for me. I bet some of my guys would have a go at her anyway, though."

Rich's arms were getting progressively tenser, the tendons standing out across the backs of his hands. I squeezed his shoulder in an effort to calm him down. "Touch either of them now and you'll regret it."

"Oh really? How's that?"

"Why don't you check your accounts and find out? I'll wait."

"What?"

Jesus God, was he really this dense? It was hard to believe this guy was related to Tony and Gianna sometimes. "Your *bank* accounts. Go ahead. You should be down by about…thirty thousand dollars across the board, at this point."

There was a stony silence for a long moment, and, when Matteo came back on, he was more than pissed, he was enraged. "You think you can fuck with me like this? You think you can steal from *me*? That's it—your mom is dead, she's fucking dead, I'm going to—"

"You touch either of our mothers and I'll make sure you're poorer than dirt in the next five minutes."

"My father will—"

"Your father is also losing money. So are all his capos—everyone I ever had access to, you get me? Everyone in the inner circle? I own their money, and right now I'm sending it to the Canary Islands. If you harm a fucking hair on our moms' heads, I will *bankrupt* you, and worse."

"What the fuck is that supposed to mean?"

"It means I'll set off financial flags that will sic the IRS on you. You might have people in bed with the Marshals, the cops, the judges, but I bet you don't have the IRS in your pocket. And I'll be sure to contact your father and let him know exactly who's to blame for his ruination. You convinced him to kill his own son, so I know you've got clout, but you'll never convince him that it was better to destroy your family fortune by harming your hostages than it would have been to be patient for an extra day."

I stopped talking and let that sink in for a moment. Matteo wasn't the sharpest knife, but he had some smart friends, and he had always craved his father's approval. As long as he was still rational and not stoned out of his mind… "Fine," he growled. "You get a stay of execution, but I gotta tell you, Leo, you're not making things better for yourself or them in the long run. I *always* get what I want in the end, and I *will* cut my satisfaction out of you and your guard dog's hides, you hear me?"

"Yeah, but not before I verify that you haven't hurt the hostages. Now, and again right before the meet. Otherwise I put you in the poorhouse."

"What makes you think I'm anywhere near those bitches right now?"

I chuckled. "Because you're a fucking sadist who takes pleasure in other people's pain. Of course you're near the hostages. You've probably been tormenting them ever since you took them. Put the marshal's mother on." I squeezed Rich's hand while we waited, to give him a little strength and also to remind him to be quiet.

A minute later, a warm, feminine voice with only a slight quiver in it came on the line. "Hello?" Rich's eyes went wide, but I had to be sure.

"Is this Mrs. Cody?"

"Yes. Is this Leotrim?"

"Yeah, it is."

"Oh God, please, is my son with you?"

She sounded so desperate I nearly cried. "Yeah, he's here with me, he's fine. We're coming to get you, okay? You haven't been hurt, have you?"

"No, honey, we're both fine."

She was probably lying for Rich's sake, but was obviously well enough to talk, so I didn't push it. "Great. Well, they're going to keep you ladies healthy until we get there, so don't worry about a thing. Rich and I'll look out for you."

"I'm sure you will, but I—"

Her voice cut off abruptly, replaced by Matteo. "You fucking happy now?"

"Thrilled," I said dryly. "You keep your hands off them, I keep my hands off your money. We'll be in town for the meet by the time our forty-eight hours are up."

"You better be, and after that? I am going to cut your throat and I'm going to make it slow, you hear me? It'll take me *hours* to saw through your windpipe, you'll scream and scream and—"

"Great, nice talking to you, bye." I hung up the phone, and Rich and I both sighed hugely.

"She's okay." He sounded incredibly relieved.

"Yeah."

"You could have asked to talk to your mom instead."

I shrugged. "Yours is the one that gives a shit. I thought you should get to hear that she's doing all right."

He glanced at me. "You know, your mom probably does care about you."

"Yeah, she really showed it with the past fifteen years of radio silence, too." I shook my head. "It doesn't matter. We're almost there."

Uncle Angelus lived in Avondale, not far from Koz Park. His home and his shop were the same place, one stacked above the other, and he worked alone except for his apprentice, Kara. His handcrafted furniture was in high demand, and his work had a waiting list years long. He'd offered to teach me woodworking in addition to artful murder, but I'd turned both of those down. A year later he found Kara, and she was in all respects a better student than I'd ever have been.

We parked a few blocks away and walked around to his back door. A camera followed our movements, but that was no surprise. You didn't survive for as long as Angelus did in this game without taking plenty of precautions. I knocked, and a moment later Kara came to the door.

"Hey Leo!" She was about my height, with dark red hair, surprisingly broad shoulders, and a sweet, girl-next-door kind of face. She wore black yoga pants and a tank top, and her slender feet were bare. "Angelus is a little busy at the moment, but if you guys want to wait upstairs in the parlor he'll be up to meet you pretty quick. He's just wrapping up some work."

"Thanks." I stepped inside and Rich followed. Kara eyed him appreciatively, and I restrained my impulse to snarl at her. She'd have my freshly-harvested balls in her hand faster than I could blink if I pushed her. "This is Rich Cody. Rich, this is Kara Kalmendi, my uncle's apprentice."

"Pleased to meet you." Kara held out a hand, and Rich smiled and shook like a gentleman.

"Same. Thanks for helping us."

"It's our pleasure! Angelus would do anything for Leo, and it gives me a chance to practice my split rib technique." She shut the door behind us—thicker than a normal door; it was probably reinforced steel underneath the wooden façade—and pointed toward the stairs. "Head up to the apartment and put the water on for tea. Your uncle will probably want a cup once we finish things down here. He—" The doorbell rang, and she frowned. "Were you followed?" she demanded.

"No," I insisted. "We just got into town and we parked three blocks away. We've both been keeping a watch on the roads on the way in too, and there's no way."

"Huh." She turned and disappeared into what looked like a closet, pushing coats out of the way. "Are you sure?" she asked, her voice slightly muffled. "Because there's a Grimaldi stooge on our doorstep, with two bodyguards for good measure."

"It's a coincidence," I said. It *had* to be a coincidence. "We rattled Matteo's cage about an hour ago. He's probably just covering his bases. He doesn't know we're here."

Kara reemerged, tucking a gun into the small of her back even as she slipped into a pair of flip-flops. She rolled her eyes and pulled on a loose denim jacket. "Sounds like

Matteo. He's so prone to overreacting; it's bad for business. But if this guy *does* cause trouble here, you're going to be on the hook to cover cleanup and expenses, you got it?" She shook her hair out so it fluffed around her face. "You go upstairs, I'll handle the goons. Angelus will be with you shortly." She headed down the hall and into the shop's showroom, closing the door behind her.

I looked at Rich. "You want to go upstairs?"

"Not a chance in hell."

"Eavesdropping it is, then." We followed as quietly as we could. The wooden floors didn't so much as creak—my uncle was a good craftsman, I had to admit. We stopped by the door Kara had left through, and I cracked it just enough to let the sound filter to us.

"Mr. Canova!" Kara was back to sounding perky. "What a surprise. What brings you here today?"

"Cut the crap and let me in," Mr. Canova—Ricky Canova, I knew him; he was Matteo's closest friend—said.

Kara tisked. "Gosh, you're not being very polite, sir."

"You're not dumb enough to try anything with me." Canova sounded confident. "Now let me in, or me and my boys will make our own entrance without asking nicely."

Kara laughed. "You think the three of you are enough? Are you sure of that? Because I'm not."

"You don't want trouble with the Grimaldis."

"And *you* don't want trouble with Angelus. Seriously, you come to his place of business, to his *home*, and you try to bully your way in with these two muscle-bound morons as your only backup? Are you insane? Do you have a death wish?"

"Bitch, I'm telling you one last time, you let me in or—"

"Kara." A familiar voice, gravelly and serene, sounded from the back of the showroom. "You didn't tell me we had guests."

"Not guests," she replied. "Matteo sent a shakedown crew, and these poor bastards drew the short straw."

Canova seemed to find his voice again, but when he spoke, he sounded a little strangled. "Oh, Angelus, hey— no, hey, Kara's got it all wrong, we're not here to—"

"Are you calling my apprentice a liar?" My uncle's steps did squeak a bit as he walked, but it wasn't from the floor. It sounded like he was wearing rubber boots. Rich looked at me and raised an eyebrow, but I couldn't explain it, and just shrugged.

"No sir, not at all, of course not. Just—it's private business, not something to be discussed on the front stoop, yeah? I—if you let us in, we can—"

Angelus came to a stop. "Can *what*?"

"You—you know, never mind, it's not—not important. Um. Just, if you've seen Leo lately, Mr. Grimaldi would kind of…like to…know about it?"

"Would he now?" Angelus sounded amused. "Is this Mr. Grimaldi the elder, or Matteo Grimaldi, the boy who would be king?"

"Hey…hey, look now, that's—"

"Because I assured Mr. Grimaldi years ago that I would not interfere in his business if he did not interfere in mine, and I have kept my word. Young Matteo, on the other hand, has made no such deal with me. But because I am feeling generous, you may tell him that no, I have not seen my nephew lately. We don't talk, Leo and I."

"Okay, great, that's great, thanks. And if, ah, if he *does* try and talk to you, if you could pass that along? Mr. Grimaldi would make it well worth your time, sir."

"I will consider it," Angelus said gravely.

"Consider it, yeah, okay. Good. Um, I think we'll be going now, so…"

"Yes, you are," Angelus said. "And don't let me see you or any of your men within a mile of my house again. Am I clear?"

"Y-yes, sir."

"Don't let the door hit your ass on your way!" Kara chirped. Said door slammed shut, and a minute later, she said, "They're clear."

Squeaky boots made their way to the hall door, and before I had the time to process what was happening, it opened to reveal my Uncle Angelus, scarier in person than any Mafioso ever could be. He stood a head taller than me, and had a scar that ran the length of his bald head and ended just above his mouth. He wore galoshes, elbow-length rubber gloves, and a heavy rubber apron. Despite his efforts to keep clean, his craggy face was dotted with blood, and his gloves glistened suspiciously. He smelled like blood and shit and pain, but he smiled genially at me and Rich.

"Curious little nipper," he said. "How naughty to listen in, eh? But I forgive you this time. I will meet you and your friend upstairs once I've cleaned up a bit. I have some news to share about your mother."

"Great," I said faintly. "We'll just…"

"Go. Make tea."

"Yep, we'll go and make tea." I took Rich by the arm and led the way back down the hall. Rich, thankfully, didn't fight me on it.

Even he knew there were some people you just didn't fuck with.

Chapter Seventeen
Rich

It didn't seem like a conversation we should be having in a homey kitchen with lace curtains and a row of matching ceramic containers with flowers on their sides, but here we were.

Kara leaned against the counter, holding a plain white mug in both hands, and I stood beside her, minus the tea because I was pretty sure I'd throw up anything I tried to consume right then. Leo leaned over the table, hands splayed on either side of the crudely drawn map. Twin crevices had formed between his eyebrows, and he glared down at the sketch of an old warehouse and the surrounding city block.

Angelus stood beside the broad oak table, absently tugging at the teabag in his steaming white mug. His hair and beard were still damp, but fortunately weren't splattered with blood anymore. He didn't reek of torture now, thank God. He looked like such a normal guy that I seriously wondered if I'd hallucinated everything that'd happened earlier.

I might have been able to convince myself of that if we weren't all standing around a map drawn according to the testimony of the man who was apparently still tied up in the basement. I really, really didn't want to imagine how Angelus had gotten the information out of him, but in the end, we had a location and detailed description of an abandoned warehouse. He'd told Angelus which room the hostages had been held in last time he'd been there, though he'd insisted there were three hostages, not two.

After a long silence, Leo tapped the paper and looked at his uncle. "We need to know who that third hostage is. Otherwise there might be someone else making a move at the same time we do, and we could trip each other up."

Angelus nodded.

"That, and…" Leo pursed his lips, glaring at the drawing. "There's a million rooms and spaces in this building. How can we be sure our moms are being held in this one?" He thumped his knuckle on the first-floor room marked with an X. "Hell, how do we even know they're still in the building?"

"Without sending someone in to look?" Angelus casually plucked the teabag from his mug and tossed it in the trash. "We don't."

"We should go in, then," I said. "Leo and I can—"

"We can't take that risk," Angelus said. "If anything happens to either of you, Grimaldi has no reason to keep your mothers alive."

"And there's no way to make sure Grimaldi gets fucked the way I want him fucked," Leo growled. "Even letting go of all their financial information isn't enough. Not now. I want to rain hellfire on them, and I'd show one of you how to do it all, but it would take ages to get it all straight."

"So what do we do?" I asked. "If we go charging in there like amateur SWAT, we could be walking into a trap."

"I can go," Kara said. "I can be in and out, verify the location of the hostages and the identity of the third one, assuming they exist, and no one will ever know I was there."

Leo frowned, but Angelus's expression didn't change. The old man turned to his apprentice. "You need any gear?"

"I've got everything I need," she said. "With the location and the size of the place, I need about three hours to get in and out. Assuming all you need is eyes on everything; if you want a video or sound, then—"

"Eyes are enough. If you can get photos or a video on your phone, do it. But time is of the essence, so let's not waste it installing surveillance equipment."

"Actually," Leo said, "it might not hurt for her to leave a couple of cameras and recording devices in place. In case the hostages move or more guards are brought in."

Angelus grunted into his teacup. "Good point."

"Uh, hold on." I shifted my weight. "Are we really talking about sending her in to recon a dangerous—"

"Is that a problem?" Kara looked at me coldly as she folded her arms across her chest. "I'm sorry, is this a 'no girls allowed' game?"

I rolled my eyes. "No, it's a 'I'm not sure I like sending anyone in alone to recon something like this' game."

She narrowed her eyes.

"You have a point, Marshal," Angelus said. "But Kara works better alone. Particularly in situations like this."

"But…" I glanced back and forth between them. "Who'll have her back?"

Kara laughed. "You mean who will slow me down? If I have anyone with me, I'll have to watch my six and theirs." She paused. "I appreciate the concern, but I know what I'm doing." She turned to Angelus. "Give me an extra hour to grab some surveillance gear. So, four hours."

Angelus gave her a nod, and Kara left the kitchen.

Leo watched her go. Without looking away from the empty doorway, he said, "You sure about this?"

"If anyone can take care of herself out there, it's Kara. She'll be fine." Angelus chuckled. "I ever tell you how I ended up hiring her?"

Leo and I glanced at each other before turning to him, neither of us speaking.

"She broke into my shop," the old man went on. "*Four times.*"

"Four—" Leo blinked. "How the fuck did she do that?"

"Hell if I know. That's why I hired her. Anyone who can get past my security is someone I want on my team. Turns out she's been breaking and entering since she was in kindergarten. Dad and brothers taught her." He looked at us. "And yet she has no police record."

"Seriously?" I asked. "How?"

"Because she's never been arrested. No one's ever caught her but me." Angelus came closer and clapped my shoulder. "You boys don't need to worry about Kara. The Grimaldis probably do, but we don't."

Leo chuckled. "I almost wish I could've gone with her just to watch her work."

Angelus laughed. "She never lets anyone see her work. That's why she's so good at what she does." He paused. "Now, how about we find some gear for you boys so you're armed up when it's time to make your move?"

Leo's eyes lit up like a kid on Christmas.

If I hadn't been wound so tight, I probably would have laughed.

Instead, I just felt queasy.

By the time we came back up from Angelus's basement—the room without the tortured man in it, thank

God—we had enough equipment to take on a small army. Leo had stuffed two backpacks full of C4, a handful of flash-bangs, and a couple of teargas cannisters. I'd picked a pistol that was identical to my service weapon, so I was already familiar with its weight and idiosyncrasies, and a fairly generic nine-mill as a backup. Leo had gone with the same models for himself, reasoning that it made sense for us to have weapons that took identical magazines in case one of us ran out of ammo. Hopefully that wouldn't be an issue, especially since we'd loaded enough spare magazines to sink a battleship. We also took a lightweight SKS rifle with a scope just in case we needed to pick anyone off from a distance.

The law enforcement official in me desperately wanted to grill Angelus about where he'd acquired some of this shit, especially the military or SWAT issue tactical gear. The Marine in me—along with the newly-spawned vigilante who wanted to save his mom and protect his sort-of-lover—told my inner cop to shut the fuck up and grab one of those Kevlar vests.

We'd lugged it all up from the basement and staged it all by the front door like luggage ready for a big vacation, and now…we waited. Two hours had gone by, and we hadn't heard from Kara since she'd left to recon the warehouse. That wasn't unexpected, of course, but it was still nerve racking. There was nothing for us to do except sit tight and wait for her intel, and then for the right moment to make our move.

Leo and Angelus were playing cards and laughing over stories from when Leo was a kid, but I wasn't taking part. I couldn't focus enough to play cards and couldn't relax enough to shoot the breeze. I envied them for being able to seize the opportunity for some downtime.

Back when I'd been in a combat zone, I'd been able to do the same thing. We'd had to be able to cut loose even when we knew there was some bad shit up ahead. It was the only way to stay sane, and the only way to stay sharp—

if you were on edge all the time, you lost your edge. My buddies and I had kept decks of cards on us for that very reason. I supposed that was why I couldn't play gin rummy anymore—one too many games interrupted by incoming fire.

As I watched them play, I wondered if Smitty still had the remaining cards of the deck that had been scattered and partially burned by a mortar. We'd all thought they were lucky somehow. Marines and soldiers had weird superstitions, and we'd decided without any debate that the cards we'd been playing before the attack—the cards we'd found in the rubble of our camp after it was all over— were lucky. After all, if Tank and Wolf hadn't gotten started fighting after Wolf accused Tank of cheating, we wouldn't have been outside trying to break them up when the first mortar had landed. We'd all gotten plenty fucked up in that attack, but we'd survived. Hard not to see some kind of luck in the cards we'd been playing.

But I didn't have any of those charred cards with me now, and I couldn't focus enough to play anyway. I was too keyed up to do anything but obsess over the plan and whether or not we could get in, get our moms, and get out safely. And then get someplace safe. Assuming such a mythical place actually existed anymore.

I was worried about Kara, too. There was no doubt in my mind she was perfectly competent; I just didn't like the idea of more people getting hurt or killed because of us.

"You're restless." Angelus was looking at the cards in his hand, but somehow I knew he was talking to me.

I squirmed in my chair beside Leo. "You think?"

"Relax." Leo elbowed me gently. "No point in tiring yourself out with nervous energy before we have to go to work."

"Easier said than done."

Leo shrugged. "Don't really have much choice."

"That's helpful."

He elbowed me again, and this time it seemed like almost an affectionate gesture. Something both playful and manly to keep his uncle from noticing how comfortable we were with touching. It made me want to wrap Leo up in my arms. Maybe even drag him off to a flat surface for a rematch. I wasn't in the mood to screw, but it would be an outlet for all that nervous energy that he'd helpfully pointed out was making me tired, and it would be something that wasn't driving me insane with fear and worry.

Not here, though. Not now.

I cleared my throat. "You, um, think it's safe for me to go for a walk?"

Angelus lifted his eyebrows. "Anywhere in particular?"

"No. Just…need to move around."

"Can't imagine why not," he said. "The neighborhood is safe enough. The Grimaldis don't know you're here, and they've been warned not to come near the place unless they want their testicles mailed to them."

I inclined my head. "But they showed up today."

"They did. And I guarantee they'll think better of doing it again." He smirked. "So as long as you're not afraid of rats or dogs…"

I got up. "Okay. I'll be back in a few, then."

Leo looked up at me. "Take your piece with you." Any other time I might've gotten annoyed that he would think for a second I'd step outside unarmed, but his tone had an undercurrent kind of like when he'd elbowed me a moment ago. A hint of subtext that his uncle would never catch on to, but resonated right through me.

Be careful. Are you sure you're okay?

I smiled as best I could and gave his shoulder a manly squeeze, followed by a subtle caress of my thumb that he hopefully felt and his uncle hopefully missed.

Then I left the house. I needed some air, and though I didn't completely trust Angelus, I believed him when he said he'd put the fear of God—or at least castration—into the Grimaldi family.

The night was cold. Or maybe that was just me. I couldn't see my breath so…yeah, it was probably just me.

I stuffed my hands in my jacket pockets and walked faster. I didn't have a particular destination in mind, but just being out and moving felt good. I couldn't relax enough to indulge in our precious downtime, but without screeching tires and flying bullets to keep the adrenaline pumping, fatigue was starting to turn into lethargy. Sleep had been elusive ever since things had gone down in that hotel hallway—had it really only been a few days?—and the constant state of near panic was wearing me down.

The panic, and the powerlessness. The utter isolation of being unable to reach out for help. I was getting paranoid to the point I questioned my own sanity. Every time I thought of a solution—contact the D.A.'s office, call the FBI—my mind shut down with "*they could be compromised too.*" I had no reason to believe they were, but after everything that had gone down, I had no reason to believe they *weren't*. If the Grimaldis were methodical and resourceful enough to plant people inside the U.S. Marshals, if they'd been playing this game for *years*, then what was to stop them from putting others inside the FBI? Or the Department of Justice? Or the local fucking loss prevention rent-a-cops? Now that I'd seen indisputable proof of Grimaldi influence, everyone was dirty until proven clean, which left me with no one I could confidently turn to for help.

I sighed into the night. How the hell was this thing going to play out? And was my mom okay? Was my brother okay? Shit, I needed to check in with Smitty at some point and make sure—

The hair on my neck stood on end.

I stopped in my tracks, senses on high alert. I held my breath and moved only my eyes.

A heartbeat too late, I realized there was someone behind me, and before I could turn around, something cold pressed against the back of my neck.

"If you scream, I'll drop you where you stand, Marshal," came a growled voice with a hint of an Italian accent.

Fuck. So much for Angelus's threats.

I slowly lifted my hands in a gesture of surrender. My pistol was tucked under my jacket, but there was no point in trying to get to it or brandish it. He'd already gotten the drop on me.

"You're Richard Cody, yeah?"

I nodded.

"Matteo Grimaldi's got a message for you."

Icy panic shot through me. If someone had already found me, then what about the others? A vision of Leo and Angelus sprawled in pools of blood beside the overturned kitchen table and scattered cards made my stomach churn violently.

The gun pressed harder against the base of my skull. "You've got twenty-four hours to give us the hacker."

I sniffed. "You too scared of Angelus to go get him yourself?"

No answer, but the gun twitched. Shit, okay. They *were* scared of Angelus. But apparently not scared enough to stay out of his neighborhood. Which explained why he hadn't shot me—they needed me to get Leo away from Angelus. Had I been Leo, I'd have smirked and taunted the asshole for being too much of a pussy to go near the old man, but I kept my mouth shut.

"Give us what we want," the man said coldly, "or your dad watches us torture your mom until she's dead."

I clenched my jaw. "My dad's already dead, fucker."

"You sure about that?"

My throat constricted.

There was some more movement behind me, and then he handed me a cell phone. On the screen was the most horrifying thing I'd ever seen—my mom huddled against a dirty wall, cradling my dad's head in her lap. He was on his side, and since he didn't have a shirt on, I could easily see the angry bruises on his arm and shoulder, not to mention the bloody bandages covering one side of his torso.

Propped up against my dad's leg was a newspaper. Undoubtedly with today's date on it.

Bile burned the back of my throat. "What do you want?" My voice was shaking, but I didn't care.

"We want the hacker," came the chilly response. "And we want him alive."

My knees were starting to shake. Fuck. This was bad.

"You might not want to take too long." The man took the phone back. "Your old man's lost a lot of blood, and I'm no doctor, but I think that bullet hole in his side is getting infected." He sounded *amused* by it. Like my father's condition and my predicament were *funny*. What the hell kind of animals did Grimaldi have on his payroll?

Then I remembered the massacre in the hotel hallway and decided I didn't really need to ask that question.

I swallowed hard. I couldn't speak. I couldn't even find any air, never mind figure out what to do with it.

"We clear, Marshal?"

"If…" I cleared my throat and managed to croak, "If I decide to cooperate, how do I contact Grimaldi?"

Another cell phone was thrust into my peripheral vision. A cheap one—probably a burner phone. "There's a preprogrammed number. When you're ready to make the exchange, you call, and you'll be given instructions. Understood?"

"Yeah." My mouth had gone dry. "Understood." I took the burner phone.

There was more movement behind me. I didn't dare turn around; I just listened while the faceless man retreated into the night. He barely made a sound.

Staring down at the phone in my hand, I wanted to be sick. My dad was still alive, and if it was true—if he had a gunshot wound that was getting infected—then I didn't have much time. Quite possibly less than the twenty-four hours Matteo had given me. And if they'd found me out here, then they knew we were hunkering down at Angelus's place. Maybe they were smart enough not to approach the house again, but obviously someone had caught our scent and stayed nearby to wait for an opportunity. Christ—if Leo had come outside with me, they probably would have shot me, taken him, and been done with it.

Shivering badly and ready to puke, I hurried back toward Angelus's house. What the fuck was I supposed to do now? Give them Leo to save my parents? Sacrifice my parents to save Leo? Fuck. Fuck!

Training and fear kept me vigilant enough to circle the block a couple of times and cut through random alleys until I was absolutely sure no one had followed me. Though maybe that was pointless. The phone in my pocket probably told them everything they needed to know. It quite possibly had a listening device in it too. Okay, so they probably knew where I was headed, and there wasn't much I could do about that. If I ditched the phone, they'd know I wasn't playing ball, and someone would wind up dead.

With my heart in my throat, I knocked on Angelus's locked front door. As soon as he came to the door, I put my finger to my lips.

Instantly, his posture stiffened.

"Did you have a nice walk?" His voice didn't give him away.

"Wasn't bad." I stepped into the house and took the phone out of my pocket. "Almost got a burrito at that convenience store down the street, but it smelled like it might kill me."

He laughed, and he was impressively convincing, sounding conversational and relaxed even as he eyed the phone in my hand. "I wouldn't eat anything from that place."

While he locked us in, I opened one of the pistol cases by the door, took out the gun, and stuffed the phone into the cutout foam. For good measure, I took the foam from another case, wrapped the phone in it, and then shut the case and latched it.

Leo stepped into the room, brow pinched like he knew something was up. I gestured for them to go into the kitchen. With the phone safely tucked into a few layers of foam and a metal case, and presumably muffled enough that we could talk, we left the living room.

I still wasn't taking chances, though. I grabbed the map we'd been looking at and plucked a pen from a cup beside the microwave.

They know we're here, I wrote quickly. *3rd hostage is my dad.*

They both read the note, and then stared at me.

"Where did that phone come from?" Angelus asked in a barely audible whisper.

"From the fucker who put a gun to my head out there," I said. "He showed me a picture of my parents. My dad's in bad shape. Really bad shape." I swallowed. "They said I have twenty-four hours to hand them Leo, but I don't think my dad's got that long."

Angelus scowled.

Leo touched my arm. "Then we're going in tonight. As soon as we hear from Kara, we're going in."

"That phone probably has a tracker in it," Angelus said. "I say when the two of you leave, I take the phone downtown to throw them off the scent. It won't be foolproof—they're going to expect you both to be smart—but whoever's watching that phone won't be watching you two."

I nodded. "Good idea."

Angelus glared at the words I'd written. Then he said, "I'm going to prepare things downstairs."

He didn't wait for either of us to respond, and left the kitchen.

Alone, Leo wrapped his arm around my waist, and I realized for the first time he'd touched me openly in front of his uncle. At this point, he probably didn't care any more than I did.

"We'll get them out," he said. "And we'll get your dad to a hospital in time."

I nodded slowly, putting my arm around his shoulders and drawing him close. I knew he couldn't realistically make that promise. There was no guaranteeing anyone would make it out of this alive. If I had to walk into this particular ring of hell, though, I was damned glad to have Leo on my side.

But with that image of my father on the warehouse floor, knowing how little time he had, I just hoped like hell I didn't have to make a deal with the Devil.

Chapter Eighteen
Leo

"Asshole goddamn motherfuckers!"

Those were the first words out of Kara's mouth when she walked back in the door three hours later, and they weren't inspiring ones. She reeked like sewage from head to toe, and as soon as she was through the front door she started stripping, every other breath a curse.

"What happened?" I demanded. "Did they make you?"

"*Make* me? No, they didn't fucking *make* me," she snarled, throwing her tank top down on the ground and starting in on her yoga pants. "What they *made* me do to get through that goddamn place was crawl through three different sets of ventilation, hide in the motherfucking boiler room for almost half an hour while some asshole decided to shoot up in private, and then exit via the sewer system. The fucking *sewers*!" She was down to her bra and panties by now, and thankfully stopped there. "Do you know how many lemons I'm going to have to go through to get the smell out of my hair?"

"Ah, Kara." Angelus shook his head. "Perhaps you went in a bit overconfident?"

If I or Rich had said it, she probably would have kneed us so hard in the balls they'd bounce into the backs of our throats. Since it was Angelus, all she did was *look* like she wanted to nut him. "I was not overconfident or underprepared. I'm *back*, aren't I? This job would have been a lot easier without the surveillance part."

"But you did get the cameras in place, right?" I pressed her.

"Of course. One close to the main entrance, one on a rafter above the back entrance, and one right down from the room they're keeping your moms in." She opened up a bag and handed over a cell phone with an open link. It wasn't transmitting, though. "You'll have to get closer for it to pick up, these are tiny cameras running on even tinier batteries," she explained when she saw me frown. "And I couldn't get in the room with your folks. It was guarded the whole time, and plenty of people were talking about it. That room's pretty secure. You're either going to have to kill a bunch of people or open up some pretty big holes to get them out."

Or exchange me for Rich's parents, but I didn't care to bring that up again. Because it wasn't an option. Rich wouldn't do that to me. After all the work he'd put into sticking by me and saving my ass, he wouldn't do that to me.

Right?

"And *you*!" She rounded on Angelus. "You've got to do something. Your reputation is slipping."

"Meaning what?"

"Meaning I saw not one, but *two* suspicious cars not two blocks away from this place on my way back that I'm willing to bet are full of Grimaldi stooges." She wrinkled her nose. "They all smoke the same rank Fortuna cigarettes, it must be their version of braiding each other's hair. Anyway, you're under watch."

Angelus shook his head. "This is an unfortunate development. For them."

"No shit," Kara agreed. "Speaking of which, excuse me while I shower and then we can get going."

"We?" Rich sounded surprised. "You want to come with us?"

"Well, I do now! We don't have to directly intervene, but we can keep our eyes on the doors after you go in, let you know what's happening outside."

"Better that you be the one to take the phone," Angelus said.

Kara frowned. "What phone?"

We clued her in to what had happened while she was gone, and by the end of it she was seething. "I swear, they did *not* learn about your being here from me. If they'd caught me in there, they would have just killed me. This is probably because we scared those pantywaist sons of bitches off earlier. They couldn't get any information directly, so they got it by spying." She glared at Rich. "Why the hell did you decide to go for a walk?"

"Why the hell did you tell me the fucking Grimaldis are too scared to show their faces here?" he countered. Kara's eyes narrowed.

"Okay, no." I stepped in between them. "We've got too much to do to start this shit. Kara, clean up and get ready to take the phone downtown. Angelus, can you stick around and be our lookout?"

He beamed at me. "I can do better than that. We will give the Grimaldis a little gift, eh? One of their own back, but carrying a little present for them. He'll make a good distraction." He hummed speculatively. "I think I left his legs intact enough to walk about a block. He'll make it before we blow him up."

Oh shit. It was a very Albanian mob solution to a problem, but—

"No fucking way," Rich said a second later, like I knew he would. His face was pale but his expression was grimly implacable. "You're not using whoever that is as a suicide bomber."

"He's a very bad man," Angelus said mildly, like that would help. "He pushes drugs to teenagers, he's a rapist, a dissolute gambler…no offense meant," he added in my direction. "But gambling, eh, it's a sickness of the mind. A weakness. The world will not miss this man."

"I'll say it again—you're not going to blow him up in the middle of his people."

"Do you even want to win this thing?" Kara demanded. "Isn't getting your folks back worth a little guts and mayhem, or are you just squeamish?"

This was going nowhere good, fast. "No human bombs," I said, and I saw Rich's shoulders relax a bit. "There's got to be plenty of other stuff to blow up around this warehouse. We don't need him."

"Ah, my nipper. Thinking with your heart, not your head." Angelus sighed heavily. "It is good that your father can't see how far you've fallen from your legacy."

My *legacy*? Abandoned by both halves of my family, wanted by no one but a dead man, and he was trying to remind me of, what, my *duty* to any of these people? "Fuck you," I said pleasantly. "Can you help us with this, or are we doing it without you?"

He shrugged. "You are still my family, even if you are a fool. And Matteo involved your mother. Dirty, dirty. This isn't the old country. Things are not done this way in America, even if you do have the police in your pockets. I'll help you." He headed for the basement door. "But first, I must take care of my guest."

Once he was gone, Kara crossed her arms. "You know he's just going to kill the guy anyway."

"I know." Rich didn't sound happy about that. "But I spent years in a place where you never knew if the next person around the corner was going to be a friend or was just getting close enough to you to take you out with them. I'm not going to deal with that shit here." *I can't*, was the subtext. Kara, for once, didn't push it.

"Fine. Your loss. I'm going to go shower, and when I get out I'll update the map of the inside of the warehouse. It isn't a complicated layout, really. Lots of rooms, I think somebody was trying to make this into an office space at one point, but they're not much more than cubicles for the most part. No doors. The only really reinforced location is the office."

"Did you see Matteo anywhere in there?" I asked.

She shook her head. "He's either in the office too, or he's holed up somewhere else entirely."

He would be there. Matteo was the one overseeing this clusterfuck, trying to keep it out of his father's eye. He *needed* to be there. "Fine. Go clean up and let's get this show on the road." She headed up the stairs, and once I was sure she was out of hearing distance, I turned to Rich. "You okay?" I murmured.

He opened his mouth to reply, but just then a single gunshot from downstairs split the silence. We both jumped a little, and Rich exhaled heavily, like he had to force his lungs to cooperate. "I just want to get this over with."

"I know." I did too. "Any suggestions for what to do once we get inside?"

This time, he smiled a little. "Actually, I do."

That smile made me nervous, but I'd asked for it. "Okay, what?"

I couldn't keep my mouth from dropping as he explained. "You aren't serious," I said once he'd finished.

"Completely serious."

Okay, this was a guy who had special codes for use with his dad over the phone. I guess I should have expected something, but *this*? "Are you sure? It could be dangerous."

CARI Z & L.A. WITT

"It'll definitely be dangerous, but everything about this already is." He had a good point. "If you get the chance, trust me, take it." Rich was calmer now, more settled since the shot downstairs. I chose to trust him. I was choosing that a lot lately—it was more than a little troubling. I didn't want to rely on him like that, and I really didn't want to rely on this plan, but every edge we could get helped.

"If you say so."

By the time we got to the warehouse, the sun was just cresting the horizon. It was really late or really early, depending on your point of view, and according to Rich one of the best times to stage an attack. "They're tired, they're wired, and if there's a shift change it's going to happen soon. Extra chaos."

"Extra guns," I muttered, but I didn't care. The guys standing guard at the front door did look pretty tired, and Matteo had a limited number of people he could use here—his father wasn't the type to let him commandeer more soldiers from their work to fix his fuck-up. This was Matteo's best chance to set things to rights. Beyond this, the Grimaldi patriarch was going to start getting annoyed. "Whatever. Is Kara done with the charges?"

"Two more minutes and she will be."

"Great." We'd ended up deciding to use Kara as our backup while Uncle Angelus took the phone—and the body—somewhere out of town to be disposed of. She was more excited for it anyway. "And you think she's got the timing down?"

"She'll be fine." Ideally, we'd all be communicating via Bluetooth and using the cameras she'd set up as we went in, but the timing hadn't worked out. Instead, we set up a schedule of events and synced our watches—actual watches, not even phones. It was old school, but I had to give it to Rich, a watch was easier to glance at on the move than pulling out my phone. Speaking of my phone…I took one last glance at the video feeds, then closed the app and put it away. It hadn't shown any new movement for the past five minutes, and I needed to focus.

I shivered a little, and Rich glanced at me with concern in his eyes. "You ready for this?"

"Fine," I said. "I'm just cold." Really cold, even through my T-shirt and bulletproof vest and jacket. Rich, on the other hand, seemed more settled than I'd have given him credit for an hour ago. "You?"

"Yeah."

"Really?"

He shrugged. "It might fuck me up a little later," he said with startling honesty, "but for now, this just feels familiar. Like settling in to an old pair of shoes."

"That are wired to explode."

He grinned. "Something like that." Our watches beeped a little warning together. "Ten seconds. Here we go."

Here we go. Into a pit of fucking vipers to rescue our people and catch Matteo. Joy. I reminded myself that this was my damn plan.

Five…four…three…two…

KA-BOOM!

The first bomb was the biggest, but even I was surprised by how much of a fucking mess it made. The parking lot to the side of the warehouse erupted in flames, sending parked cars flying into the air. As the ringing in my ears subsided, I heard shouts come from the back of the warehouse. Men streamed into the lot, guns drawn, yelling at each other unintelligibly as they looked for us. Rich and I were already on the move, though.

One shot from each of us took out the guards, and I yanked the door back so Rich could enter and clear the room. *Pop-pop-pop.* I followed him in and saw two more men on the ground, one of them still groaning, but we couldn't linger here. We had to get to the office, fast. It was time to split up. Rich hadn't liked that part of the plan, but it was two of us and over twenty of them. We needed to maximize our efficiency. He went left and I went right.

And I walked straight into the path of two guys I slightly recognized running down the hall. I heard a flashbang grenade go off nearby and groaned inside my head. Right, that *had* been the plan. Less than a minute in and I was already fucking this up. I fired at the men and they darted into opposite rooms while I fumbled at my waist for a grenade.

A bullet took me in the shoulder—it hit the vest, but the momentum knocked me back against the wall. Fuck, fuck, fuck, I needed this grenade *yesterday*. Another bullet punched through the cheap plasterboard by my head, and I fired off a few more rounds as I finally got to the grenade and threw it down the hall.

Instead of a flash, white smoke began to spray from it. I'd grabbed a tear gas cannister by mistake. It was working on the guys—I could hear them both retching—but now I had to go *through* the damn stuff. Brilliant.

One man staggered out of the cloud, and I shot him through the head. There was no sign of the other guy—he must have gone back the way he'd come. Shit. I needed to move.

My watch beeped. I glanced at the time—ah, distraction number two in three…two…

BOOM. The west side of the warehouse shuddered, rocked by the bundles of C4 Kara had planted there. She'd assured me it wouldn't be enough to make the place collapse, just give people something to think about, and she was right. Two more capos ran for the front door through the dissipating tear gas, and I shot both of them in the chest and sped past them as they fell. I needed to get a move on.

The map said I should turn left up here. I did—the way was clear, but I checked the rooms as I went anyway.

All empty. No prisoners. At the next hall I took a right, and was immediately body checked into the wall. *Fuck*. It was Carlo Paolini, a guy I used to play cards with. When he saw it was me, he grinned like a maniac.

I tried to bring my gun up but he got my wrist in a crushing grip and banged my hand repeatedly against the wall. I couldn't hold on. The gun skittered away, and a second later his hand found my throat. I couldn't reach my backup gun, and I couldn't fucking *breathe* either. I clawed at Carlo's face while I kicked and scraped at his legs with my feet. He grunted, but just widened his stance and lowered his head to the side of my neck.

"If Matteo didn't want you alive, I'd have killed you already," he hissed in my ear. "Maybe if you stop struggling, he won't make your momma watch when he cuts off your—" His breathless rant ended as quickly as it had begun, his head falling back even as his grip on me lost its strength. Carlo fell away, only to reveal Rich behind him, wiping the blood off a double-edged knife on his pant leg and reaching for me with the other. He put a hand on my shoulder as I coughed.

"You okay, Leo?" he asked tersely. The darkness of his clothing hid the blood, but I could smell more on him. He'd had at least one up-close encounter as well.

"Fine," I managed.

"Good. We're almost there."

We were, he was right. I needed to pull myself together. I took a deep breath, picked up my gun and nodded. "Let's go."

The main office was close to the center of the warehouse. We rounded two more corners without trouble but then I stopped Rich before he took the last one. "Hang on." I pulled out my phone and checked the surveillance. The room looked unguarded. I hadn't had any texts from Kara to indicate the hostages had been pulled out, though. "Fuck. We're gonna get ambushed in there."

"Then we play it like we planned."

"I don't like this plan."

"You'll get over it." Or I'd be dead.

We entered the hallway and stopped to the side of the closed office door. *You ready?* Rich mouthed at me. I swallowed and nodded. He turned, kicked the door in and entered. I followed right behind him, gun at the ready.

God damn. The place smelled as bad as Uncle Angelus's basement. Matteo was there, along with Ricky and two other guys, each of them holding a gun on the individual hostages. Rich's mother was still cradling her husband's head, but he'd gone from white to gray, and there was a lot of blood on those bandages. At least he was unconscious, but her face was a stony mask of tension. And my own mother...

She looked odd, in Sketchers and blue jeans and a lavender blouse, like some Middle American housewife. Gone was the gloriously long brown hair I remembered, replaced by a bland bob cut. She looked at me like she didn't even recognize me. I could say the same.

"Leo." Matteo grinned widely at me. Oh, this fucker was high as a kite. I could see it in his eyes, bloodshot and wild. "You made it."

"No thanks to you."

"I told my boys not to rough you up, but they can be a little overzealous. But still, here you are." He clapped his hands together. "And Marshal! I expected you to keep that fucking phone on you."

"I don't like being told what to do," Rich said in a bored, cold tone I'd never heard from him. Before I knew it, he'd grabbed me and jerked me in front of him, taking my gun away so smoothly I hardly even registered it. "I brought him to you. Now hand over my parents."

"Looks to me like he brought himself."

"Do you want to argue semantics, or do you want me to shoot him through the head before you get a chance to torture the information you need out of him?"

I gulped. My heart beat frantically in my chest. "Rich…"

"Shut the fuck up. Well, Mattie? I don't have all damn day."

"We'll do a little exchange, then." Matteo motioned to the man holding his gun on Rich's father. "Pick him up and go over to the marshal." The big guy complied, even though getting Rich's father away from his wife was like ripping apart Velcro. She sobbed a little as he was taken from her.

Before Matteo could say anything else, I felt a heavy boot kick me square in the ass, sending me sprawling toward the far wall. I landed with a crash next to Rich's mother, whose hands fluttered nervously as she reached for me. "Oh, honey, are you okay?"

"He's fine, Mom. Don't waste your ammo on him." Rich refocused on Matteo. "And my mother?"

"Let's not get ahead of ourselves," Matteo said lightly. "After all, I might have Leo here but I don't have the information I need yet. I'll give you your mother when I'm sure my money and the organization's data are safe."

"That wasn't the deal," Rich snarled, taking a half-step toward Matteo. All the men in there aimed their guns at him. Rich's mother pulled me closer, one hand patting my shoulder while the other trailed down my back.

"It's *my* deal now, Marshal, and I say take your father and run for it. You might get out of the warehouse alive." Matteo smirked. "Although, I gotta say, your dad probably won't make it to the nearest hospital. He's—"

Between one breath and the next, Rich's mother reached under my jacket and pulled my extra gun out from the small of my back, fired one shot over my head, then twisted and fired another behind her at Matteo, who had just enough warning to jerk Ricky Canova in front of him and catch the bullet with his buddy's forehead. At the same time, Rich turned and shot the man holding his

213

father, catching his dad's limp body as his dying captor sagged to the ground.

Rich's mom fired at Matteo again, but he was already running for the door, barreling past Rich and into the hall before she could get a bead on him. I surged to my feet to run after him, but a second later a third explosion rattled the building from somewhere in front of us. That was the final one, not just there to provide a distraction but as a warning that the cops were coming.

I didn't care. I could still get him.

"Leo!"

I ran out of the room and down the hall, past the bodies we'd left behind.

"*Leo!*"

I ignored the voice and kept going. I didn't know which way Matteo had gone, so I just picked a direction and sprinted as fast as I could. Matteo was *not* allowed to escape, he just wasn't.

The air was thick with smoke, and several of the cubicles had collapsed under the stress of the explosions. I fought my way over the rubble, scraped myself on a board full of nails but ran on. He'd be here. Just a little further and I'd be at the exit, and I'd find Matteo—

I found the exit, but Matteo wasn't there. There were three bodies instead, each one with an enormous spray of blood behind them—shot with a sniper rifle. Kara's work, but I didn't have time to appreciate it. I slammed my shoulder against the door and out of the building, and saw—

Nothing. No Matteo, no Kara. She'd probably taken off the moment she blew the last bomb. And no Matteo.

"Fuck," I whispered, feeling my guts twist into a Gordion knot. "Fuck!" It couldn't end like this, couldn't put me at the head of a goddamn massacre without giving me the thing that made it worth all the nightmares. "*Fuck!*"

I dropped back against the dirt brick wall, all my energy suddenly gone. I could still ruin Matteo, still ruin the whole Grimaldi crime family—and I would—but taking their money was a hollow victory beside the prospect of taking out Matteo. He didn't deserve to live, after what he did to Tony.

"Leo!" Someone crouched in front of me, and it took me a second to realize it was Rich. "Leo, we have to get out of here, my dad needs a hospital." Vaguely, I heard sirens growing louder and louder. "We'll get him," Rich promised me, and I reached out and squeezed his hand so hard I had to be hurting him, but he just let me do it. "I swear, we'll find Matteo again. Just come with me right now."

Moving like I'd aged fifty years in a minute, I let Rich get me to my feet and guide me over to the idling SUV I hadn't even noticed pull up. My mother was driving. *Good.* I didn't want to deal with her, didn't even want to look at her. I got into the back, behind Rich's parents, and stared out the window at nothing as we left behind the smoking warehouse and all of its victims.

Chapter Nineteen
Rich

"He's out of surgery." My mom released a long breath. "They said it'll be a while before we can see him, but he's in recovery."

I slumped against the wall in the hospital room where I'd been pacing for the last hour and a half, not to mention hiding from anyone who might care that we were here. My body was exhausted, and every step I'd taken had hurt like hell, but I'd kept going because I didn't want to fall asleep. I could feel the nightmares already, and I wasn't about to give in to them yet. The only reason I'd stopped now was I didn't want to make my mom follow me up and down the floor. Or raise her voice so I could hear her, which would potentially wake up Leo, who was sleeping on the bed in the room. Not as a patient—a nurse had given us this room to keep a low profile, and Leo had finally surrendered to fatigue about half an hour ago. At least one of us could sleep.

Voice soft, I turned to my mom. "So, he'll be okay?"

She hugged herself, glancing back at the door she'd come through with tired, worried eyes. "He should be. He lost a lot of blood, and he had the beginnings of an infection."

I winced. "But they can treat it?"

Mom nodded. "He'll be in the ICU for a little while. We'll just have to wait and see."

Wait and see. As if there was time for that. Hell, maybe there was. It felt like forever since my life had had any semblance of calm instead of this constant balls-to-the-wall bullshit. I wondered if this was how it would be for the rest of my life.

Apparently oblivious to me, my mom sighed. "I just can't believe this." She swallowed hard. "He went outside to talk to you on the phone, and then there were suddenly men everywhere. They grabbed me, and I heard the gun go off…" She shuddered violently, voice wavering as she whispered, "I thought your father was dead."

"So did I." I put my hands on her shoulders. "But he's alive now. We all are."

Her eyes met mine, and she might as well have said out loud, *but for how long?*

As if I could answer that.

She pulled in a breath through her nose, and her shoulders seemed to solidify under my hands. The helplessness in her eyes shifted to determination. "So what happens next?" *Who else do I have to shoot?*

I couldn't help laughing quietly. "Leo and I will figure it out." I wondered if I sounded even a little bit confident, because with the way things had been going, I sure as shit didn't feel the part. "You just stay here with Dad."

It was hard to say if the answer was a relief, or if it frustrated her. My mom had always had a hell of a poker face, and she was deploying it now. "How will I reach you?"

"You won't. I'll get in touch with you. Dad will be here for a few days at least, so that's how I'll find you."

Her lips tightened with maternal worry, but the practiced stoicism of being a marshal's wife—and now a marshal's mother—came through. "Okay. I should, um, get back to the waiting room. In case they have any updates."

"Good idea." I wrapped my arms around her and kissed the top of her head. "I'm glad you and Dad are okay."

"Me too. We've been worried sick about you, baby." Her shaking voice let some of that worry come through, and it broke my heart almost as much as the words did.

"I know. I'm sorry."

"It's part of the job." Right back to stoic. She let me go. We held each other's gazes. Then without another word, she headed back up to wait for an update on my dad.

I started pacing again before lethargy could pull me to my knees or down onto the gurney beside Leo. The walls in this room had been closing in for the last couple of hours, and now they were suffocating. I didn't dare wander the hospital, though. It had been risky enough feeding a bullshit story to the nurse who'd given us the room. After all, we weren't exactly inconspicuous in battered tactical gear that smelled like blood, smoke, and tear gas. Fortunately, nurses and cops tended to look out for each other, and apparently that courtesy extended to marshals too. I'd assured her that the "situation" was under control but that I couldn't disclose details, and that had been enough.

We were out of sight now, but people had seen us come in. Question was, how safe were we here? And for how long? Once it got out that there was a rogue U.S. Marshal, that would set off some alarm bells. If the Marshals, the Grimaldis, or Chicago P.D. caught wind of a couple of guys decked out in tactical shit who came in with minor injuries and a man nearly dying of a gunshot wound? Yeah, that would raise some questions.

For the millionth time, I kicked myself for even staying here at the hospital. We were sitting ducks here, but hell, I'd needed to be sure my dad was all right. And anyway, we'd both been running on fumes. Risk be damned, we'd needed the downtime. That, and I'd been worried about Leo when we'd arrived. He'd been out of it. Distracted. I'd freaked out that maybe he had a concussion or some other hidden wound, but then his mother had tried to talk to him, and...yeah. Okay. He wasn't hurt. He was just pissed off. Glad she was safe, but irritated by her presence.

A nurse had checked both of us out, and she'd let us take this room to lay low and get some rest. Nurses were saints. Seriously.

A quiet murmur pulled me out of my thoughts, and I turned to see Leo gingerly sitting up. He grimaced as he rubbed his shoulder.

"You okay?" I asked.

He grunted, swinging his legs over the side of the bed. "Any word on your dad?"

"He made it through surgery."

Leo lifted his gaze, brow pinched. "So he's good?"

"As good as can be expected."

He nodded slowly. Then, sighing heavily, he raked a hand through his hair. "I can't believe we fucking failed."

"What?" I stepped closer and touched his face. "Leo, we didn't fail. We got our parents out."

"And Matteo's still alive," he snapped. "And he fucking knows we're coming for him. How do we get to him when—"

"Leo." I put my hands on his shoulders, just like I had with my mom a few minutes ago, and though he wouldn't look at me, I fixed my gaze on him. "We'll get him. I'm not stopping until—"

"Why the hell do you even want to keep going?" He finally met my eyes. "You've done your part. Your parents are safe."

"But you're not."

"Neither are you as long as you stay involved."

"And neither of us will be until we take Matteo down." I pulled him in and kissed his forehead. "You're not getting rid of me, so stop trying."

He relaxed a little, and gave a soft, humorless laugh. "Getting rid of you is the last thing I want to do. I just don't want anything to happen to you."

"Pretty sure I'm okay so long as you've got my back." Our eyes met, and when he smiled, a little zing went through me, a feeling reminiscent to that moment we'd shared in the missile silo. Like we could pretend the rest of the world wasn't burning down and steal a few minutes for nothing but pleasure and each other.

"You know I have your back," he whispered. "Always."

"Me too. And we're going to see this through all the way to the end."

A faint smile flickered across his lips. Then he put his arms around my neck and pulled me in for a kiss. I sighed into his embrace and opened to his kiss, not feeling the least bit guilty about this momentary indulgence. If I'd learned one thing in our short time together, it was that chaos and hellfire were always lurking just around the corner, and if we had the opportunity to steal a moment to ourselves—whether it was a tender kiss or a wild fuck—I'd hate myself for letting it pass us by. God knew when or if we'd have another one.

Leo drew back and met my eyes. "So what happens next?"

"Our parents are safe. I say we get in contact with Angelus and Kara, and we'll figure out our next move from there."

He frowned, but nodded. "Okay. So do we—"

The door opened, and we both tensed, but then I relaxed. Leo absolutely did not because the person who'd joined us was his mother.

221

"This is the best I could find." She offered up a pair of Walmart bags. "Will it work?"

I glanced inside the first bag. Jeans. A sweatshirt. Socks. "Yeah. This is great. Thank you." I looked at Leo, and he glared back at me. Rolling my eyes, I hissed, "Just take it."

The glare intensified.

His mother cleared her throat. She set the bags down on the gurney, gave her son an unreadable look, and left again.

As I peeled off my shirt, Leo kept his glare fixed on the door. I sighed. "Just put it on."

"I can't believe you put her up to this." He still didn't reach for the clothes.

"She was the only one in our little group who wasn't hospitalized or"—I gestured at our clothes—"dressed like Tactical Timmy."

He pursed his lips. "You know she's going to think I owe her for this, right?"

"Pretty sure we can settle up after this is all over." I pulled on the shirt, and damn, the cheap, soft cotton felt amazing. It was clean and dry. Couldn't ask for much more. "Just get fucking dressed, and then you can ream me out later for sending your mom to Walmart."

Leo huffed. I thought he might keep arguing, but he kept his mouth shut and stripped off his clothes. He was moving gingerly, but so was I. An alarming bruise covered one of his shoulders, and my blood chilled. Thank God he'd been wearing Kevlar, because I didn't think that bruise had come from hand-to-hand combat.

We put our battered vests on over our T-shirts, then hid them under oversized hoodies. There wasn't much we could do about our shoes except hope no one glanced down and noticed smudges of blood alongside burn marks on our dirty sneakers.

Someone knocked at the door, and again, we both tensed.

222

"Boys?" Mom poked her head in. She looked us up and down, eyebrows jumping, then said, "Your dad's awake and in his room if you want to come see him."

The marshal and the Marine in me knew we needed to get the fuck out of here. That it was a risky move and an unnecessary delay.

The son in me desperately needed to be sure my dad was okay.

Leo squeezed my elbow. "There's no reason we can't step in there for a minute."

I looked in his eyes. "You sure?"

Mute, he nodded.

I swallowed, glancing back and forth between him and my mom. Then I cleared my throat. "Okay. Just for a minute, though, and then we need to get out of here." *And maybe that minute will give me time to figure out where the hell to go.*

Except…damn it. As much as I wanted to see my dad and take some time to think, we didn't have time. The longer we stayed here, the better the odds of someone noticing us.

I stopped. So did Mom and Leo.

"What?" Leo asked.

"On second thought, we should…" I moistened my lips. Then I exhaled. "Mom, tell Dad I wanted to come see him. But we"—I gestured at Leo—"need to get out of here before we draw attention."

Mom's jaw tightened, but then she nodded. "Okay. I'll tell him." She glanced up the long hallway. "There's a couple of security guards near the elevators. You might want to go out a different way."

"Good to know." I gestured sharply for Leo to follow me, and we doubled back the other way.

"Be careful," Mom called after us.

"We will," we both replied, and walked as fast as we could without breaking into a jog.

The back stairs took us all the way down to the parking garage, and we casually walked across it in plain sight of the cameras before doubling back, this time using vehicles for cover. Once we'd reached the end of the garage, we slipped out and hurried across the street to another parking lot.

"Tag, you're it," I panted. "Time to work your car thief magic."

Leo worked fast like he always did. In a matter of minutes—around the time three Chicago P.D. cars were pulling up to the hospital—we had a battered old sedan purring and blasting heat. Okay, it was kind of rattling and there was definitely something wrong under the hood, but it was functional. That was all we needed.

We slipped out of the parking lot, and as the hospital faded behind us, Leo exhaled. "I don't want to jinx us, but that seemed a little too easy."

"You think?" I watched the side mirror, expecting a tail at any moment. Maybe I was just getting paranoid. Maybe I was getting smart. So far, though, no one had followed us, but I didn't imagine that would last. "We're going to have to move quickly." I licked my dry lips. "Like I said, first we get in touch with Angelus and Kara. Then…"

Leo gave the silence a few beats before he glanced at me. "Then?"

"Then…we make a plan." I faced him. "That's as far as I've gotten. I promise, I'll think of something."

"No you won't." He took a hand off the wheel, reached across the console, and squeezed my leg. "We will."

We exchanged glances, and smiled faintly. If not for all the bruises and scrapes on both of us, not to mention the dark circles under his eyes, I might've even chuckled at his cheesy romantic gesture. Right now, it was exactly what I needed.

We drove in circles for a while to make absolutely sure no one had followed us. Then we slipped into a public library that had just opened, and did a search for abandoned buildings. Once we'd found one, we jotted down the address, erased the browser history, and took off again.

The building we'd chosen was a dilapidated house that made all the other dilapidated houses on the block look like something off House Hunters. Mint green paint was falling off gray, cracked siding in big chunks, and the roof was sagging on one side. The porch didn't look safe at all, so we went around to the back. We didn't even have to jimmy the door—the lock had been pried off, taking a slab of wood with it.

The door creaked open, and we entered carefully. The kitchen had been gutted of any appliances, and there were a few broken dishes scattered on the floor, which was so covered in dirt and mold, the linoleum's pattern was impossible to see.

"We should be okay here," I said quietly. "We're out of sight, we're out of the..." I shivered, and when I exhaled, blew out a thin cloud. "Okay, not out of the *cold*, but..."

"It's better than being out there," he agreed. "So now we—"

"Hey!" Two bearded guys in ratty coats stormed into the kitchen.

"What the hell are you doing?" the black man demanded.

"This is ours," the white guy said. "Get out."

Leo bristled. "We just need a place to—"

"I don't care." The white guy jabbed a gloved hand at me. "This place ain't—"

My pistol in his face shut him up right quick. "We're not here to kick you out," I said evenly. "You let us lay low in here, there won't be any trouble. Got it?"

He stared at my gun, his hands up and his eyes wide. "Y-yeah. No trouble."

The black man stared too. "Okay. Okay. Just…okay."

They both backed toward the door, exchanged wary glances, and then disappeared from the kitchen.

Leo exhaled. "Anyone shows up, we're going to get them killed." He nodded at the now empty doorway. "We can't stay here long."

I sighed, creating another cloud in the cold air. "I know. So let's get in contact with Angelus, make a plan, and get moving."

Chapter Twenty
Leo

Rich was right, we needed to get moving, but I wasn't going to deny him the chance to snatch a catnap either. We'd been going nonstop for what felt like days—actually, yeah, it *was* days—and he was the one who'd been handling the emotional fallout from his mother getting kidnapped and his father, so we'd thought, being killed. The guy needed the rest, and me…I needed some time to think.

We ditched yet another set of clothes and I ran them a few derelict houses down, and then managed to convince Rich that the world really wouldn't end if he caught a little shuteye. "You can spell me as soon as you wake up," I assured him, because of course *that* was what he was worrying about. Me. The self-sacrificing son of a bitch needed to learn to put himself first. "I'll keep a look out, don't worry."

He just nodded, trusting me. Like I deserved it. Hell…maybe I finally did, after everything we'd just gone through. The thought made my head spin.

"Are you going to call Angelus?" he asked.

"Yeah, but I'll keep it brief." We still had burner phones from the kits Kara had outfitted for us, and I was pretty sure they weren't being tracked. Yet. Christ, with the Marshals on our tails it was hard to say how long it would last. That was part of the big, too-heavy problem that loomed on the edge of my vision, the one I didn't want to think about but wouldn't be able to avoid.

First things first, though—I needed to call Angelus. I dialed his personal number into the burner phone one moldy, trash-filled room away from Rich's sleeping form, my eyes on the street. Two rings later, my uncle answered.

"Alo?"

Just hearing his voice made me fume. "So, when were you planning on telling me my mother doesn't live in Albania anymore?"

He sighed heavily. "I thought you would probably figure that out, nipper."

Yeah, well, it hadn't been too hard. She'd never have pulled a Jennifer Aniston on her hair if she'd been living in Albania. Plus, I'd overheard her introduce herself to one of the doctors at the hospital as "Mrs. Browning." A few quick Google searches later and I'd found "Valerie Browning," resident of Indianapolis, Indiana, wife of a tax lawyer—and good God that was ironic—and mother of two little girls. I had half-siblings that I'd never met— never would meet, either. My mother hadn't just abandoned the family she'd made with me and my father, she'd gone off and birthed an entirely new one to replace us with.

"You told me she went back to the old country."

"She did." I could almost hear his shrug. "Briefly. But there was no life for her there anymore, not with the reputation she'd developed. A whore for an Italian mobster…who would have her after that? So I helped her return to the U.S., found her a new place to live and an identity to inhabit. You should be happy for her. She has flourished."

Flourished, while I'd foundered and broken against the rocks of low expectations. "And you would have gone on letting me believe this for the rest of my life?"

"For the rest of mine, certainly." Angelus sighed again. "I don't like that we had to deceive you, Leotrim, but surely you can understand why. How could Valmira make a fresh start with you in her life? I promised her I would look out for you, and I did so."

"Look *out* for me?" My voice rose without me meaning it to, and I heard Rich stir. I forced it down again. "You called me once a year and taught me some skills with a fillet knife that I'll never forget—or use—and you're calling that looking out for me?"

"Mmm. You are too tender. You always were too tender, my nipper. You should be grateful that you learned so many things the hard way, because otherwise you wouldn't have lasted nearly so long."

So it was a *good* thing I'd been separated from my father, abandoned by my mother and ignored by my uncle for most of my life. "Got it. Thanks for clarifying the situation."

"Don't hold a grudge, Leo. I can still be of use to you."

"No, I don't think you can." One way or another, I was done with my family. All of it. "Don't contact me again. Ever."

"Now, Leo—"

I ended the call and resisted the urge to break the phone against the windowsill. Fucking, goddamn, sanctimonious asshole—who did he think he was, manipulating my entire life like that? And Valmira. *Valerie.* If I never saw the woman who had given birth to me

229

again, it would be too fucking soon. Now my dilemma was more potent than ever.

The thing was, I knew my family was shit. I'd known that since I was eight. I hadn't gone into this situation expecting to come out with any satisfaction beyond cold, hard revenge against Matteo and his entire clan.

I checked the account algorithms—money was flowing nicely, good. Matteo would be sweating bullets right now, his father would be displeased, tensions among the Grimaldis would be rising…all of which gave *me* more power. The question was: how did I use that power? I had the uncomfortable feeling that I was going to spend it all on Rich.

If only I hadn't met his family. I could have kept my eyes on the prize better if I'd never had to meet his parents, who were—well, I couldn't really speak to his dad, but his mother had probably literally saved my life. He had a family that was worth a damn, and that was something worth protecting. For his sake.

You owe him this.

I owed him a lot more than this, but this was what I could do. It would mean giving up my ultimate goal, but unless I wanted to light the fuse on my very own bottle rocket straight to Hell, I had to protect Rich's family. That meant bargaining for Matteo's life, because we needed a Grimaldi to identify the dirty marshals who were threatening Rich's parents even now.

Fuck me. Angelus was right, I was too tender for my own damn good.

I needed to find Matteo, fast. Faster than the Marshals could get to him, because now that his value was in the toilet I figured they wouldn't think twice about eliminating him to save their own skins. His father might not bother to intervene at the rate I was bleeding his empire dry, either. Where was Matteo's safe place when everyone else had failed him?

The same place Tony's had been. With their sister, Gianna. She had been more mother than sister to both of them growing up, and even though her father had dismissed her from the family after she married an outsider and left the family business behind for fashion, old habits died hard. She would know where he was. The question remained, though—would she tell me?

There was only one way to find out. I dialed the message service that Gianna and I had set up years ago. Three new messages. *Beep.*

"What the hell are you doing, Leo?" Yep, that was her—she had a voice like an angry opera singer. "What was that shitshow in the warehouse? Didn't Tony teach you the littlest thing about handling these sorts of operations on the sly? You can't make such a big mess, not if you expect my father to look the other way. You—" I could hear the faint tone of another call come in on her phone. The message ended. *Beep.*

"He's here." She sounded subdued. "I told him not to come to me, I don't want to see him, but he knows I'm— I'm *weak*—when he's with me in person. I always was with my brothers. I look into his eyes and it's too easy to see him as a five-year-old again, begging me for a taste of my ice cream cone. He used to be so...but now he's here, and he won't leave, and my husband is here. My *children* are here, and he *won't leave*. You can't come here, Leo. I won't have them put in danger. Give me time to work this out." *Beep.*

"I found the money you left me." She was the only member of the Grimaldi empire that I wasn't draining dry, but I couldn't afford to leave her funds in their original accounts either—if things came to a head, the Feds would only freeze them and ultimately claim them and leave her with nothing. I'd sent her a coded email a week ago, before this all got so out of hand. Looks like she'd decoded it just fine.

"I told my brother I would set up a new account for him, and arrange to get him out of the country, if he goes to stay in a safehouse for a while. It's not one associated with the family, because our father is looking for him now and he's on the warpath. This place is off the family's books. A place of Matteo's that our Dad doesn't know about." She rattled off an address on Lake Geneva, a resort town a few hours south of Chicago. "Matteo should be there by tonight. He's got at least two men meeting him there, but I'm not sure of that number. Leo…" Her sigh sounded suspiciously like a sob. "I wish it had never come to this. I wish there was some other way out, but there isn't, is there? I tried so hard to get out. I wish Tony had come with me. I miss him so much. I'll always miss him. I'll miss both of my brothers." Her breath hitched. "I just wish…" The message ended.

I put the phone down and closed my eyes for a moment, letting it all sink in. One way or another now, there was no going back. There was no one left for me in my old life. Without Angelus and Gianna, I was completely adrift.

You've got Rich.

I did, but not for long. I was going to fix things for him and then I was going to let him go. That was all there was to it.

Probably I was making a lot out of nothing, anyway. I pulled myself together and headed back into the other room. I touched Rich's shoulder and he came awake in an instant. "What's happening?" he asked in a gravelly voice, wiping sand from the corners of his eyes. I wanted to run my hand through his hair. I clenched my fist instead.

"I've got a location for Matteo. His father hasn't found him yet, and neither have the Marshals, but if we're going to be there first we need to be fast."

"We? As in, just you and me?" he clarified.

"Yeah," I said grimly. "It's just us from here on out." Maybe that was reckless, maybe I should have gone crawling back to Angelus and asked him to loan us Kara for the operation coming up, but I couldn't quite make myself do it. When I cut down a relationship, I scorched the ground and salted the earth it had grown in.

"Okay, then."

"You're allowed to disagree with me on this," I said testily. "I know I—"

"Leo." Rich shook his head. "If you don't trust them, then it would do more harm than good to have them along anyway. I'm fine with this. Really."

"Matteo won't be alone."

"I know. We'll make it work."

Yeah, we would. We had to. And now it was time to talk about the elephant in the room. "We can't kill Matteo."

Rich looked at me carefully. "Why do you think that?" I knew he knew what I was getting at, but apparently he wanted me to spell it out for him.

"Because we need him, to get the Marshals off your back. To make your family safe. And to turn evidence against his father." I could still take down the Grimaldi empire, at least, even if I couldn't kill Matteo.

It felt like such a betrayal of Tony not to seek revenge with every atom of my being. Was I really going to forget him so fast that I didn't even bother to kill the man who'd killed him, just to make a lawman happy? Tony had been everything to me for so long. How could I do this to him?

I wasn't really a religious person, for all I'd grown up surrounded by the trappings of Catholicism. I didn't believe in life after death, I didn't believe that Tony was looking down on me from heaven or up at me from hell, judging me. The only person judging me was myself, and Rich. I suspected that, as generous as Rich was, even he would have something to say if I threw his parents to the lions for the sake of vengeance. He was the only ally I had left. I couldn't afford to alienate him.

At least, that was what I was going to try to believe about this whole thing. There'd be time to hate myself later.

Rich shut his eyes for a long moment, and when he opened them again they shined with gratitude in a way that made me feel uncomfortably like I wanted to see that expression over and over again. "Thank you."

"Don't, please." Happily, he didn't push it. Instead he stood up, stretched, and then froze as he looked out the window behind us. "What?" I asked.

"The black SUV coming down the road." Any residual sleepiness was gone in an instant, one hand going to rest on his gun even as he turned and grabbed up the nearest duffel bag. "It's a government car."

I rolled my eyes. "Of course it is. Christ, you guys don't know how to be subtle."

"Black is classic."

"Shiny black SUVs in this part of Chicago are classically *dumb*, yeah. They should be driving a beater."

He shrugged. "The better to intimidate you with."

Well, it wasn't going to intimidate me, but it did light a fire under my ass. "We have to get out of here and find Matteo before it's too late."

"You're right." I went to grab the other bag, but Rich looped a hand around the back of my neck and pulled me in for a quick kiss. My lungs trembled in my chest, but I did my best not to let on how much it affected me. I kissed him back, lingering—this might be the last time we ever touched like this, and I deserved a second to savor it, damn it—then pulled away.

"We have to go."

"Yeah." He nodded toward the back door, and I led the way to our rusting brown sedan. I hoped it lasted as far as Lake Geneva.

It was a race against time now. By now, every law enforcement agency in the country had caught wind of what had happened at the warehouse, and they'd all be gunning for Matteo. So would his father's men. Whoever got to Matteo first would have all the bargaining power. It was going to be us. It *had* to be us.

And if he and his buddies decided to fight back? Well, fuck. Matteo didn't need both his kneecaps. Hell, he didn't even need one of them.

And I was sure I could find a fillet knife somewhere.

Chapter Twenty-One
Rich

If there was one thing I was learning in my crash course of dealing with Mob families, it was that they didn't do things by halves. When I thought "safe house in Lake Geneva," I imagined a remote cabin surrounded by a thick forest and protected by a couple of thugs in ghillie suits. Or maybe an inconspicuous suburban split level, complete with the white picket fence and windchimes so nobody would notice the sniper perched in the second story window. Maybe even another missile silo because why the fuck not?

I did *not* think of a lavish multimillion-dollar house next to a six-boat dock on a sprawling stretch of lakeshore.

Under the cover of some thick brush in a green belt beside another property, Leo and I stayed low and surveyed the massive estate. According to a website we'd checked on the way here, the house sat on roughly forty acres, and most of that was a manicured lawn ringed by a thick enough band of trees to offer the illusion of privacy. On the surface, it didn't appear all that secure, but I had no doubt there were motion sensors, cameras, dogs, drones, dragons, and whatever else a Grimaldi could afford to protect his lair.

We hadn't been able to find any public information about the house itself except a Google Maps image that didn't show us anything we couldn't see from here. The structure was three stories, probably with a full basement below, judging by the stairs leading down beside the back deck. It was built out of ugly beige stone and surrounded by floodlights that would probably make the place visible from space after dark. Though the sun was still up, lights were on in several windows. Matteo hadn't even bothered to close the curtains except on one third-floor room, which had blackout curtains on every window. His bedroom, I guessed.

A stone path wound about a hundred feet down the gently sloping lawn from the house to the lake shore and a long dock, and beside that, half a dozen boats bobbed on the lake's gentle waves. Two were basic outboard motorboats like the ones my dad and I would take out fishing, but the other four probably each cost as much as a normal person's house. Especially the enormous, sleek speedboat. Was this lake even deep enough for boats like that? Did it need to be? I supposed it didn't matter; a boat like that served primarily as a dick extension as far as I was concerned.

"I take it subtlety isn't a priority," I muttered as I scoped out the scene through binoculars.

Beside me, Leo snorted. "Are you kidding? They didn't get that rich so they could live in a trailer park. Plus, it doesn't raise eyebrows when they bring in contractors for Fort Knox-level security."

"Good point. Hadn't thought of that." I lowered the binoculars and turned to him. "You think you can get past a security system like that?"

Leo rolled an incredulous gaze toward me. "You haven't known me very long, but I think you *have* known me long enough you don't need to ask that question."

"Okay, fair, but it's still a valid question if we're going to—"

"Yes, I can bypass their system." He looked out at the house again. "What I need to know is how many men he's got. Gianna said at least two, but I don't want to go strolling in there and find an entire SEAL team."

I frowned. "We don't have much time. We may have to go in blinder than we'd like."

Leo made an unhappy noise. After several solid minutes of silence, he said, "I've got an idea."

"Hmm?"

"There are motion sensors and cameras down by the dock. With boats that expensive, there's probably all kinds of shit, but I think if we can get under the dock undetected—"

"Like, swim in?"

Leo nodded. "I saw a sportsman's store on the way in. About thirty minutes back the way we came. They'll have wetsuits, and probably something waterproof we can put our weapons in." He paused. "You ever scuba dived?"

"Not since I was in the Marines, but I can remember how to do it."

"Good. They had a diver down flag in the window, so I guarantee they've got gear."

"You planning on tapping into the Grimaldi's money to pay for all that?"

Without even looking at me, he said, "I didn't say we were buying any of it."

Oh Lord. "Okay, so hypothetically, we steal a bunch of dive gear and swim up under Matteo's dock. Then what?"

"Then we make some noise."

Somehow, I could tell he was zeroing in on that speedboat.

"So, draw everyone out of the house."

Leo nodded. "While they're dealing with whatever chaos we've left for them, we go inside." He turned to me, a wicked grin playing at his lips. "And when they come back in, we'll be waiting."

"You really think Matteo will be flushed out that easily? Or that *all* of his security will come out?"

"Of course not. But he'll have us between him and at least some of his muscle."

I arched an eyebrow. "You are aware that it's not a good idea to fight a two-front war, right?"

"Well, ideally we'll take out one front before the other one realizes there's shit going down inside the house." He turned to me. "Long as there's enough noise on the dock, they won't hear what we're doing inside."

I shook my head and picked up the binoculars again. "You are way too optimistic for someone who's been through this past week."

To my surprise, that got a quiet chuckle out of him.

We both silently observed the property for another long moment. If he was anything like me, he was calculating every possible angle we could use for our attack. Every maneuver, its pros and cons, and anything Matteo might have thought of to keep the place secure.

Two guys in suits carrying pistols came out to do a perimeter check. I looked at my watch. Twenty minutes since they'd last made their rounds. Forty since the time before.

"They are way too predictable," Leo said under his breath. "I'm gonna guess they're relying on their security systems." He huffed a laugh. "Idiots."

"Don't they know there's a hacker coming after them?"

"I'm pretty sure they're more worried about the cavalry showing up, not us."

"The cavalry?"

Leo shrugged. "FBI. Cops. Whoever they think might've been tipped off by now after what happened at the warehouse, not to mention whoever gets called in once the rich neighbors hear World War Grimaldi happening over there." He motioned toward the house. "They're expecting a big fight, so they're not keeping their guard up for the little guys."

"Build a fence to keep out the bears, and don't notice when the weasel sneaks under it."

He shot me a look. "Are you calling me a weasel?"

"In the most complimentary way possible."

He held my gaze, then laughed, which made me laugh too, and some of the tension palpably eased. He bumped my shoulder, and I bumped his in return. My buddies in the Marines had been like this too—making jokes right before shit hit the fan—and I was glad I'd reached that point with Leo. It kept us both relaxed, and being relaxed kept us focused.

Now we just have to get those assholes in the house un*focused.*

Instantly, a thought dropped into my head, and I sat up. "I've got a better idea than swimming in."

"Yeah?"

"Yeah." I squinted at the property in front of us. "Once we're on land, we're not going to have the mobility we need in wetsuits, and we won't have time to kick off dry suits. Plus there's the risk of hypothermia, especially since we'll have to swim in from far enough away that no one sees us, *plus* stay as deep as we can so we don't disturb the surface." I turned to Leo. "But I'd bet money we can find another motorboat like one of those"—I gestured at the dock—"and hide in plain sight."

Leo blinked. "Explain to me how that isn't the most insane fucking idea ever."

"Because if we go puttering by in a boat like a couple of drunk fishermen, they might come out and tell us to get away from the shore, but they won't suspect anything. Our guns don't get wet and neither do we because we'll be wearing hip waders."

His eyes lost focused and he nodded along slowly. "And we should still be able to get pretty close to the dock like that."

"Exactly." I scanned the scene again. "And as long as we're going in via the dock, we should disable the boats too. Anybody makes a break for it, they'll be dead in the water."

Leo nodded. "That's easy enough."

I glanced at him, and I could see gears turning in his head. I wasn't sure I wanted to know what he planned to do to the boats bobbing behind the safehouse, but it probably wouldn't be as simple as sugar in the fuel tank or jamming a prop. Nothing involving Leo was ever that mundane.

"What about when we get into the house?" he asked.

"We'll have to play that by ear because we can't see inside. We don't know the layout or manning."

"Which means shoot first and identify later."

"Yep." I swallowed. "It'll be just like clearing a house in a combat zone."

He turned to me. "Can you handle that?"

"I handled the warehouse. I can handle this." I squeezed his arm. "We've got this."

"I will never understand the appeal of fishing." Leo wrinkled his nose as he situated himself in the boat. "Everything's wet, it's fucking cold, you sit around half the day with a piece of string in the water, and if you're lucky, you get to gut a goddamned trout."

"You forgot the beer." I tapped the red Coleman cooler with my boot. "There's always beer."

"Don't kick that, Rich. And anyway, there isn't enough beer in the world to make fishing fun."

"Well, good thing we're not actually going fishing." I fired up the motor, and as we puttered away from the boat launch, added, "Especially since we don't have any beer."

He laughed dryly and fussed with the zipper on his camouflage parka. It was almost comical, seeing him decked out like a serious fisherman. He was the last man on earth I'd have ever pictured in drab green hip waders, a red flannel shirt, and a camo jacket, and the camouflage baseball cap complete with colorful fly fishing hooks was a hilarious touch. As was the glare he kept shooting me from under the bill. Probably the only thing keeping him from being in an extra sour mood was knowing this was all part of bringing down Grimaldi. And the fact that everything from his hat to the boat was stolen.

I was dressed about the same, and to anyone who saw us, we were a couple of idiots out fishing after dark. No one had to know about the guns lying at our feet or the improvised explosives in the cooler.

The night was almost completely black. There was a half moon in the sky, but as long as the thick cloud cover didn't break up, we'd be good. Besides that faint overhead glow, there were just pinpricks of light and beacons of ostentatious wealth dotting the shoreline. The largest of those obnoxious glittering scenes belonged to Matteo, and we motored toward it like it was a lighthouse.

"Are you sure you want them to see us?" Leo asked as Matteo's house drew closer. "Shouldn't we just skip to the stealthy part?"

"You want to know how many men he's got or not?"

He huffed, pushing out a thin cloud of breath. "Okay. But still."

"And it'll get their guard down," I said over the motor. "Like somebody who keeps catching a racoon or a neighbor cat going through their garbage stops being jumpy when they hear stuff rustling outside."

CARI Z & L.A. WITT

Leo must have accepted that explanation because he didn't question it any further. I just hoped I was right. Everyone in that house would be on high alert. If some movement and noise turned out to be a couple of drunken fishermen, Matteo and his thugs would still be on high alert, but they'd be more likely to brush off any additional noise as those fishermen again. In theory, anyway.

"Okay, we're almost within earshot." I tried like hell to sound serious, but his groan made me laugh. "Time to play drunken idiots!"

He covered his face with one gloved hand and swore.

I just chuckled, took a deep breath, and started belting out the lyrics to *Africa*. I didn't even have to try to sound drunk—I was a *terrible* singer, and I was fighting so hard to keep from laughing that, yeah, I sounded pretty trashed. The silence of the lake worked to my advantage, too, and my voice echoed off the Grimaldi house as we got closer.

"I think you've got their attention," Leo muttered. "I see movement."

I did too, and watched the house from the corner of my eye. I was about to start another verse when Leo loudly cut me off.

"Would you just watch where you're going?" he slurred. "You're gonna ground us again, you fucker."

Under normal circumstances, I'd have laughed, but three very large black-clad men carrying very large black guns were trooping out onto the back deck. Another broad silhouette filled a downstairs window, and some lights went off upstairs. At least five people total, then, including Matteo.

One of the men came down the concrete walk, rifle aimed at us. "This is private property!" he shouted. "Get the hell out of here."

"Whoa, hey!" Leo made a big gesture of putting up his hands, though he kept his face shaded by his cap. "No need for guns, man, we're just—"

"You're getting out of here is what you're doing. Now."

In my best backwoods Minnesota accent with a drunken slur, I called out, "Sorry. We got turned around. We're just—"

"I don't fucking care," he bellowed back. "Get out of here or I'll shoot a hole in your boat." He aimed, and I suspected he wasn't joking.

I gunned the engine and, as the boat pulled away, shouted, "Asshole."

"Rich," Leo hissed.

"What?" I shrugged. "He won't buy it if I'm polite."

Leo rolled his eyes, but even in the darkness, I didn't miss the hint of amusement.

I sped up the boat.

"And get away from those boats!" the armed guy shouted. "You put so much as a scratch on—"

"Shit!" I cried, and our boat grazed the hull of the speedboat. The larger craft listed heavily, and the screech of metal on fiberglass was impossible to miss. "Fuck! Sorry! Oh, sorry about that!"

There was shouting and cursing, and I could hear boots coming down the concrete path and onto the dock.

Leo moved lightning fast. He flipped open the Coleman cooler, grabbed one of the improvised explosives from inside, and—using long strips of duct tape he'd pulled off a roll before we'd left the shore—taped the device to the speedboat's hull.

"Okay, go! Go!"

I shouted another slurred apology as men poured onto the speedboat, and I got us the hell out of there. A few gunshots cracked through the night, and the splashes were a little closer than I'd have liked, but none hit us or our boat

We motored a safe distance away, then cut the engine and watched. There were flashlights bobbing all over the dock, which seemed a bit excessive now that the blinding floodlights had come on. The men were thorough, I'd give them that—they were all over the boat, the dock, and the shoreline. More than once, flashlights pointed our way, but they seemed to lose interest in us pretty quickly.

One by one, the bobbing lights left the speedboat and the dock, and the men returned to the house. I could see two large shadows outside on the deck, but the others went inside.

Leo and I pulled a couple of oars from under the seats. We took off our jackets and, making as little noise as possible, paddled back in the general direction Grimaldi's house. If anyone saw us, we were cutting a lazy path toward the next house over.

"So there's a minimum of six people," Leo whispered. "Three on the deck, two upstairs, one in the kitchen."

I'd only seen five, but I'd go with his count over mine. "How much time do we have before the bomb goes off?"

Leo checked his watch. "Sixteen minutes, forty-two seconds."

That didn't seem like enough time, but it would have to do. "Let's move."

In near-silence, we paddled toward the edge of the yard. We carefully grounded the boat, gathered our weapons, and climbed out. I didn't like the distance between the green belt around the property and the house, but logistics were what they were.

At the edge of the green belt, we stripped off the bulky hip waders and each put in a pair of earplugs.

"Should've put these in before you started singing," he grumbled.

I just chuckled and slid mine into my ears.

Leo took out his phone. He shielded it with his jacket so the glow wouldn't give us away, and rapidly tapped the screen. He swore a few times under his breath, but after a moment, said, "We're in."

I nodded and watched the security guys milling around on the deck. One was smoking a cigarette. The other looked bored. Good.

"Time?" I asked.

"Less than a minute."

We crouched low in the shadows, and waited.

Less than a minute later, an explosion lit up the night, and the speedboat reared up in the water before toppling onto the cabin cruiser beside it. I gaped at the sight for a split second, but there was no time to marvel at how much bigger it had been than I'd anticipated, or to wonder what the fuck Leo had put in that explosive.

"Let's go!" he hissed, and took off in a soundless run across the grass.

I followed, staying low and watching as men poured out of the back of the house. If they were smart, at least two would break off and check the perimeter, knowing damn well the explosion could be a diversion.

They *were* smart—four broke off.

As Leo and I stayed motionless in the shadows, two men jogged around our side, weapons drawn. Neither of us made a sound. The men muttered at each other and walked right by us, obviously scanning the outer edges of the property rather than thinking someone had already made it to the house.

The instant they turned the corner to start around the front, we were in motion, creeping toward the rear entrance. Halfway there, Leo stopped and crouched. I stayed partly upright, watching his back while he secured another explosive—hopefully a smaller one this time—to a basement window.

Then he tapped my leg, and we kept moving.

Two men were stationed on the back deck, illuminated by the billowing flames their boys were trying to extinguish on the dock.

Without hesitation, we dropped them. Leo took out the closer one. I took out the other. Before they'd even hit the deck, we jogged past them into the house. I spared one a glance, and knew that if I survived this, I'd be spending a lot of nights debating the morality of dispatching men who were probably just doing their job and weren't actively threatening me. Right now, the cold hard fact was that there were a lot more of them than us, and our only hope of getting through this was to mow down every threat that showed itself.

Inside, while Leo swept the room, I shut the door and barricaded it. It wouldn't hold off all of them, but it would slow them down by a few seconds.

"Company," Leo said sharply. We pressed our backs to the wall, staying still and silent as boots clomped down the hall. As soon as the first showed his face, Leo dropped him. The second wisely hesitated, but I caught his reflection in the oven door, and was able to come around the corner and catch him by surprise.

Leo glanced back. "The boys outside are on their way back in." We didn't bother keeping our voices down now. They knew we were here, and they knew where we were, and anyway his ears were probably ringing from the gunfire just like mine were. The earplugs we both wore would only do so much.

"Someone's coming down from upstairs," I said.

We pressed our backs together and waited.

A second later, the house was alive with gunfire. As soon as I was sure the guy on the stairs was down for the count, I turned to help Leo with the other men. Everything was chaos. I couldn't hear anything anymore, though I felt Leo grunt with the force of a round hitting his chest. He stumbled back, recovered, and fired again. Thank God for Kevlar.

It was over in a matter of minutes. Maybe less. It simultaneously felt like forever and a flash. Guns blazing. Drywall exploding from errant rounds. The momentary helplessness while I reloaded. Covering Leo while he did the same.

When the dust settled, we were the only two left standing. Leo leaned against the wall, holding his side gingerly. No blood seeped between his fingers, but he was probably tender. I'd seen him take at least one round, possibly more. I'd been hit twice, the second nearly knocking the wind out of me, and I would absolutely be black and blue before sunrise. As if I wasn't already.

"You good?" he croaked.

My hearing was still iffy, but I could make out the words. "Yeah. You?"

Wincing, he nodded. "Let's check the rest of the house and the yard." He pushed himself off the wall. "Make sure everybody's down. Then we find Matteo."

We went through the first floor, guns drawn as we checked every room, nook, and cranny. There were a lot of people down here, but aside from us, every one of them was dead on the floor.

Carefully, we made our way up to the second floor. Leo checked the first room while I covered the hall. Then I checked the next room while he covered the hall. All clear.

Leo turned to me and mouthed, "Third floor?"

I nodded, and we started in that direction.

A split second too late, I was aware of movement just beyond my peripheral vision. Before I could turn, an arm went around my neck and something cold and hard pressed against my temple. Fear shot through me. This was the second time someone had gotten the drop on me and put a gun to my head, and something told me this one wasn't just to make me hold still so someone could deliver a message.

My hearing was starting to come back, and through the cotton still stuffed in my ears, I heard a growled, "Put the gun down."

I held it up to show I didn't have my finger on the trigger.

Leo rounded the corner and froze, gun still drawn. Watching us over the weapon, he narrowed his eyes and clenched his jaw. "Don't think I won't fucking kill you, Grimaldi."

"You sure you want to do that?" The gun against my head jabbed it roughly. "Because if I go down, I'm taking him with me."

Leo stayed still, but the ripple down the front of his throat gave him away.

Matteo laughed wickedly. "You're so predictable, Nicolosi. Spend a little time with a pretty boy, and now you've got a soft spot for him."

Leo's jaw worked. His eyes flashed with fury, and I could almost hear some snide comebacks on the tip of his tongue, but he wisely kept them to himself. Instead, he growled, "It's over, Matteo. The Feds know everything, and your only options are how much you cooperate."

I could feel Matteo tensing, and I winced as I imagine his finger curling around the trigger.

"You've got a choice, Nicolosi." Matteo said coldly. "Option one? You get on the phone right now and undo all the shit you've done to my family's accounts. Every cent goes back where it came from. Or, option two"—he jabbed the muzzle of the pistol against my head—"you can try putting all the pieces of his brain back into his skull."

For long seconds, Leo was still, eyes flicking back and forth from Matteo to me. I held my breath. I was pretty sure Matteo did too.

Then, Leo relaxed. No, that wasn't it. He gave up. Resignation seemed to crash over him, and he lowered his gun. "Fine. Give me a phone." He swallowed. "Actually, it…it'll be faster on a computer."

Matteo huffed. With a sharp nod, he indicated the stairs. "Don't do anything stupid unless you want me to paint the wall with this asshole's brains."

I tried to swallow, but couldn't. The helpless look Leo shot me didn't help. As I was frog-marched down the stairs behind Leo, I was absolutely convinced my minutes were numbered. Once Matteo had what he wanted, he'd have no reason to keep me alive. Which meant I really had nothing to lose except—

Except Leo.

Damn it.

As we rounded the corner at the bottom of the stairs, I briefly considered going out in a blaze of glory and taking down Matteo, at the very least distracting him long enough for Leo to make a break for it, but there was no point. Matteo would shoot him in the back before he made it to the end of the hall.

Matteo walked us past the blood and bodies and into the relatively intact living room. There, he took out a laptop, turned it on, and logged in, all the while keeping his pistol trained on my head. I watched Leo, desperate for some sign that he wasn't really giving up. That he wasn't surrendering to the Grimaldis in the name of saving me.

But he wouldn't look at me.

When the computer was logged in, Matteo handed it to Leo, and Leo sat on the couch. Leo's hands moved so fast they blurred across the keyboard. His brow furrowed with intense concentration. After a solid three minutes, he sat back, shoulders sagging. "All right." He swallowed hard. "It's done. Check your account."

My heart sank. *No. No, no, no…*

Matteo loosened his hold on me and took out his phone. Leo avoided my eyes, and I tried not to get sick. We'd come this far, and Matteo was going to win? Was there even any way to get out of this alive now?

Then Leo met my gaze. His eyes flicked toward Matteo, who was focused on the screen. I held my breath, trying like hell to read his mind.

Barely moving at all, Leo made a subtle gesture of touching something in his pocket. A heartbeat later, a loud *thump* shook the whole house, and somewhere, glass shattered.

Without a second thought, I seized the opportunity, batted Matteo's weapon away from me, and tackled him. We both went down, and he hit the floor with a grunt and what sounded like a kneecap cracking on hardwood. Once I had the upper hand, he was easy to subdue—I twisted his arm behind his back, dug my knee into his spine, and growled, "Game over, Grimaldi."

He swore in Italian, but stopped struggling. I pulled a couple of zip ties from my back pocket and bound Matteo's hands. Then with Leo's help, I got up and jerked the asshole to his feet. To Leo, I said, "Did you really give back all the money?"

"No." Leo smirked. "Just moved it over from Daddy's account, and didn't bother covering my tracks." He gave Matteo's head a condescending pat. "So guess who's gonna see his son ripping him off without—"

"You son of a bitch!" Matteo snarled. "I should shoot you both in—"

"Actually you should shut the fuck up," I said.

He stared at me. They both did.

Looking Matteo right in the eye, I said, "The Feds are on their way right now. One way or another, you're going to prison, at the *very* least for assaulting and threatening a U.S. Marshal. So if you don't want to be in the general population along with God knows how many guys who are more than willing to shank an inmate on your old man's order, I would suggest you start talking."

He stared at me with icy hatred, but slowly, that ice melted in favor of fear. In favor of the dawning realization that there was no way out.

Dropping his gaze, he exhaled hard, and his shoulders fell as he said, "What do you want to know?"

"Whatever you've got," I said.

We sat him down at the dining room table and brushed some drywall dust and shattered glass out of the way. In a drawer, I found a notepad and a pen, and I sat across from Matteo while Leo loomed over my shoulder, gun still in his hand.

Looking Matteo right in the eye, I uncapped the pen. "All right. Start talking."

Chapter Twenty-Two
Leo

The list we ended up with went on for pages and pages. I was kind of amazed Matteo could remember that much, but in actuality a lot of it was just extrapolation. If one officer was identified as compromised, it was more likely that his partner was too, even if Matteo didn't know for sure. If over half of a unit looked dirty, then it was probably safest to assume the entire unit was unsafe until further notice. Rich had been quietly stunned to learn that two of the guys he'd been working with back when he was supposed to be securing me were on the Grimaldi's payroll. Getting caught in the crossfire had been an accident—a hazard of doing business with us untrustworthy sons of bitches.

"That's it?" Rich pressed when Matteo finally stopped talking. "You're sure?"

"Yes."

I smacked him hard on the back of the head. "You *sure?* No more cops or marshals you're conveniently forgetting?"

"God, motherfucker! I don't know anything else!" Matteo insisted. "Papa's the one who runs point on turning law enforcement, not me!"

"You mean he doesn't trust you with it." I sneered at him. "Does he trust you with anything?"

Matteo grinned evilly at me. "He trusted me enough to kill Tony on my say-so, didn't he?"

I couldn't help it. I dove forward, punching Matteo right in his smirking shithole of a mouth. His hands flew up as his head snapped back, but they didn't stop me. It wasn't enough to hit him once. So I did it again. And again. He flailed at me, trying to kick me off, but there was fire in my veins now and I wouldn't be moved by him, not by this sick, sorry son of a—

"Leo!" Strong arms pulled me back, clamping my fists to my side. "Leo, stop! We need him alive—we need him *alive*, Leo, *stop!*"

I hung my head for a moment, shuddering in Rich's grip. Shit, when had I lost my breath? I glanced down at my knuckles and blinked when I saw how bloody they were. "Damn." My hand hurt. I tried to shake it out and hissed between my teeth at the pain. "*Damn* it." Matteo was on his back, moaning softly, his face a bloody mess.

"Sorry," I said. "I'm sorry, I'm fine." Rich let me go, carefully, and I stepped away from both him and Matteo. My hand *really* hurt now. What the hell had I done to it?

"Go put some ice on that," Rich said gently. "I'm going to call this in."

"Good luck finding someone to report to who isn't a dirty fink." I turned and left the room before the temptation to jump on Matteo and finish him off overwhelmed me.

I carefully navigated my way to the kitchen, skirting debris and giving the bodies a wide berth. I hated killing for a lot of reasons, but most of all because of the sordid aftermath of it. When the shooting was over and you'd won, there was still so much left to take care of. Dead bodies were heavy, smelly, messy, and ugly reminders of your own near-and-dear mortality.

At least the kitchen was relatively clean. I opened the freezer and pulled out an icepack—houses associated with the mob always had decent first aid supplies, that was just smart planning—wrapped it in a towel and placed it on my right hand. I sat on a bar stool and stared at the marble floor, waiting for the pain to subside. I'd have a hard time driving the beater with my hand giving me hell, but I didn't have a choice. I couldn't stay here.

The Grimaldis were ruined. It was only a matter of time before they figured that out. I had their money, and that was most of their power right there. The big old Mafia families had downsized over the past few decades when it became clear that blood, while thicker than water, still wasn't a match for a plea deal with the Feds. Lorenzo Grimaldi had restricted the depths of his know-how to his sons, and Tony had been in far deeper than Matteo. When he'd had Tony killed, he'd cut his own throat without realizing it.

Matteo was a valuable witness. His information would ensure his father's demise. His information would protect Rich's parents and rebuild Rich's career. A lot of law enforcement officers were going to go down after this, but Rich wouldn't be one of them. He was going to rise up. It was almost a shame that I wouldn't be around to see it.

I couldn't stay. I *couldn't*, not after the role I'd played in all of this. I wasn't the big fish anymore—instead, I was the turncoat, the one who'd made all this carnage possible. Mafiosos and cops alike would be gunning for me. Matteo didn't know everyone on his family's payroll, and until the Feds could make his father talk, I'd be vulnerable. It wouldn't take much to kill me when my guard was down. They could doctor my food, shoot me up with bad drugs—hell, even just shove me into traffic. Then there'd be one less rat to deal with.

Rich would take me running hard, but there was no help for it now. He was going to be hurt no matter what happened next, whether I stayed and got assassinated or ran and left him behind. Of those two options, the choice seemed clear. I wanted to live, so I had to go. Right?

Only my stomach churned at the thought of leaving Rich.

"Fuck me," I muttered into the hazy, death-filled silence. "Fuck. Me."

"I would, but this isn't really the time or place for it."

I whirled around on the stool and looked at Rich, who stood in the doorway all casual, hands in his pockets, like he wasn't standing in a mass grave. "Where's Matteo?" I demanded.

"Sleeping it off. Don't worry, I tied him up. He's not going anywhere."

"You should make sure. Don't leave him alone, he's a sneaky bastard."

"Leo." Rich came over and stood in front of me, not quite close enough to touch. "What's going on?"

"I'm apparently instructing you on how to take care of a prisoner, which—it feels kind of weird to me, I have to say. You're usually so good at this."

"Leo." Damn that tone. That was the "I'm not going to let you piss me off no matter how much you want to" tone. "Forget about Matteo. Tell me what you're thinking."

I sighed. "I don't think you want to know that."

"I know that I do." Finally he touched me, just his hands on my shoulders, sliding down until he could squeeze my upper arms. A light touch, gentle so I wouldn't spook. I wanted to jerk back anyway—Rich knew he was the only person to touch me with any sort of affection in months, I was programmed to respond to it by now.

I should have told him to fuck off. That we were done. I was leaving, as good as gone.

But you don't want to go.

No, I didn't. But I had to. "I think it's time for me to get out of here." It didn't come out as forcefully as I intended it to, but it had the same effect. I glanced up just in time to see Rich's eyes go wide.

"Why? Why leave now?" he asked. "After you've won?"

I shook my head. "What have I won? Matteo's alive, Papa Grimaldi is alive, my only family has been lying to me for years, I'm still a marked man…if this is winning, I'd hate to see what losing feels like."

"It feels like a bullet," Rich said bluntly. "Which is how you know you've won. Leo, if this is about your safety, then believe me—the guys coming to us are people I…" He paused, then deflated a little. "They're people I'm *supposed* to trust with my own life, which is supposed to make them almost good enough to protect yours. Now, I don't…fuck, I don't know."

"Either way, you don't need me anymore." There. Fine. I'd said it. And as soon as I did, it was easier to go on. "Seriously, I'm just going to bog things down from here on out. Matteo is the new star witness. He can give you everything you need and more to take out the Grimaldis and all the dirty cops and judges and Feds. I'm just the money man. Which, fuck, if I go in they're going to hold the cash in probate or whatever the equivalent is in this kind of thing. What a waste."

"You're not just the money man," Rich argued. "Leo. Look at me. C'mon."

Fucking fine. I tilted my head up just enough to see him from under my eyelashes. Rich looked beat—he was probably bruised to hell and back underneath his Henley. What the man needed was for his life to get back to normal, and that was never going to happen as long as I was still in the mix.

"We need you for corroboration," Rich said softly. "Matteo's words are just words without evidence to back them up. That's what the money trail is—hard evidence. That's going to be important."

"I can leave you the financial info and you can get some forensic accountants on it." It would probably take a team of them a solid month to parse through everything I'd done, but they'd get there eventually. "Also…you get that I'm still going to be a target, right?" This was the part I'd been trying to put out of my mind. It wasn't working. "Maybe not from dirty cops, but when the Grimaldis go down there are going to be a lot of wise guys who managed to keep their records clean put out of work. Some of them are going to want revenge." I shrugged, then winced as my own bruises reminded me that my entire *body* was going to wish for an ice pack in another hour. "It's better to keep you out of that. For everyone."

Rich crossed his arms over his chest. His lips were thin, annoyed. I waited for him to curse me out. "You're wrong."

"Your parents—"

"Are going to be fine from here on out," he said. "Dad's got a protective detail he can trust, plus my mother is heavily armed. They'll figure something out for my brother too, so I'm not worried about him either."

"*You* will be safer if I'm not around." I was absolutely sure of this part. "It's time for you to get your life back together. Go back to being a marshal."

"I never stopped."

I rolled my eyes. "You know what I mean. An *official* one, working on official cases with witnesses who aren't going to bring the Mafia down on your ass. It'll be better for you." I paused, wondering whether I should add the next part, then thought *to hell with it*. "It'll be better for your mental health to get some stability, too. Fewer nightmares. Fewer freak-outs. You can't tell me that doesn't appeal."

When I glanced up at Rich again, his expression made him look like he'd been flayed open. His face was raw, pained. He stared at me like he was looking at his own bloody heart. He ran a hand over his face. "I hear what you're saying. And if you want to go because you don't think I'm going to be able to protect you anymore, or because neither of us can trust anyone, then you should go. I understand. I didn't do a great job of it this last time around."

"No, that's not what I—"

"But if you're leaving because you want to make *me* feel safe, then listen up. Not having you with me will in no way improve my life. I want you to get through this trial and come out the other side, not just because it's the right thing to do, but because when you finally emerge from it you'll really be free. Not just on the run, but *free*."

"Free under a new, assumed identity," I interjected.

"Maybe. Maybe not. We won't know until Matteo goes to trial and we see who comes out of the woodwork. Leo, look." Rich shut his eyes for a moment and tilted his head toward the ceiling. The tendons in his neck stood out as sharp as knives. I wanted to trace them with my lips.

"If you don't trust the rest of the Marshals or the cops, then trust me. Let me take you to another safehouse, somewhere no one knows about. Personal witness protection. I'll clear it with my boss, just…don't run away yet. See this through with me. Then maybe stick around to see what's on the other side."

Was he saying what I thought he was saying? "Rich…I'm not the sort of person you should pin any hopes on," I warned him. "I'm a criminal. I've got a shit family and a shit background. I'm a murderer. I'm the fucking scum of the earth, okay?" At least Tony, he had been the same as me—classier, way more powerful, but he knew the score. Guys like us didn't get futures with men like Rich. "You're too good to go to waste."

"Nothing about you could ever be considered a waste," Rich said earnestly. I was tempted to hit him for sounding like that, but I didn't want to bust my other hand on his jaw. I opened my mouth to yell at him, but shut it abruptly as I made out the sound of sirens closing in.

I was up in a flash. "I can't stay here." I dropped the ice pack and flexed my hand with a wince. It still hurt, but I was pretty sure I hadn't broken anything. "I can't let them find me here, they'll shoot first and—"

"I know." Rich was touching me again, grounding me. I was annoyed that it worked. "Head back to our car. It's far enough away that no one should be canvassing out there. Once I'm done here, I'll meet you. We can head for the new safehouse together and figure out our next moves." He tilted my chin up with a finger. "It won't be forever, I promise. The D.A. is going to have to move fast on this to catch people, so it should all be over soon."

I had to smile. "You want to send me back to the getaway car."

"To *wait* for me," he emphasized. "Not to drive away. If you even *can* drive with your hand like that."

"It really hurts," I admitted.

"You think that hurts, you should see Matteo's face."

I perked up a little. "Yeah? Not so pretty now?"

Rich scoffed. "He was never pretty."

It was a dumb thing to get moved by, but it worked. I threw my good arm around Rich's shoulders and drew him into a fierce, dirty kiss. His hands found my waist, pulling me in close. I was so tired, it shouldn't have been possible for me to get hard, but my body was definitely thinking about trying it.

God, Rich, you asshole. Look at what you've done to me. "Fine," I growled as soon as the kiss broke. "I'll wait. But if you're not there by dawn, I'm out of here."

"Deal. I'll join you soon." The sirens were getting louder. "Go, Leo."

I went.

It felt cold outside, colder still when I finally reached the car and shut the door behind me. I groped in the back seat for a hoodie and pulled it on over my head. I stared straight forward, into the night, and listened to animal movements and the sound of the wind in the trees.

Now was the time to go. Screw what I'd told Rich, I never thought clearly in his presence. I could leave now and he'd never find me. I'd just email the account info, all the dirty money's dirty little secrets, and be gone, off to Puerto Rico or the Virgin Islands, or hey—the Maldives were nice. Or maybe the Seychelles, that was a haven for money laundering if I ever saw one. I could set up a new betting business, live off my hard-earned Mafia cash for a while. Maybe for the rest of my life. I could be far away. I could be free.

I could be alone.

"Fuck me," I said again with a sigh, then tilted the seat back as far as it would go and curled up into a ball.

Rich better get here soon, or I'd freeze before sunrise.

Chapter Twenty-Three
Rich

Minutes after Leo had left the house, the living outnumbered the dead by probably five to one. Local law enforcement swarmed the place, the Feds hot on their heels. Paramedics came to take Matteo, as did some agents who weren't to leave his side. The coroner or the M.E.—I didn't even know what Lake Geneva had—came to scrape up all the dead goons. The bomb squad was called in to make sure there weren't more explosives on the dock or in the house. I didn't tell them there'd only been two bombs because I wasn't about to explain how I knew.

In under an hour, this place had gone from a hideout to a warzone to a ghost town to being utterly packed with people wearing silver badges or FBI jackets. Voices echoed throughout the house that had seemed huge, but now felt about as claustrophobic as some of the hidey holes my boys and I had hunkered down in during our combat tours. Where you couldn't breathe without both your chest and back pushing against something, whether it was rocks, sandbags, or your buddy.

Cold sweat prickled the back of my neck. My skin crawled under my clothes, especially in places where the fabric was stiff from dried blood—whose, I wasn't even sure anymore. I'd taken off my Kevlar vest to let a paramedic check where I'd been hit. Just bruises on top of bruises. Enough I wouldn't be sleeping comfortably for a while, but nothing to worry about.

Sleep. As if I'd be doing any of that in the near future. Not after all the flying bullets and dropping bodies and Leo being in danger and the punch of a round—*what if those had been armor-piercing?*—and an explosion and—

"Mr. Cody?" A woman's voice nudged my consciousness. I shook myself and met the eyes of the detective who'd been asking me questions. Detective Lansing, wasn't it? My head was so scattered I couldn't hold onto anything. Not anything in the present, anyway.

"I'm sorry." I swallowed a wave of nausea that almost caught me off guard. "I…what were you saying?"

She scowled. "I asked if you know the whereabouts of Leotrim Nicolosi?" She motioned toward the room where Matteo had been minutes ago, before the paramedics had wheeled him out. "He told an officer that Nicolosi was here."

"I don't know where he is." I looked her in the eye when I said it, and didn't flinch because it was true. I knew where Leo had *said* he was going, but he was as slippery as he was jumpy. He'd been itching to run before I'd talked him down, and, for all I knew, that was exactly what he'd done.

I should have been panicking over losing my badge. Even after everything that had happened, when all was said and done, Leo was my witness and my responsibility, and regardless of how things had gone down, it was on me to keep him safe. If he was on the wind, then I'd take the fall.

But I didn't care about that. They could have my badge. I just wanted him to be all right. Alive and safe, at least. I knew he was far from all right, but I needed him to be safe and protected, and I trusted absolutely no one but myself—not even Leo—to keep him that way.

I shouldn't be here. I should be there. Wherever he is. What if Grimaldi has more men coming? What if they find him? What if they're—

"Mr. Cody." Lansing put a firm hand on my arm. "Are you okay?"

"Yeah, I'm…" Shaking. All over. And about to throw up. My vision was darkening around the edges, and I recognized the feeling of sliding into a panic attack. Or a flashback. Or both. I closed my eyes and tried to breathe, but there were too many people in the room and they were taking up all the air. There wasn't enough left for me. I couldn't get…I couldn't…

I shook off the detective's hand and brushed past her, darting for the back deck. I made it to the railing by the skin of my teeth and heaved over the side into the manicured bushes. Even while I was getting sick, I told myself the heat of the desert sun on my back wasn't real. That it was nighttime and I was on the other side of the world.

That didn't help. Memories of cold, dark nights in the mountains crashed through my head. Fear. The scream of an incoming mortar. The too-close flash of tracers. The absolute certainty that I was about to die, and the crushing realization that while I hadn't died, the man beside me had. I was pretty sure only the acid in my mouth kept me from smelling the acrid sweat and coppery blood that had saturated our uniforms by the end of that mission.

Stay here. Stay in the now. Fall apart later.

I squeezed my eyes shut, and told myself it was the puking that had made me tear up like this. God, this was so not the time. Leo needed me. The fucking Marshals needed me. We'd been compromised and he was out there alone and what was I doing? Throwing up in the bushes because shooting it out with Grimaldi's goons in the house had triggered everything I never wanted to think about from my time in the Corps.

Get it together, Rich. Get it fucking together because Leo fucking needs you.

I spat in the bushes before taking some slow breaths. My stomach was far from settled, but I managed to pull my focus into the here and now instead of leaving it to fall apart in the past.

"Mr. Cody, are you sure you're all right?" Detective Lansing was beside me. How long had she been there?

I nodded, eyes still shut. "Yeah," I croaked. "It's, uh, been a long night."

"So I see."

"Listen." I turned to her and blinked some tears out of my eyes. Hopefully she interpreted those as being from vomiting too. My voice was shaky and hoarse as I spoke. "I need to get out of here. I need to get in touch with some contacts at the Marshals' office and see if anyone knows where Nicolosi is."

She scowled. "I still need a statement from you about—"

"And you'll get it," I said more firmly. "But I've got a witness on the wind, and—"

"And he's a suspect in all this." She gestured at the house.

"Either way, I need to find him and get him someplace safe. Whether he ends up on trial for this or not, I need him as a witness against Grimaldi."

She eyed me skeptically.

"Leave me your card." I pulled out my wallet and pretended not to notice one side of the worn black leather was darker than the rest, and I definitely tried not to think about whose blood it was. "I'll leave you mine and my boss's." I slid both cards free and offered them to her. "We're on the same side here, all right? If you want to call my boss and check out my story, fine, but I have *got* to go find my witness before something happens to him."

Cops understood. They knew what a delicate and crucial operation WITSEC was, and a marshal protecting a witness had more leeway than your average officer.

Detective Lansing considered the cards for a moment before she took them. "Let me give him a call."

I wanted to fidget with nerves—hadn't we wasted enough time?—but I waited while she took my boss's card and called him. I twitched and shifted, only partially listening to the conversation while my mind shot ahead to where Leo was, if he was all right, if he—

"All right, Mr. Cody." She sighed with annoyance as she lowered her phone. "Your story checks out. Your boss wants you to get moving. So…" She made a shooing motion. "Go."

She did *not* look happy about it, and I didn't wait around in case she changed her mind or decided to second-guess my boss. There was no way in hell I was walking through that bloody battlefield of a house, so I went around the side yard toward the front. The night was getting brutally cold. I shivered, wishing I'd put my vest back on; at least it provided a layer of protection against the biting wind.

Near the front of the house, two officers milled around beside a window, and a small perimeter had been established in yellow police tape. As I got closer, I could see why—the charred, gaping hole where a basement window used to be. I swallowed as the phantom *thump* of that explosion echoed in my head.

It wasn't enemy fire. It hadn't targeted me. That had been Leo, not an enemy.

Still, fresh nausea rolled through me, and I had to swallow again—harder this time—to keep from puking. Again.

I made it past the house and onto the driveway, and broke into a jog. The sooner I got away from this place, the better, and damn it I needed to get to where Leo was *right now.* At the end of the long driveway, it took a moment to collect my bearings, but once I did, I hurried down the road toward where we'd ditched the car.

Fear and PTSD made the walk a hell of a lot longer than it needed to be. I was still reeling from the gunfight, still shaky from being so close to a fiery explosion, and also fixated on all the worst-case scenarios that could be playing out right now. A Grimaldi goon could have caught up with Leo and killed him. Or—possibly worse—could have taken him to answer to Papa Grimaldi in person. Someone could be tailing me. They could have planted a bomb in the car. For all I fucking knew, there was a Reaper drone quietly following me and waiting for just the right moment to—

Okay. Dude. Don't think about that.

I shivered as much from the fear as the cold, and couldn't help walking faster. I'd been way too close to some drone strikes in the Sandbox. One had been close enough to leave my ears ringing and my skull throbbing for days. Another—friendly fire while we'd been sleeping in an abandoned house—had ended a buddy's military career, and it was up for debate if him surviving had been a blessing or a curse. He'd never been able to sleep after that. Two years later, he couldn't take it anymore. Which meant I guess I could say the drone strike did kill him. It just took a while.

But the Grimaldis didn't have Reaper drones. Neither did the Marshals, whether they'd been compromised or not. I was just letting my nightmares crash into my reality, and my fight-or-flight instinct was on a hair trigger because I could no longer see the lines between then and now, real and dreams, here and there.

By the time I reached the car, I was drenched in sweat and almost hyperventilating with fear.

And there was no one in the car.

I broke into a jog, murmuring a panicked "No, no, Leo, no," into the night. Where the hell had he—

Wait.

No.

There.

The passenger seat had been laid back, and there he was—curled on his side, chest moving slowly and evenly as he slept.

I almost wanted to yank the door open and bitch him out for falling asleep instead of being vigilant, but I was so relieved to see him alive, I didn't give a damn. He was here. He was okay. No one had beaten me to him.

I gave the dark parking lot a slow sweep, making absolutely sure no one had followed me. If they had, I couldn't see them, so all I could do was hope for the best.

I tapped the glass. Then again, harder this time. That was enough to jostle him out of what must have been a sound sleep, and he stiffened, head snapping toward me. In his hand, just barely visible in the low light, was a pistol that had been partially tucked under him. Good thing I hadn't startled him, and thank God he hadn't been completely careless when he'd racked out.

Once I was sure he recognized me, I went around to the driver side. He unlocked the door, and I got in.

"Hey," he said sleepily. "Are you—"

I shut him up with a tight hug. I desperately wanted to kiss him, but that could wait until I *hadn't* been heaving my guts out in the middle of a badly-timed flashback.

He tensed at first, but then wrapped his arms around me too. "Hey. You okay?"

"Kind of. I think. I…" I sighed, burying my face against his neck. Now that the panic was dissipating, it was like the bottom had fallen out of my ability to hold myself up. The memories I'd been trying to suppress came crashing in. The fear of what could have happened, what had happened, and what might still happen bombarded my senses. Literally the only thing I was sure of right then was

271

that Leo and I were both still alive, and I held onto him for dear life because I needed to be sure this was real. Because for all I knew, it would change in…hell, in thirty seconds or twenty-four hours or—

"Easy, Rich," he whispered, stroking my hair. "Jesus. You're shaking."

I was, wasn't I? All over. Uncontrollably. So hard my teeth tried to chatter. Fuck, I was crashing. Coming apart.

"Fuck." I held him tighter. "I'm sorry."

"Sorry? For what?"

"You were depending on me to keep you safe, and you need someone who's got his shit together enough to—"

"What?" Leo drew back and looked in my eyes in the parking lot's dim light. "If you hadn't noticed, I *am* safe. I can't imagine anyone could have kept me safer than you have since this whole thing started."

I ran a badly trembling hand through my sweat-dampened hair. "You need to be with someone who isn't going to fall apart when the bullets start flying."

"Do you *hear* yourself?" He took my hand. "You kept your head together when it counted. We both made it out alive and Matteo's in custody now, right?"

"Yeah, but look at me now. I barely fucking made it back to the car because I was losing my shit."

His thumb ran across the back of my hand, and that gentle affection felt so alien right now. As if nothing but violence and chaos had ever existed at all. "Rich, anyone would crash after something like that. PTSD or not. But you held it together in the moment, and we won."

"We did. And now you're in even more danger, and you will be until all this is over." I rubbed my eyes with my free hand. "I need to find a marshal who isn't dirty and let them take you someplace safe, because—"

"Whoa, whoa." His voice turned sharp and his grip tightened on my hand. "That wasn't the deal."

"Come on. Before you left the house, you wanted to run so you—"

"I wanted to run so I didn't put you or anyone else in danger, not because I didn't feel safe with you." His voice softened again. "To tell you the truth, I don't feel safe with anyone *but* you."

I searched his eyes. "Even when I'm…"

"Yeah. Even when you're a mess after the fact." He started to draw me in, but I stopped him with a hand on his chest and turned my head a little.

"I, uh…got sick. Before I came here."

"Oh. Okay. Thanks for the warning." He didn't pull back, though. Instead, he gathered me in his arms and held me like I'd held him when I'd gotten into the car. Smoothing my hair, he whispered, "We can pick up that part once we find a place to hunker down."

To my surprise, a quiet thrill ran through me. I wasn't sure why. I was too sore and exhausted to even think about sex, and anyway I was dubious that there was a safe place on earth where we *could* hunker down. But maybe I needed to know that Leo still wanted me even while I was a goddamned train wreck. Even if getting intimate wasn't in the cards right here, right now, it was still on the table.

I closed my eyes and relaxed into his embrace, resting my head on his shoulder and sighing.

"I mean it," he whispered. "I wanted to run because I freaked out. But at the end of the day, there's no place I feel safer than with you."

I held him tighter. "Me too." I swallowed. "I think…I think our best bet is going to be to get somewhere safe and lay low until you need to testify."

"Any ideas?" He pulled back and met my gaze. "*Is* there any place safe?"

I thought for a moment. "About the only place I can think of is Smitty's missile silo."

"You really want to bring this back to his front door?"

"No. But I'm not sure where else we can go. Every safehouse I know about is compromised, and I don't know who I can trust within the Marshals."

Leo nodded slowly. "So I guess…" He hesitated. "Back to Colorado?"

"I think so, yeah." I paused. "I need to get in touch with my dad, though. So I think we should find some cheap, no-name motel that takes cash, catch our breath, and figure out if Smitty's place really is the best place to go."

"Okay." He exhaled. "Okay. Let's do that." He touched my face. "Are you going to be okay to drive?"

I thought about it, and to my surprise, I'd stopped shaking. I still felt kind of jittery, but I was steadier. "I think so, yeah."

He eyed me uncertainly. "If you're not, pull over and we'll switch."

"I'll be okay." I managed to smile, and though I didn't dare kiss him on the mouth, I cupped his face and pressed a kiss to his forehead. "Let's get out of here."

Leo nodded. He settled back into the passenger seat while I put on my seatbelt, and when I turned the key, I swore my heart sped up as the engine turned over. The headlights came on, slicing through the darkness, and I pulled out of the deserted lot and onto the empty road.

This wasn't over. The Grimaldis would still be gunning for Leo, especially leading up to the trial, and it was impossible to say who we could trust within the Marshals.

But we had a plan. The best plan we could have under these circumstances.

And as long as I could keep Leo safe, then maybe I could make it through this too.

Chapter Twenty-Four
Leo

If I never had to have another conversation with my lawyer again it would be too soon.

All I'd done since we got to our shitty hotel room on the outskirts of Chicago was talk on the damn phone. Well, no, that wasn't completely true—Rich had talked on the phone first, breaking the news to his boss that he'd run away with the witness again and handling that heat, then going on and on about what having Matteo in custody would do to the case against his father. I'd taken the opportunity to have a scalding hot shower and eat a cellophane-wrapped banana nut muffin that someone had left in the mini fridge in the corner. Now my stomach was gurgling, and not in a *yum, delicious* kind of way.

Once Rich was done with round one and went to take his own shower, I got on the phone with my lawyer. The conversation started "public perception of fleeing," continued onto "destruction of public and private property" and ended with "better show up for the trial this time, because so help me *God*, if I have to figure out a way

275

to accommodate one more self-important Justice Department official I will resign in protest."

I liked my lawyer—I'd picked her and was paying for her myself, and she'd represented a number of my old contemporaries—but she was more comfortable handling her clients on a smaller, less public scale. "You know I couldn't have stuck around after what happened in the hotel," I reminded her. "I'm lucky to be alive right now."

"I know. I apologize." She'd heaved a sigh. "We'll work this out. I'll let the rest of my team know that we'll be pulling some all-nighters leading up to this."

"But having Matteo as the primary witness will be a good thing for me, right?"

"Maybe. We'll see. I'll be in touch." She'd hung up after that cryptic response, and a few minutes later Rich came back into the bedroom. In nothing but a T-shirt and sweatpants, I could see a lot more of the damage he'd taken back at Gianna's house. There were dark bruises on his arms, one high up on his shoulder and extending toward his neck—shit, he was lucky he hadn't cracked his collarbone. It must have come from a bullet. Even his bare feet looked bruised, and he walked like he was easing his way across a sheet of ice. At least his hands weren't shaking anymore.

Small comfort.

"It's not my feet," he assured me when he saw me staring at them. "I took a shot right above my hip and strained some muscle in my groin. I'll be walking better later." *Everything will be better later.* That was what Rich wanted me to believe, I knew it, but I wasn't sure he was right.

Rich was injured, he was dealing with some major PTSD, and what he probably needed more than anything right now was a fucking break. If I had any kind of backbone when it came to him, I'd insist on a new marshal to watch over me until trial. Rich had done enough. He'd *suffered* enough.

I didn't trust anyone else, though, and I was pretty sure Rich didn't either. And I truly did believe that he would keep me safe better than anyone else. Nobody else had any reason to like me. Another marshal would do their job and put their life on the line to keep me safe—if they weren't a turncoat asshole like too many that we'd met so far—but they wouldn't care like Rich did. And I needed that kind of care right now.

You're such a selfish little asshole.

I was. I knew it. But there was a reason behind my selfishness, too—no one else would look out for Rich the way I planned to after this, and he was going to need that. Cops, Marshalls, FBI—it was all a brotherhood. Most people would see Rich as the victim in what had happened to his team, but *some* people? People who had known the turncoats, who had been friends with them without joining their side? They might see Rich as an enemy. If he was with me, at least he could put off that confrontation for a while.

"Did your boss okay our new trip?" I asked, sitting up with a wince. Ugh. Rich wasn't the only one recovering from a rough night. I'd taken two rounds to the gut and my abs were screaming at me.

"He didn't like it, but he couldn't come up with a better alternative, and he's busy making sure my parents and brother are good and safe. Hell, he flat out said he didn't blame me for not trusting anyone enough to show my face in the Marshals office."

"Or telling him where we're going?"

Rich barked a laugh. "No way in hell was he getting that out of me."

"Good. How about Smitty, what did he say?"

Finally Rich smiled. "He told me to get our asses back there, pronto. He was bored and he wanted a rematch at poker."

"He must be a closet masochist, then."

"Or not so closeted." Rich sat down next to me and kept going before I could pry at that interesting reveal. "I figure we leave here tomorrow morning and try to make it there in a day. I'll order us a pizza or something tonight."

"Okay." We stared at each other for a moment, and Rich broke eye contact first.

"Are you positive about this, Leo? Really sure?"

I huffed. "You've got to stop asking me dumb questions, Rich. The answer's not going to change. I'm completely sure I want you to see all of this through with me." I leaned in and bumped my nose against his jaw. "Is your mouth clean now?"

He turned his head to face me. "Yeah."

"Good." I kissed him, gently because I wasn't up for starting anything right now and neither was he, but it was still one of the best kisses I'd ever had. It reminded both of us that no matter what we'd just gone through, we'd come out the other side together. We were alive, and for now, we were safe, and safety was surprisingly sexy. I would have kept going if not for my face's intense urge to yawn.

"How about we sleep before we eat?" I offered as I pulled back. "Just sleep. But together."

He smiled. "Sounds good."

We settled down on the bed together, and I rolled into little spoon position without a second thought. As Rich wrapped an arm around my waist and snuggled in behind me, I spared a moment's consideration for the fact that, while I knew he liked to be the big spoon, I didn't know his favorite food—practically all we'd been eating since we met was fast food or prepackaged crap. I knew he preferred a Para Ordnance to a Glock, but I didn't know if he had any pets he was feeling guilty over neglecting, or whether he was allergic to cats like Tony had been. I knew he had friends, comrades-in-arms, but I didn't know how long he'd served or when he'd enlisted in the Marines. I'd met his parents, but I didn't know where he'd grown up.

The list of things I knew about Rich Cody could fit on the palm of my hand. The list of things I didn't know was almost too vast to consider.

The one thing I knew for certain, though, was that I wanted to know more. More of who he was, beyond his job. More of what he planned, once he was done with this gig. More of everything about him.

Going back to Smitty's would give me a chance to learn the things I wanted to know. I'd have to take advantage while I could, because after the trial, well…that was too far away to be real yet.

Better to live in the now than worry about the future. Or, as the Mafia put it, *enjoy today, because tomorrow you might be dead.*

Words to live by.

The End.

About the Authors

Cari Z. is a Colorado girl who loves snow and sunshine. She writes award-winning LGBTQ fiction featuring aliens, supervillains, soothsayers, and even normal people sometimes

Cari has published short stories, novellas and novels with numerous print and e-presses, and she also offers up a tremendous amount of free content on Literotica.com, under the name Carizabeth. Follow her blog to read her serial stories, with new chapters posting every week.

Want to follow along or get in touch? No problem!

Website: http://cari-z.net
Email: carizabeth@hotmail.com
Twitter: @author_cariz

L.A. Witt is an abnormal M/M romance writer who has finally been released from the purgatorial corn maze of Omaha, Nebraska, and now spends her time on the southwestern coast of Spain. In between wondering how she didn't lose her mind in Omaha, she explores the country with her husband, several clairvoyant hamsters, and an ever-growing herd of rabid plot bunnies. She also has substantially more time on her hands these days, as she has recruited a small army of mercenaries to search South America for her nemesis, romance author Lauren Gallagher, but don't tell Lauren. And definitely don't tell Lori A. Witt or Ann Gallagher. Neither of those twits can keep their mouths shut…

Website: www.gallagherwitt.com
Email: gallagherwitt@gmail.com
Twitter: @GallagherWitt

Made in the USA
San Bernardino, CA
28 August 2018